Rappahannock Voices

Other Anthologies of the Riverside Writers

Riverside Currents (2001)
Riverside Echoes (2003)
Riverside Reflections (2005)
Riverside Revelations (2008)
Rappahannock Review (2011)

Rappahannock Voices

An Anthology of Stories and Poetry

Riverside Writers

A Chapter of the Virginia Writers Club

∞ INFINITY
PUBLISHING

All rights reserved. No part of this book shall be reproduced or transmitted in any form or by any means, electronic, mechanical, magnetic, photographic including photocopying, recording or by any information storage and retrieval system, without prior written permission of the publisher. No patent liability is assumed with respect to the use of the information contained herein. Although every precaution has been taken in the preparation of this book, the publisher and author assume no responsibility for errors or omissions. Neither is any liability assumed for damages resulting from the use of the information contained herein.

Copyright © 2014 by Riverside Writers

ISBN 978-1-4958-0012-2

Printed in the United States of America

Published March 2014

INFINITY PUBLISHING
1094 New DeHaven Street, Suite 100
West Conshohocken, PA 19428-2713
Toll-free (877) BUY BOOK
Local Phone (610) 941-9999
Fax (610) 941-9959
Info@buybooksontheweb.com
www.buybooksontheweb.com

Introduction

A noteworthy short story, essay, fable or poem becomes transformative when it engages the reader in a powerful dialogue about the human condition, its fluctuations and its enigmas. Stylistically, a well-honed work sings. Structurally, it unveils a mesmerizing voice. Thematically, it offers wisdom capable of exacting change.

The anthology, *Rappahannock Voices*, represents the exemplary efforts of the Riverside Writers to give their audience something worthwhile to ponder. From various backgrounds and professions, this diverse group treats an array of timely themes that astound us with intriguing insights. Some of the authors address our frailties or the battle scars of past wars, while others contemplate historical roots, occupational choices, marital and family challenges. Still others reflect on life's fleeting nature or lovingly pay tribute to a spouse or in-law.

The nonfiction and fiction writers invite us to confront heartrending stories, enlivened through memorable narration and dialogue. The poets enthrall us with their skillful manipulation of both free and formal verse, sometimes surprising us with an evocative villanelle, sonnet, or simultaneous poem. Especially rich are the syntactical arrangements in service of musicality. Regardless of the genre, the authors rely on metaphors and symbols to suggest the fluidity of time by placing us in the mainstream of life's ongoing flow.

A wordsmith is challenged to arrange and rearrange the elements of a creative work until the polished product resonates. The contributors to *Rappahannock Voices* achieve this goal by exploring life's victories or defeats in finely tuned prose and poetry. Ultimately, each piece captivates the mind and spirit.

I commend the Riverside Writers for producing notable work that deepens our understanding of humankind. I applaud their ability to advise us to exercise prudence in the choices we make and to appreciate the gifts we frequently overlook. I compliment the group's enthusiastic support of one another's growth through critique sessions, monthly meetings, and annual festivals. A collaborative spirit soars to the surface of this remarkable anthology.

Carolyn Kreiter-Foronda, Ph.D.
Poet Laureate Emerita of Virginia, 2006-2008
Faculty Member, Statewide Programs
Virginia Museum of Fine Arts

Tinnitus
by Carolyn Kreiter-Foronda, Ph.D.

The ringing like a claw starts,
    a sequestered racket
        that hisses in sleep

and hums in a spring-fed swamp,
    spatterdock's *clair de lune* hearts
        bobbing like vessels.

Easing my kayak beyond the stream's
    fringe, I paddle through
        the after-hush of dusk.

Feverish, the stars. The moon coy
    above a quilt of clouds,
        the wetlands in an uproar—

owls, raccoons, minks sounding
    an alarm as jarring as a howl
        in the hoarse throat

of night. The feathery dark swells
    to a crescendo, a choir
        of spring peepers

in search of mates. Lowering
    my head, I count the times
        their vocal sacs fill

and empty, these cross-bearers
    olive-green, tan and gray,
        colors I see every time

my ear whistles. The din—
    the maddening noise—calms
        among the scent

of half-opened cow lilies,
    seductive in these elusive
        headwaters.

O canopy of bald cypress,
    sycamore, sweetgum,
        dance for me

until my hearing heals
    in the defining hour,
        windless, serene.

"Tinnitus" previously appeared in *Delaware Poetry Review,* Vol. 4, No. 1, 2012.

Contents

Seasons of Life
J. R. Robert-Saavedara, *Time* 3

Childhood
Julie Phend, *Babies Burp* 4
Rod Vanderhoof, *The Girl with the Curly Hair* 4
Rod Vanderhoof, *My Summer on the Prairie* 6

Youth
Rod Vanderhoof, *The Water Skier* 9
Michelle O'Hearn, *Yopo Experience* 11
Ron Russis, *Coming Down* 12
Donna H. Turner, *Growing Up with Dreams* 13

Love, Marriage, Family
John M. Wills, *Our Hearts* 15
Ummie, *Rebirth* 16
Larry Turner, *Miracle* 17
Larry Turner, *Six Children* 18
J. Allen Hill, *Metamorphosis* 19

Middle Age
Andrea Williams Reed, *We Endure* 25
Joe Metz, *Dern Hills – The Aftermath* 26
Juanita Dyer Roush, *Today I'm Deaf* 29
Madalin Bickel, *The Album* 32
Andrea Williams Reed, *Blood and Sugar* 33
J. R. Robert-Saavedra, *Towards the End* 34

Departing
Michelle O'Hearn, *Doomsday Daddy* 36
J. R. Robert-Saavedra, *As Death Works* 37
Larry Turner, *Stories the Night before Jim's Funeral* 38

Larry Turner, *Stickers for Grandma* 41
Thomas J. Higgins, *This is It?* 44

People You Might Meet

Thomas J. Higgins, *Danny the Cowboy* 49
Thomas J. Higgins, *While Walking through the Park* 51
Norma E. Redfern, *They Called Her Violet* 52
J. R. Robert-Saavedara, *The Vagabond* 53
Ron Russis, *Bill and I Knew* 54
Ron Russis, *Two Pints a Day* 55
J. R. Robert-Saavedara, *The Fifth and Last Winter* 56
Joe Metz, *Ballad of the D & L Diner* 57
Larry Turner, *How Do Mermaids Mate?* 59
Jennifer Anne Gregory, *Chuckles* 61
Dan Walker, *The Structure of the Poop* 63

The World of Women and Men

Ummie, *Seed Planting* 71
Ummie, *Hit and Run* 72
J. R. Robert-Saavedra, *I Want to Kiss You* 73
J. R. Robert-Saavedra, *To Claudia* 74
Michelle O'Hearn, *In Different Places* 75
Ron Russis, *Heels* 76
Donna H. Turner, *Valentine's Day Surprise* 77
Anne Heard Flythe, *The Profane Egg* 81

Family and Other Creatures

Jim Gaines, *Play Time* 85
Ron Russis, *Sunday Swimming* 86
Ron Russis, *Go Fetch a Switch* 88
Maxine Clark, *The Clay Girl* 90
S. Kelley Chambers, *Family Night* 93
Greg Miller, *Sink or Swim* 95
Stanley B. Trice, *Sisters* 100
Fred Fanning, *Dreadlocks and the Three Fishermen* 108
Andrea Williams Reed, *The In-Law* 111

Ron Russis, *Closing Days* 112
C.A. Rowland, *Interview with a Rabbit* 113
Michelle O'Hearn, *Icicle Days* 119
Ron Russis, *Now That You Ask…* 120
Anne Heard Flythe, *Acorns as Vocabulary* 121
Ron Russis, *Signs* 122
Larry Turner, *Triceratops: A Dinosaur Mystery Solved* 122
Jill Austin Deming, *The Goose* 124

City, Town, Country, Nature

City
Michelle O'Hearn, *A Moment to Own it* 127
Stanley B. Trice, *Boxcars* 128

Town
Juanita Dyer Roush, *You Call That a Massage?* 138
Madalin Bickel, *The Five and Dime Fork* 144
Andrea Williams Reed, *House on Route 17* 148

Country
Ron Russis, *In the End, I Couldn't Sell* 149
Norma Redfern, *Midwestern Corn* 151
Rod Vanderhoof, *Father and Son* 152
Madalin Bickel, *Cold January* 156
Kelly Patterson, *Night Chase* 157

Nature
Michelle O'Hearn, *Old Rag Cottonwood Stag* 158
Ummie, *Portrait* 159
Jill Austin Deming, *The Quickening* 160
J. R. Robert-Saavedra, *The Tree* 161
J. R. Robert-Saavedra, *Sunrise* 162
J. R. Robert-Saavedra, *Ignored* 163
Julie Phend, *Camping in the Woods of Wisconsin* 164
Jill Austin Deming, *The Pond* 165
Anne Heard Flythe, *Matters of Gravity* 167
Kelly Patterson, *Frisky* 169
Jim Gaines, *Pastime* 170

Far Away and Long Ago

Rod Vanderhoof, *Only in America* 173
Jim Gaines, *Long Distance* 174
Jim Gaines, *Beachcombers* 175
Rod Vanderhoof, *Hawaiian Surfer* 176
Madalin Bickel, *Route Sixty-Six* 177
Rod Vanderhoof, *My Man in Pamplona* 179
Steven P. Pody, *The Thorny Branch* 180
Ummie, *Birth of a Nation* 182
Greg Miller, *Betsy and George* 182
Michelle O'Hearn, *At Home with Mrs. Madison* 186
Madalin Bickel, *Ain't Nothin' Left* 188
Madalin Bickel, *Collapse of the Silver Bridge* 189
D.P. Tolan, *Passages of Josephus, 1853* 190

Composing Dancing Acting Writing

Julie Phend, *When I Get to be a Composer* 201
Rod Vanderhoof, *My Evening with Igor Stravinsky* 202
Ummie, *Way Back* 205
Michelle O'Hearn, *Her Flowering Audience* 206
Kelly Patterson, *The Actress* 207
Joe Metz, *Casey's Part: A Fantasy* 209
James Gaines, *A Whimper and a Bang* 214
Larry Turner, *Shape Up, Sylvia!* 215
R. L. Russis, *Michael McDonald's Reading* 216
Rod Vanderhoof, *How I Became a Poet* 219
Jim Gaines, *Lines on the Iowa Writers Workshop* 220
Elizabeth Talbot, *Breaking Good* 221

Crime and Crime Fighters

John M. Wills, *Black Mask* 231
Darrin E. Chambers, *First Damned Day* 234
Elizabeth Talbot, *Second Chances* 236
John M. Wills, *Why I Became a Cop* 243

War's Legacy

Rod Vanderhoof, *Private First Class Michio Kobiashi* 249
Rod Vanderhoof, *As the Lights Come On Again* 251
J. Allen Hill, *A Walk in the Park* 253
Ron Russis, *PTSD* 260
Juanita Dyer Roush, *The Man He Might Have Been* 261

Seeking Something More

Anne Heard Flythe, *Ophidian Vanity* 265
Ummie, *That Brass Ring* 266
Larry Turner, *Among the Anthropophagi* 267
Jim Gaines, *Forbidden Planet* 268
Joe Metz, *My Time with the Cosmic Forces* 270
Chuck Hillig, *Your Beliefs Can Sabotage Relations* 276
Larry Turner, *Bump in the Night* 282
Larry Turner, *Hallelujah Carol* 284
Joe Metz, *The Apostle Peter* 285
J. R. Robert-Saavedra, *Of People and Flowers* 287
J. R. Robert-Saavedra, *Life's Cellar* 287
Rod Vanderhoof, *The Unknowable* 288
Anne Heard Flythe, *Overlooking the Aegean* 289
Fred Fanning, *Nothing Personal Just Business* 289
Michelle O'Hearn, *Heavenly Gardens* 297
Steven P. Pody, *Sonnet of the Imperishable Minimum* 298

Contributors 299

Index 313

Preface

As president of Riverside Writers, the Fredericksburg chapter of the Virginia Writers Club, I am very happy to invite you to enjoy the poetry and prose offered in our sixth anthology, *Rappahannock Voices*. Riverside Writers first began to publish anthologies during my previous presidency, with *Riverside Currents* appearing in 2001 with iUniverse. Since that time, the subsequent volumes were entitled *Riverside Echoes* (2003, iUniverse), *Riverside Reflections* (2005, Infinity Publishing), *Riverside Revelations* (2008, Infinity Publishing), and *Rappahannock Review* (2011, Infinity Publishing). The volumes have grown in quality, as more and more Fredericksburg area members have been able to take part in our Monday critique groups led by Larry Turner and in our monthly meetings and readings, as well as in specially organized workshops sponsored by Riverside. In November of 2013, Larry Turner was recognized by the Virginia Writers Club with an Outstanding Achievement Award for his ongoing work as a premier writing mentor.

The contributors to these six volumes have all been chapter members possessed by a drive to hone their writing abilities and to discover new frontiers in their respective genres. The latter cover an especially wide range in both poetry and prose, spanning many varieties and themes of verse and unrhymed poetry and prose that stretches from historical to humor to crime writing and science fiction. It is a distinctive feature of the Riverside anthologies that writers from so many diverse paths can combine to produce a cohesive and worthwhile union of their efforts. As the roster of members has changed over the years, we have seen some of the original pioneers pass on and many other new faces join our journey. The anthologies also allow the reader to enjoy the development in the style and focus of those writers who have gone the distance from the beginnings all the way to *Rappahannock Voices*. To all of us involved in the evaluation of submissions and the editorial process of the anthologies, it has also been a joy to see so many who made their beginnings with us move out into the publishing world with works that appear widely in print and on the internet. We can say with assurance that these volumes have been a spawning ground for the careers of people who have gone on to produce impressive collections and books. Perhaps the authors of some of the pieces you read in *Rappahannock Voices* may in a few years be known in the most distinguished circles of American publication.

Riverside is proud to be among the most active branches of the Virginia Writers Club in encouraging its members to polish their work until it is ready for print and to help them take that sometimes daunting step from sharing their work with an intimate group of friends to the launching of a book. Since the establishment of the chapter in 1998, we have stepped up to become an integral part of the statewide organization founded in 1918 in order to bring together folk of all races, creeds and genders in the pursuit of literary excellence. Personally, I was honored to serve as one of the four state presidents of Virginia Writers Club that our chapter has furnished to date. The statewide club serves as a nexus for the work of all the individual chapters by allotting grants for writing workshops and activities, serving as a data base for all the activities in different parts of Virginia, conducting writing contests, and promoting the Young Virginia Writers Club to find and develop new talents emerging in our schools. I would like to urge all who are interested in these endeavors to contact the club at its online website, www.virginiawritersclub.org, at our Riverside website, www.riversidewriters.com, or at any of the other chapter websites accessible from the state online chapter menu. While sharing one's writings may at first seem to be fraught with embarrassment or trepidation, a new contact will quickly grow to learn that there is support, expertise, encouragement, and friendship to be gained in this fellowship, and nothing to lose but the rough edges of one's words. We invite all who aspire to our goals to join us and be part of the next anthology that will follow *Rappahannock Voices* and to discover the wonderful things that you can contribute along with us.

Jim Gaines
President, Riverside Writers

Acknowledgments

We wish to thank the members of Riverside Writers who contributed their poems and stories. We also thank the many people who reviewed the submissions and the following members of the Anthology Committee, who devoted many hours to the planning and preparation of the book.

Andrea Reed, Chair
Larry Turner, Editor
Judy Hill
Greg Mitchell
Elizabeth Talbot
Rod Vanderhoof

Cover photograph "Looking Back" by William Charnley
Used by permission

Seasons of Life

Time
by J. R. Robert-Saavedara

As time flows
And seasons pass
As rain drops fall
And are then absorbed
So does Life flow
And it is cast
Like iron
Into a mold.

So our Life grows
And shapes acquire
Through hours, and days
And years past
Always taking shape
And always molding
Some with love
And some with hate.

As time flows
And as life develops
Some grotesque
Others with beauty
It is ours
And ours alone
To hold
And to Love
As mother does child.

Childhood

Babies Burp
by Julie Phend

It's not impolite when babies burp
'Cause that's the way they eat.
They drink and burp and slurp soft food.
If I did that, they'd call me rude!
But when babies burp,
it's sweet.

The Girl with the Curly Hair
by Rod Vanderhoof

"I've seen this curly haired little girl before," said an old lady in the elevator. "I know . . . she's Little Orphan Annie. She's so cute." The elevator door opened and the lady left.

Grandpa, who's Little Orphan Annie . . . does she have curly hair?

Orphan Annie's in the comic strips, darlin' and, yes, her hair's curly.

Who had the curliest hair you know, Grandpa? What was she like?

Well, her grade school teacher said, "She greets all the new kids, asks where they're from and makes them less lonely in a brand new place."

Tell me more!

Okay, she danced in a high school musical called, "Chicago," and sang in Hungarian.

Hungarian? Who sings in Hungarian, Grandpa?

The Hungarians, of course.

Oh, Grandpa! What else? I want to know.

"She's great at rugby?" her college coach said. "She plays scrum-half and is our best all-around player. As captain, she's the brains of the team. And watch her make an open field tackle."
That's good, Grandpa! What else?

Well, she toured the great Egypt of old,
sat astride a humpback camel, an action bold.
She watched the dizzy Dervishes whirl,
shopped the ancient Khan Bazaar, a well-traveled girl.
She sailed in a *faluka* along the Nile,
rode a horse named Cleopatra, for just awhile.

What happened then, Grandpa?

She did what little girls do, darlin'. She grew into a beautiful woman, found her guy, married him and now has her own little girl.
With curly hair, Grandpa? Like mine?
Yes, darlin', with curly hair, just like yours.

My Summer on the Prairie
by Rod Vanderhoof
(The 1930s)

*I almost remember my summer on the Canadian prairie,
but it's so long ago.*

I peer through the car windshield into the dark,
looking for Grams and Gramps's house.
I see a yellow light.

"Is that it Daddy? They always leave the light on."

"Not yet."

"When Daddy? When?"

We finally arrive.

"Hi, Grams and Gramps,
I'm here for the summer.
Are you glad to see me?"

*No answer.
They don't hear me, I guess.*

The next day I play with Zippy.
I run him out to the wheat field near the railroad tracks.
I throw an old rubber ball.
Zippy brings it back again and again.

One morning I don't see Zippy.
"Where is he, Grams?"

"He broke into the hen house and
killed the chickens.
Gramps shot him."

I barely remember Zippy.

At night during a deluge of rain
I hear the cannon blast from
a lightning strike,
splitting an oak tree,
killing a cow standing next.

I'd nearly forgotten the lightning.

A big bull charges Gramps who
swings himself behind a post.
The bull smashes his arm.
He is sheet white.

I run to Grams.
"Come quick,
Gramps is hurt."

I open the car door and
help Gramps into the passenger seat.
Grams enters the driver's side.

*I run to the kitchen for my coat and hurry back,
but they're gone. They forgot me, I guess.*

The doctor places a cast on Gramps's arm,
leaving town for a few days.
Gangrene sets in.

Now Gramps is dead.
Grams is alone.
She's selling the farm.

"I'm sorry, Grams. I wish I could make things right.
I'll help milk the cows,
feed the chickens,
pick the apples and cherries.
I'll be the man of the farm and boss
the plowing and planting and harvesting."

She doesn't hear me, I guess.

Daddy comes.
We drive home.
I gaze ahead into the dark, seeing only the
occasional lights of a lonely farmhouse.

*I barely remember that summer.
It was so long ago.*

Youth

The Water Skier
by Rod Vanderhoof

After the evening squall
but before dark,
the lake is a black mirror.
I swing wide right
out of the wake to
flat, pristine water.

Skis chatter.
Rope pull is strong, steady.
I'm exhilarated by projectile speed and
moist, cooling air.

The driver swerves heavy left to
match a twisting shoreline.
I am the snap at the end of the whip—super fast.

Trees loom ahead at water's edge.
Hunched over, I duck below the
leaning trunk and branches
of a sweet gum.

Risky!
Dazzling!
Spirited!

I drop my right ski and,
with both feet on the left,
I slalom.

I pull a hard left turn.
A million dense droplets
explode skyward in a
soaring rooster tail.

I slam hard against the
wake's right ridge and
launch into the air
landing with a gunshot
Ka-whap!

I cross the froth,
catapult off the left ridge
and slap
Ka-whap!
onto solid glass.

Finally, I coast,
then cut sharp right and send
iridescent spray towering
against a darkening sky.

I follow the ski boat wherever it takes me.

Yopo Experience
by Michelle O'Hearn

Naturally residing
    inside the human brain
DMT it is named
The Amazoas experimented
    to break open the power
    of the Yopo plant
Traversing all the jungle and
    overcoming biting ants.

Without degrees and
    without laws
An addict administers
    the juice
According to the desired
    cause;
Definitive answers from
    subconscious claws
To stretch and reach
    a believer.

Embrace it and
    face it
but the mind could still break it.
No test or trial
    can fix the denial of
Actions and visions attained.

Coming Down
(After Getting High)
by Ron Russis

I rode the light, the smoke, the cloudy dawn,
the pipe taking me, propelling me head-
long, along the dragon's tail, into things
I'd always suspected, now my learning
they all were true, of colors that spoke and
of pigs that flew, of changing and faceless
faces, of all those invisible places
where only we gods could go... And so I
got high and like Art's daughter I tried to fly
and flapped my wings, but they were clumsy, crude,
awkward things and in spite of my best efforts,
and for all I tried, like Galileo's balls,
I dropped near straight to ground, my arcing
just a bit with that speeding shadow marking
my impact destination – that sidewalk spot –
a shrinking point of failed trajectory
and the landing strip for this, my short-lived trip,
an impetuous, impromptu flight of seduction,
in love with the haze within which I swam,
a blissful oblivion, unaware of the gravity...
But, with my ETA confirmed, still on schedule
to point of arrival, although it wasn't much distant
from point of departure, from where I'd begun,
from where last I'd stood – except for its being
sixteen floors down – this unannounced flight
abruptly arrived, the impact so sudden
and me so high I never knew I died...

Growing Up with Dreams
by Donna H. Turner

When I was young, I was very idealistic, very religious, and felt the whole world was mine. High school was a time of fun but a chance to prove what I could do for myself and the world. Yes, I was a disadvantaged kid. Yes, there were times when I was not certain of who I was or where I was headed, but for all of that, I was positive about the world.

My mother was a single woman trying to raise two children on her own. We lived in a low-rent housing project, which for me seemed paradise—especially compared with some places we had lived earlier. The apartment had two bedrooms, a full bathroom with a bathtub, and in the kitchen what to my eyes was an enormous refrigerator with a freezer on top. Every once in a while, Mom would splurge and buy a carton of ice cream. It never lasted long in the freezer; we devoured it before it had a chance to melt.

Even as a little child, I was positive about life. I figured that a person could direct his or her own life choice. Personally, I could get out of my background by being a person who made the right choices. I began to think I could get an education, make something of myself and become that teacher I always wanted to be.

Many adults were there to help show me the way. The experience of my early life had taught me marriage was a punishment, not a partnership. I can remember that when I heard our youth pastor was getting married, my thirteen-year-old self tried to talk her out of it. Why would anyone choose to get married? I couldn't fathom it. Now, more than sixty years later, she and I are still connected. Her marriage has lasted sixty-some years, and my own nearly fifty-five. It was in the home of another pastor friend that I learned married life could be normal and healthy.

I often wondered why the small group of young people in our church were marked for "saving." There certainly were a lot of kids who weren't so lucky. A classmate of mine had three children by the time she was sixteen. When I asked her why she was pregnant again, she said she was running out of money and her welfare payment would be raised when she had another baby. I look back and remember feeling great sadness for her. There was no reason she couldn't have had a better life, but she ended up living her life with three or more children, living in another project if she was lucky.

I did well enough in high school that I was granted a scholarship in one of our Presbyterian colleges, and a woman from our home church offered to give me money for what the scholarship wouldn't cover. There it was: A four-year free ride! But when I told our relief worker, she said, "Oh, no. You can't do that. It's your turn to care for your mother." I was crushed beyond words. So I got a job to support my mother and me.

When I got married at age twenty, my mother went back on relief. Eventually she married again, this time to a bus driver. She led her own life and then retired to Florida with her husband where she sang country songs at the VFW.

Why did I decide to get married at the age of twenty? Well, Larry had something to do with it. We met at a college group in our church on Sunday nights. The group served dinner and was a place to "hang out" as they say today. I'd never met anyone as smart as Larry. I was smitten with his intellect first; love came a little later. He was the most moral person I ever met. When he said he believed in something, he did. He had a dream about his life, and I was convinced that he would achieve it. Soon he wanted me to be a part of that dream, and I was glad to do it. Being a faculty wife at a Christian college was something I would like to do. I wanted to have a family, and that too was in our plans. A good life. A comfortable life. That's not a bad dream for a girl from the wrong side of the tracks, even though it was not my original dream.

Love, Marriage, Family

Our Hearts
by John M. Wills

A cute little blond girl down the street,
caught my eye and imagination.
I desperately tried to grab your attention,
clumsily and doggedly inviting you to play
in childish sport and 6th grade pickup games.

You saw right through me and looked away,
yet your smile and attitude held me tight.
Rebuffed and rebuked at every attempt.
Ignored and chided I endured for years,
and graduated to writing notes to show you I cared.

Then one day you stopped to talk.
Shocked and elated, What a glorious day!
So much in common but not yet a match,
dissimilar families, roadblocks to circumvent.
Still, feelings of the heart diminished the worries.

Finally, a cold day in November
warmed when our two souls made promises before Him.
Some bitter feelings remained,
but rings entwined to prove the strength of two.
Husband and wife forever together.

Three little babies affirmed our bond,
each one a treasure and gift from above.
Growing like flowers among many weeds,
their harvest was bountiful.
Grandchildren fell like stars from the heavens.

Weeks spent apart, many filled with danger,
death so near made each moment precious.
Decades passed as did grudges.
Words unneeded as eyes spoke clearly.
Your heart was mine and mine was yours.

Forty-five years seems so long,
yet each day together seems too short.
Strong when together, even stronger apart.
In my wildest dreams, I would never have thought
that cute little blond girl would own my heart.

Rebirth
by Ummie

I found you
I heard you
I listened
We touched
I was
Reborn!

Miracle
by Larry Turner

Someday you will find yourself
in a debate over miracles.
Someone will offer a definition:
A miracle is a violation of natural law.
Do not accept this!
It is intended only to define miracles
out of existence. *Worse yet,*
it is dishonest: If you point out
a miracle, natural law instantly
changes to fit it. *Worse yet,*
it excludes miracles like sunrise and childbirth
and less frequent but equally
impressive miracles.

But here is a miracle that fits that
strict definition: Despite derision from
psychologists, sociologists, comparative zoologists,
a young couple stands in the presence of family,
friends, and community
and promises to love each other for a lifetime
in a unique and exclusive way.
This is not a miracle.

Some actually do it.
This is.

Six Children
by Larry Turner

We never spoke of making plans to wed.
No bended knee to offer you a ring.
The topic of our dialogue instead
Became how many children we would bring
Into the world, and six is what we chose.
Back in the 1950s, no one thought
Too many kids would bring the planet woes.
But in a decade, overcrowding caught
The world's attention. Though we would agree,
We looked at our two sons, and we were sure
That if we had a third child, he or she
Might add, not to the curse, but to the cure.
If you, my third son, wonder why you're here,
Your brothers gave us faith for future year.

Metamorphosis
by J. Allen Hill

Impossible to turn a reptile into a mammal, you say? Well, I advise you not to wager too high a sum on the question as I'm here to tell you the story of how it happened one summer day in Fairfield, Connecticut.

It happened on Chuckie's sixth birthday—a June birthday – a milestone birthday. Grandma had sent a check in recognition of the fact that he would be old enough to attend school in the fall. And I had promised him—also in deference of his newly advanced age— that he could spend the money on anything he wanted. The problem was Chuckie had his heart set on buying his very own pet: a snake. No amount of logic, cajolery, persuasion, argument or ice cream could convince the boy otherwise.

He was shown pictures of an attacking rattler, its fangs dripping with venom, danger and evil. "Not that one," he said. The engulfing white mouth of a moccasin, the entangling coils of a giant python, the seductive beauty of the coral, the copperhead—all were rejected. Chuckie was adamant and stood his ground, all sturdy three feet of him. "I want a boa constrictor, a boy one."

I had misjudged him and I knew better. Chuckie at six already read voraciously and had checked his facts. Male boas are smaller than females. Acquired young, housed in a tank and fed a restricted diet, their size can be controlled.

A promise is a promise, so we donned our best birthday clothes and made a trip to Mr. Paulie's Pet Shop. George Paulie was a kind, grandfatherly man, wise in the ways of animals and children. I was counting on him to change Chuckie's mind.

The shop was an emporium of animalia; feathered, furred, and scaled, it had them all. Alex, an African gray parrot, guarded the front door greeting customers with a raucous shout of "G'day Mate," always ready to flirt and perform. A wire pen that sat just inside of the front door was usually filled with scampering puppies no child could resist. If he should tire of these, the left wall was lined with cages of everything cuddly and furry: dogs and cats, bunnies, hamsters, guinea pigs, ferrets, mice and rats. The middle of the store was packed with aviaries of singing, talking, chirping, chattering birds and glass tanks of sand dwellers such as hermit crabs, tortoise, lizards and tarantulas. Bubbling aquariums lit up the right wall with the flashing bright colors of tropical fish. Of course, we had to visit them all, petting, cooing and cuddling, scratching ears and rousing the night dwellers from sleep.

An hour after arriving, Chuckie finally asked, "Mr. Paulie, where are the boa constrictors?"

I was gesturing wildly trying to hint to George that I needed his help here. But instead of listing all of the unwelcome properties of owning such an animal, George engaged Chuckie in a long informative discourse on snakes – boas in particular – as he led the boy to the back of the store. It soon became evident that Chuckie knew almost as much about boas as George did so George didn't try to discourage him. I fumed and sputtered not realizing at the time how wise this man really was.

A series of glass tanks were lined up against the wall exactly at the eye level of a three-foot tall boy. Each contained a single or pair of reptiles in its own specialized habitat. Chuckie proceeded from tank to tank his nose pressed against the glass. Back and forth. Back and forth he walked the line, finally stopping in front of the last tank, its sole occupant awake and curious. Nose to nose the snake and the boy. Small beady black snake eyes stared into wide little boy blue ones. Chuckie didn't move a muscle. For a full five minutes no one said a word, the only sound a low hiss coming from the tank. Suddenly the snake flicked its tongue, reared back and struck the side of the glass. Chuckie jumped two feet into the air.

"Mama, what would you think about a puppy?" he asked, and that is how we changed a reptile into a little brown shelter dog named Shaggy. But that is another story.

WE ARE ADOPTED

The puppies in the pet shop all had their papers. Well, all puppies have papers, but these had the AKC kind and Chuckie did not have enough money for one of them.

"There's another place we can look," I told him. "We can look at the animal shelter."

Chuckie pulled out his Roy Rogers wallet and carefully counted his money. "Can I afford a shelter dog?" he asked.

"I am sure you can. They are free."

Chuckie's eyes were wide with excitement for the entire twenty mile drive to the shelter. He deflated as we pulled into the parking lot of a shabby gray building with no windows and a scarred red door. Animal shelters are a universal gray green color inside, smell of pine oil and antiseptic, and ring with the din of bored animals behind steel bars. This one was no different.

Chuckie grabbed my hand as we walked slowly up and down the rows of cages. He surveyed each occupant carefully. I wondered if he knew some of these would not be here tomorrow. I did not attempt to explain this to him.

"They all want out so bad, Mom. We can't take them all." He was stating both a fact and making a wish.

"No. We have room for only one."

Again we toured the rows of cages. Warm tongues licked our outstretched fingers and tails of all descriptions beat a hopeful welcome.

Chuckie stopped in front of a large collie. Reaching his chubby arms through the bars, he squeezed the dog tightly around its ruffed neck. "Lassie dogs are nice."

The Lassie dog wet down Chuckie's ear with his tongue, but as the arms squeezed tighter and tighter, the poor dog panicked and pulled away. He slumped off into the corner of his enclosure, disappointed that the boy was not suitable.

"I guess he doesn't like me," Chuckie sighed.

"His card says he belonged to an elderly couple, son. They had to give him up because they were moving into a small apartment. He's just not used to children."

We stopped in front of a floppy eared beagle with quiet soulful eyes. Boy and dog carefully looked each other over.

"His ears are ragged," Chuckie said as he studied the dog. "His eyes are drippy and his nose is runny." The beagle didn't offer a paw or a kiss. He made no sound.

"He's so sad, Mom. I think he better get out of here soon. Should we take him?"

My son had the heart of a Good Samaritan. With instincts like his, we could become the home for all the halt and lame animals of the world. I read the card affixed to the beagle's cage.

> Name: Grumpy
> Breed: Beagle Mix
> Age: 12 years
> Reason for surrender to shelter:
> Death of owner

This sturdy old fellow had been someone's sole companion and now he had lost both friend and home just when he needed them most.

"He's quite old, son, and not very well," I ventured. "I really don't think he could keep up with you. It would be hard for him." But I was tempted. I smoothed his grizzled back and scratched behind his ears. For a moment he closed his eyes and tilted his head in satisfaction. Then, grumbling deep within his chest, Grumpy resolutely turned his back on us and walked away. He knew his field days were over and he had made the decision for us.

"You're probably right, Mom. I run very fast." A hollow ache formed in my chest. Oh my. This wasn't going to be easy.

The silver poodle yapped shrilly. I thought my ears would snap. The spotted hound lunged repeatedly against the bars.

"He'll break his ribs," worried Chuck.

The golden spaniel paced and whined – paced and whined. *Very nervous*, I thought. Of course, who could blame her.

They came in all colors, shapes and sizes; all ages and conditions – these waifs of over breeding, thoughtless owners, broken homes. And we had room for only one.

"Mom, I don't know how to pick one."

"I know how you feel, sweets. I think this has been a hard day for us. Maybe we'd better go home and think about it. We'll come back tomorrow."

Tomorrow. Oh jeez. Tomorrow the ranks would be thinned.

"Okay."

We were weary with our stretched emotions. As we turned to leave, we spotted one cage we had missed.

She was very dignified. A brown furry mop of ragged matted fur, she sat still and straight and shined her eyes at us. Her upper lip curled into an unmistakable grin. She snizzled a welcoming hello. Her tail – her whole bottom – swept the floor in greeting. Another snizzle, a snurf and a whuff clearly said, "Take me home. You won't be disappointed. I promise."

Amazing. We didn't know we knew how to speak dog.

Riverside Writers

I read her card:

> Name: Shaggy. *Appropriate*, I thought
> Breed: Long haired poodle. *Questionable.*
> Age: 2 years. *Hmmm.*
> Reason for surrender to shelter:
> Allergies in household

As I read, Shaggy increased her sales pitch. She offered to shake paws. She executed a little dance on her hind feet, accompanying herself with more whuffs and snuffles. Her smile flashed again and again.

We could not leave without her. She had staked her claim.

It didn't take long to fill out the adoption forms. A small donation was asked and solemnly supplied from the Roy Rogers wallet. The warden handed us Shaggy's chain and a small red dish, her only possessions.

Shaggy led us to the car. She seemed to know which one it was. Politely waiting for Chuckie to scramble into his usual spot in the back seat, she hopped into the front seat next to me. Turning around twice and neatly scrunching her tail into a hollow in the soft upholstery, she rolled her eyes once in my direction, clearly stating, "Let's get this show on the road."

With a turn of her head and a soft whine, she promised Chuckie a real romp as soon as we reached home. As we pulled away from the shelter, Chuckie slapped a kiss on Shaggy's eye and she slopped one on his. "She's ours, now, Mom, huh? Really ours?"

"Well, son, I think it's more a case of us being hers."

Middle Age

We Endure
by Andrea Williams Reed

We endure the excessive change of seasons,
burning sun in summer and chilled to the bone in winter.
We endure the cross boss, jealous co-workers,
and demanding clients that put food on the table.
We endure traffic, to get where we're going.
We endure a family gathering to keep peace.
We endure the awkward moment with a former lover,
to prove we are the better person.
We endure the gum stained bleachers
to cheer on our little ones.
We endure the technical delays of a concert
to hear the sound that takes us away.
We endure the 90 minute wait in line,
for the 90 second roller coaster ride
that takes us upside down.
We endure the illness that takes us away
from people and things we love.
We endure…

Dern Hills – The Aftermath
(A parody of Dylan Thomas' *Fern Hill*)
by Joe Metz

Now as I was gray and grouchy under the ceiling fans
About my dusty home and crabby as the grass was long,
    The night above the condo cloudy,
        Time let me growl and grumble
    Sullen in the cataracts of his eyes,
And honored among Fraternal Orders I was Sergeant-at-Arms on Tuesdays
And once upon a time I lordly had the Stars and Stripes
        Trail with honor and glory
    Down the ragings of a beachhead fight.

And as I was arthritic and hair-free, famous among pharmacists
About the neighborhood and railing at the cost of drugs,
    In the sun that is hot too often,
        Time let me age and be
    Wrinkled with no mercy in its means,
And pale and knobby I was father and grandpa, the kids
Yelled in my ears, their dogs in the mini-vans barked clear and cold,
        And our Sundays rang loudly
    With the clamor of unholy screams.

All day long my nose was running, it was swollen, the pollen
Count high as the house, the smell from the freeway, it
        Was smog,
    And exhaust fumes, stinky and murky,
        And smoke from burning grass.
    And nightly under the hidden stars
As I tried to sleep some kids were blasting their room away.

All the moon long I heard, blessed among DJ's, Led-
     Zeppelin,
     Encores by the Eagles, and the Stones
         Strutting into the dark.

And then to awake, and the condo, like a freezer white
With the frost, come back, the goose bumps thick on my
shoulder; it was all
     Whining, it was "drat 'em, I'm fadin'!"
         The sky clouded up again
     And the lightning flashed round that very day.
So it must have been after the birth of my simple life
In the last bedding space, the well-bred doctors walking
     white
         Out of the overcrowded ER's
             Into the yields of praise.

And honoured among Moose and Elks in smoky lodges,
Under "Daily Special" signs and happy that my heart was
strong
     For bingo that came Thursdays over and over,
         I damned my winless cards,
     My fingers raced through the house high play
And nothing I dared, even four-card trades, let my time
allow
In all this number churning so few "N's" and "O's"
     Before some Mom, plump and placid,
         Bellowed "Bingo" in her place,

Nothing I cared, in my shortening days, that time would
         yank me
Up to a poorly staffed nursing home with a by-pass in my
chest,
     With rates that are always rising,
         Nor that trying to sleep
     I should hear jets from the airfields

And wake to a nurse forever blessed with ice-like hands.
Oh as I was gray and grouchy at the mercy of his means,
    Time held me mean and vying
Though I filled my "Depends" like a sea.

Today I'm Deaf
by Juanita Dyer Roush

I am deaf. Most of my life is spent trying not to be deaf. I work at not being disabled but at declaring by my actions and lifestyle that I have abilities. I work a fulltime job in a demanding but rewarding position, interact on a regular basis with family, friends and acquaintances, attend plays, book signings, poetry readings, and things that others attend.

This morning I broke one of my BTE hearing aids. They are not pretty, even though my insurance company pays nothing towards their purchase due to relegating them to the category of "cosmetic," but they are important to me.

I have a "good ear" and a "bad ear" and can't hear out of either of them. My journey into a quiet world started when I was 42 years old and found that, due to a genetic condition probably caused by a gene from each side of my family colliding and blessing me with deafness. It has been a slow process, and for that, I'm thankful.

I try not to put myself into situations where my deafness is obvious such as, large rooms and big crowds where interaction with others is expected of me. Sometimes my situation can be funny (or at least others think so) when I give an obscure answer that has nothing to do with the question. It is embarrassing and a little bit intimidating to be the object of laughter. Most people don't know I'm deaf until they are told.

This morning while inserting my hearing aide, it broke in my hand. It is Sunday morning and I'm sitting here debating whether to go to church or not. It wouldn't be such a dilemma if sneaking in and out of the building without having to talk to people was an option. Today I'm sorry to say that my church is a friendly church which is usually a positive attribute to find in the House of God. Everyone wants to talk to me before and after services though. I could hide out in the restroom until the service starts and then quietly slide into the pew, or sneak out and go to a Sunday school classroom and close the door until everyone else is out of the church. But what about my husband who has been sitting in the car drumming his fingers on the steering wheel impatiently waiting? The good thing is, I won't be able to hear what he says about my disappearances.

That takes care of church, but the biggest dilemma is the family gathering after church. My family can be brutal. They are a loving bunch, but teasing is a part of the whole family thing. Experience tells me that I am going to get to be the brunt of it today.

I remind myself that there are so many other blessings in my life such as sight, the ability to walk and talk (although not about the right subject today), and I can even dance, but the music is remembered inside my mind. I have a wonderful family and great friends.

For now, I need to get up and get a shower and dress and go face the world to prove once again that I am not disabled. Being deaf doesn't change who I am inside or change the fact that I still have feelings that are perhaps too close to the surface today.

I do believe in healing – that Our Lord God still heals. My prayer is, "Lord, I wouldn't be at all adverse to You proving Yourself through me today with Your healing touch – because today, I'm deaf."

Tonight I'm Deaf
(on being made to feel disabled)

Tonight I'm deaf.
Oh, I've been deaf for many years now,
Somewhere between hard of hearing
And lucky to find any sound

I work hard to be "normal"
Working twice as hard to hear as "normal" people
Most people don't even know I'm deaf ...one on one
But in a crowd, I lose my lip reading advantage.

Hearing aids can only do so much
And when you are limited to only wearing one
When no sound comes through the other at all
Life can be difficult at times

And tonight, I'm feeling sorry for myself
Made to feel like the village idiot over and over
Is disheartening, all joy is sapped
I'm an intelligent person... but who cares?

People are not interested in anyone else's harangue
They are only interested in what I can hear
I deal with it all the time so sometimes I forget
But tonight, I failed – and Tonight I'm deaf.

The Album
by Madalin Bickel

It lay quietly on a stack of boxes
waiting to be safely stowed;
white leather with gold script;
thick pages with one large photo
encased and protected forever.

The ivory gown in peau de soie
draped around the bride.
Imported lace and beads gracefully
framed her face.
In one the groom actually smiled
at her beauty or her innocence.

The smell of gardenias and
white roses seemed a whiff away,
but nearly fifty years had escaped
along with all her dreams.
Her mother gazed back with a
younger face than her own.

The girls were dressed in gold silk,
the men in tails. Another time,
another place when life held hope.
The ghosts of so many danced before her eyes.
Even the groom was gone - first by choice
then by death.

The last page once made her cry.
Now it caught her breath.
The wedding over, dyed shoes laid aside,
the mothers of the bride and groom sat
and shared a cup of tea,
a smile on their ageless faces.

Blood and Sugar
by Andrea Williams Reed

Too much sugar in the blood,
Fatigue replaces desire.
Doctor visits filled vacation days.
Injections instead of desserts;
Granddaddy's eyes grew dim.
Moods change like the river's tides,
Appetite yet to be satisfied;
Constant in affection for loved ones.

Towards the End
by J. R. Robert-Saavedra

Staring at the fireplace
In the family room
I hear songs of long ago
From a campfire far away.

Young, eager voices then
Falsettos and new basses
Innocent voices of youth past
In a forest meadow lit by campfire light.

So much future
So much hope
Some dead early
Some, hanging on.

Slowly then
And much faster now
These ghostly figures
From the flames they rise.

Their presence makes me warm
Their Love fills my heart
The sandman closes my eyes
Silently they stand guard.

My wife arrives,
She touches my arm,
She helps me to bed,
She tucks me in.

The new morrow alights
With a clean slate
The sun kisses my cheeks
The wind dances with the trees.

The squirrels scamper
So beautiful the birds sing
I sip a red wine
Then close my eyes.

I recall faraway lands
Long forgotten names
The joy of youth
The adventures then.

Focused on love
I search for a face
A warm tropical night
Blue eyes beneath the moon.

Butterflies dance
The hummingbirds hum
The sun shatters red on the clouds
The night veil drops.

The night turns cold
My angel of a wife arrives
She turns the porch lights on
Then helps me into the home.

Staring at the fireplace
In the family room
I hear songs of long ago
From a campfire far away.

Departing

Doomsday Daddy
by Michelle O'Hearn

Doomsday occurred in this year past
Ending my world as I knew it.
The comfort of Daddy is gone
12.21.12
Only his sense of humor
Would have chosen
the Mayan doomsday he told us
Not to believe in.
69 years is not enough time
For the world to enjoy
Such a vibrant and loving life.

The visit I promised this spring
Never to come.
I heard you say that you love me
And I know you heard it in return.
This year has been devastating
But you taught me how to fight;
To kick and scratch to survive.
Cancer didn't win. You did.
And in my heart you will forever abide
In Heaven we will be home
Together;
A reunion that will force this world
To sing
For that visit in Spring.

As Death Works
by J. R. Robert-Saavedra

Where have you been?
    The widow asked of death
Why do you ask? Said death
Such a long time I have waited
    The widow said.
Her family said it was time.

Death's sleep was interrupted
By a prod and a pull
It is not time yet
    Death yelled
The abortion team said
    It is a success.

Death met the hard worker, in mid step
At the office on his way to a meeting
Wait! What are you doing?
    He asked of death.
At the funeral his friends whispered:
    He led such a full life.

In the city's dark ghetto streets
    A weapon's bang can be heard
The young child the bullet hits
    Bleeds slowly to death
The police said
Such a waste these drug wars are

As the young successful co-workers
Were in a car driving too fast
They ran into death waiting at a bend of the road
At the funeral parlor through sobs and tears
    Their friends whispered "they were so young."

Riverside Writers

In a far away land the Soldier turned the corner
    As death turned the corner
What are you doing here?
    In unison they both said
As the family sobbed someone said
    This war has to stop.

Stories the Night before Jim's Funeral
by Larry Turner

I. Flying Saucer over Pinehurst

Among the ancient Celts, so I've been told,
when an epic battle had been fought,
bards from both sides gathered to agree
upon a common version of the feats
that had occurred upon that bloody field.

One December evening, high above
the Pinehurst home of Marion and Jim,
a flying saucer hovered. There its crew
of aliens observed us earthlings
and reached agreement that our family
had gathered from all corners of the land
in order to select definitive
versions of the stories that we shared.

II. Shoes Beside the Door

When they arrived at Jim and Marion's,
the women who came first may have been friends,
who had been on their feet preparing for
our dinner at the church and planning for
tomorrow's funeral. Perhaps they were
Jim's granddaughters, who chose to wear
unfamiliar heels to show respect, but found
such footwear pained their unaccustomed feet.

For whatever reason, they took off
their shoes. When out of state family
arrived later, they saw those shoes and judged
that such must be the custom of the house
and took off theirs as well. Marion
was at the kitchen stove preparing snacks.
Returning to the living room, she found
a row of shoes beside the door, while folks
were walking comfortably in stocking feet.

III. Dead Men Tell No Tales

The oldest remaining family member,
I was asked to start sharing our memories
of Jim. I started prior to my birth.
Our mother told the story to me, so
it must be true. When Jim was three years old,
he took his dog and got lost in the woods.
Our parents could not find him anywhere.
The sheriff brought out trusties from the jail
to aid the search. When Jim at last turned up,
he said he and his dog were never lost,
that they were "hunting wabbits" in the woods.

Whenever Jim gave his account, it was
the State Police, not trusties from the jail,
who helped to find him. As for me, I don't
believe Ohio State Police had yet
been founded at the time all this took place.
Since I am still alive, and Jim is not,
my version of this childhood story stands.

I also told the family members how
the school had made Jim shift his handedness
from left to right, and how that change had caused
his lifelong stutter. Jim had long denied
he had ever been left-handed, but among
his children and grandchildren gathered there

Riverside Writers

so many were left-handed that it gave
my tale an added credibility.

IV. Charlie Cornelius and His Physique

That night the painful truth sank into me:
Never again can I phone my brother Jim,
the way I did one Sunday afternoon
a year or so ago. When he picked up
the phone, I asked him, "Where does Charlie Cornelius
keep his physique?" He answered instantly:
"In his wheelbarrow."

It happened in the last year of the war,
I was eight years old, and everybody
was growing victory gardens.
Charlie Cornelius, who lived across the street,
had planted his on the lot next door.
While gardening, he took off his shirt,
which shocked my proper mother. Even worse,
she caught a glimpse of his pot belly,
and said, "Look at Charlie's physique!"
I saw nothing. "Where is it?" I asked,
"In his wheelbarrow?"

V. Jim's Love Affair with Cars

Jim inherited our father's love
of automobiles. When our dad was only
eleven, his father phoned him from town
to say that he had purchased their first car.
Dad should walk to town and drive it home.

Dad gave Jim a Ford convertible
as a high-school graduation gift.
I remember Jim out for a drive
in his convertible. The top was down.
Four of us went with him, plus our dog,

who ran around the back and even on
the trunk. Going round a bend, the dog
slid off. Jim had to stop to bring him back,

Some years later, Jim decided it
was time to trade. I went with him as he
drove back and forth between the
Ford and Plymouth dealers. Finally the one
who handled Plymouths offered him a price
so low he scarcely could believe it:
nine-hundred fifty dollars plus his car
if I remember right. The Ford dealer told Jim,
"I can't match a price like that." When Jim
returned to the Plymouth dealer, the man said,
"I was sort of hoping you wouldn't come back."
"Well, that's okay," Jim responded. "Why don't
we say an even thousand bucks?" *What kind of way
is this to bargain for a car?* I thought.

Stickers for Grandma
by Larry Turner
A simultaneous poem
suggested by the October 2, 2011 "Dear Abby" column

Martha Speaks

Why traumatize a child by bringing her to a wake?

A four-year-old had no business there.

Was my sister too cheap to find a sitter?

I'm sure Cousin Ruth meant well when she pulled stickers out of her purse to keep Joy quiet. God knows she carries everything else in that monster of a bag!

Suddenly I looked up to see Joy pasting stickers on Mother's hand, and even on her face.

What disrespect! I'm certain all the family and friends were shocked and saddened to have their grief mocked that way.

At least my daughter Eleanor tried to correct things by removing the stickers. She's only eighteen, but she knew what to do.

Joy threw a tantrum and refused to move.

Joy was out of control. Gently I picked her up and carried her away from the casket.

I'm glad that Mother couldn't see how Mary and Joy disrespected her body in front of all her friends and family.

I never want to see Mary or Joy again!

Mary Speaks

Why traumatize my daughter over a small thing like stickers?

Joy had to learn she'll never see Grandma again. Age four is not too young to begin to learn the finality of death.

The two of us flew here from California. What else could I have done with Joy?

How sweet of Cousin Ruth. How did she come to have stickers in her purse? Did she put them in especially for Joy, or did she just happen to have them there?

Suddenly I looked up to see Joy pasting stickers on Mother's hand and face.

How precious! I'm sure everyone chuckled and was touched to see Joy paying her respects to her Grandma that way.

Everything was fine until Eleanor stuck her nose in and removed the stickers. Why can't Martha make her daughter behave?

I calmed things down by letting Joy put a couple of stickers back on Mother's hand.

Joy is my daughter. Martha and Eleanor had no business undermining my parenting.

If only Mother could have seen! Mother loved Joy. She would have been delighted at what Joy was doing to say goodbye.

I never want to see Martha or Eleanor again!

Riverside Writers

This is It?
by Thomas J. Higgins

There are tubes down my throat. I want to talk, but my mouth will not open to utter aloud the words that I am thinking. I feel like I don't have the strength to move any part of my body. I am very weak and although I see light, I realize my eyes are closed. Occasionally I hear a familiar voice and make a feeble attempt to open my eyes and see a family member. They are leaning over me, trying to comfort me and smiling, but I see sadness in their eyes. I try to reach out and tell them that I love them, but the body fails.

I am sure I am in a hospital bed, because when I do open my eyes I can see bags of liquid hanging on a rack above my shoulder. I hear distant voices in the hallway and announcements on the PA system in the room.

I believe all of my family is in the room. I am very cold but am unable to ask anyone for a blanket.

Am I dying? Is this it? Family members are saying they love me and embracing me. Why can't I return the love? They can't hear me telling them how much they have meant to me, and how proud I am of them and what they have done with their lives.

I feel so helpless.

I don't recall having extended pain, as I am sure that I have been administered pain killing drugs. I am thankful for this. I am a sissy when it comes to pain. I am not afraid of dying, as I have had a good life, but I feel so low and sad right now.

What's going on now? Everything has shut down. I don't hear or see anything. No light. No nothing and I feel even colder. I have just lost my five senses. I am dead? Well I am still thinking. I guess the brain is still turned on.

Now I hear loud excruciating noises. Am I having another MRI? After a few minutes it is strangely quiet. I can see a flicker of light and now feel the sensation of warmth and moving through that tunnel of light that I heard about, from people who have talked about near death experiences. I begin to hear beautiful violin orchestral music, similar to Percy Faith and Andre Kostelantz. I know they have passed away and must have made it to this place. And the guy on PBS- What's his name? Oh yes, Andre Rieu. I think he is still alive. I must be in the right place; no heavy metal or rap music, thank the Lord.

I believe I have now come through the tunnel of light and no longer have the sensation of moving. I don't feel extreme heat, so I think I am in the right place. I open my eyes and see beauty all around. It's like the beginning scene of Rogers and Hammerstein's musical play, "Carousel" where Billy Bigelow is sitting on a stepladder and polishing the crystal glass stars and throwing them back to earth one by one.

I see a handsome and young man coming toward me. "Tom, I have been expecting you. Just call me Peter. Let me go back to my desk and get your file. Having looked it over, I feel we definitely have some things to discuss."

Well, it looks like we are on a first name basis. This is encouraging. Hopefully I can stay here in this place which I assume is heaven. It's beautiful. I hear music in the distance in harmony with the tinkling of the ever moving glass chandeliers and hanging mobiles that reflect the rainbow colors. I feel light breezes and the air smells fresh. I touch some of the hanging crystal. This takes care of four of my senses.

I wonder if people eat up here. I just realized that I have not seen anyone else here, other than Peter. I am curious as to what he has in my file. Will it be a list of all the sins I've committed on earth? Will I see any of my loved ones, who hopefully arrived here earlier? How about the people I did not like?

So many questions, but I feel good physically and there is no stress. I am still concerned; however, there is

Riverside Writers

no one around. I always loved being with people. Peter comes back with a file which looks very thin to me. I wonder if this is bad or good. Now I do feel stress building up.

I get up enough courage to ask, "Where is everyone?"

Peter's reply, "They're all at lunch."

Well now I guess I am operating on all cylinders. I am ready to find out the contents of the file in Peter's hand.

People You Might Meet

Danny the Cowboy
by Thomas J. Higgins
An excerpt from the book,
How Far is it From Richmond to Heaven?

Danny has been in a wheelchair all his life. He lives in a group home for special needs folks. His means of communication is tapping his right foot on the floor or making a single syllable sound. He does attempt to point to his picture/word board placed under his clear plastic tray, but this is difficult because his arms are atrophied and folded up toward his shoulders. His body is small and unsteady. This, however, does not keep him from being happy, smiling, and laughing most of the time.

I did one-on-one mentoring with him for a few years, while working part time with the Community Service Board. We became buddies. Often I took him out of the group home and pushed him in his wheelchair around the subdivision to get some fresh air instead of sitting and watching TV.

One Saturday morning we decided to go to a movie. I wheeled him into the theater, and asked him if he would like to sit in a regular seat. He made his single-syllable sounds and was almost jumping out of the wheelchair. I picked him up and sat him in the seat, moved the wheelchair out of the way, and sat down beside him. He was in seventh heaven. We were just two regular dudes sitting together watching a Saturday morning flick.

There were times when I worked part-time and stayed overnight. I was responsible for six residents living in the group home. Most of them were independent as far as their hygiene was concerned. Staff would help Danny with bathing and putting on his pajamas at night.

It was not easy trying to get him dressed after his shower. He would sit in his wheelchair and I on the commode seat top, that enabled me to be on a more even level with him. Putting on shirts was especially difficult when trying to get hands, arms, and elbows into the sleeves. As time went on I became more proficient getting him dressed. However, it never failed. I always worked up a sweat.

One particular evening while helping him get dressed he leaned over, smiled, and gave me a hug with his small rigid arms. That made it all worthwhile. This hug from a person who can't talk, had just communicated volumes to me! He was saying thank you for helping me. Thank you for caring that I am clean. Thank you for being my friend.

At night when I put Danny in bed, he lay very still in a fetal position. After covering him up, I usually put a tape or CD on his radio to lull him to sleep. In the morning he got out of bed and crawled around on his knees pulling out clothes he wanted to wear. His favorite clothing—cowboy hat, cowboy shirt, and cowboy boots. He also selected video tapes that he wanted to pack and take to his day program.

I have not worked with Danny for over fifteen years, but see him on occasion at the Community Service Board day program where I am a board member. When entering the room, he sees me. I hear noises made by his laughter and jumping up and down in the wheelchair. What a treat to see that big cowboy smile.

My wish is to be his friend forever. He is surely mine.

While Walking through the Park
by Thomas J. Higgins
An excerpt from the book,
How Far is it From Richmond to Heaven?

One Sunday afternoon in May I took Pat, Benny, and Jeff from the Wolfe Street group home to Alum Springs Park. It was a beautiful, warm and sunny day. We ate a picnic lunch and decided to take a little hike through the park for exercise.

After a short walk we came upon the crystal clear water making its way down the stream. I came up with the terrific idea of taking our shoes and socks off and wading into the water. I couldn't get any takers except Pat. While Benny and Jeff sat down by the stream, Pat and I made our way into the water. It was ice cold, and the rocks hurt our feet. We stayed for about two minutes! Pat and I helped each other back up to the bank where the others were sitting. We had mud and leaves all over our feet as we sat down.

I didn't have anything with which to wipe our feet. I decided I would take Pat's socks and try to wipe off his feet. What a mess! After I got him somewhat cleaned up, I got ready to clean off my feet with my socks.

At that moment, Jeff who was sitting to the left of me said, "Wait Tom". He grabbed my left leg and bent my knee so that he could reach my foot. Without hesitation, he took his clean hands and began wiping the mud and leaves off my foot.

I got cold chills as the story of Jesus washing the feet of his disciples rushed to my mind. I looked up, saw the gently swaying trees and blue sky, and silently thanked God for this very special moment with my friends in the park.

They Called Her Violet
by Norma E. Redfern

Eyes deep purple in light
Streaked with lavender plum,
fringed with blue-black lashes.
Lips like a small open blossom
Barely a smile settled on her face.
Freckles sprinkled softly
Across her cheeks and nose.
Tall, lean and slim as a cat.
It was her time of pleasure.
Yearning desire, seeking for more.
The knowledge of her heart,
The essence of her soul
Giving her spirit a new wish
In search of the source.
She waited and watched.
Like a willow in the wind
She walked with the moon's rays
Bending, swaying through her mind.
He said he would come,
Not till the moment was right.
Would she wait in vain?

The Vagabond
by J. R. Robert-Saavedara

A vagabond
With boot off
Sitting on a trash can
Scratching his toes.

From the streets of the city,
With a smiling face
Staring at the speeding world
Passing him.

The smiling face with rotting teeth
Framed in scraggly beard;
Crowned with a baseball cap
Does not mind, does not care.

He turns, and peers into the trash,
Picks-up his mail.
And goes on smiling, laughing
At the speeding world going nowhere.

Bill and I Knew
by Ron Russis

...I'm all about survival – and survive I will...
And as my brother would tell you, were he here,
"Those are some pretty-meaty dogs you've got;"
and I knew first-hand they'd gut out the same
as a bear, a deer or some farmer's hog; and I
knew from past experience that any kind of meat
feels good going down into a long-empty belly;
and I knew that the wide-eyed hungry can't taste
the difference between beef and pork or dog and
cat, all they know is how good not being hungry
feels and the way those hot juices heat one's gut,
how those chunks swell the belly round to full.
Yes, Bill and I knew full-well what the average
joe might do, what unexpected circumstances
could drive one to – whether these good people
wanted to believe it true or not, Bill and I knew;
we knew too well... and I grinned back at the man,
the policeman he'd brought with his writ to search,
my hunger pangs sated, my once empty belly full.

Two Pints a Day
by Ron Russis

He coughed as he swallowed, then said,
"There's too much coffee in that cup,"
as he added a third double of bourbon.
I could only watch in surprise, and we
were all amazed at how much he drank
and how he held his drink, and I don't
mean just the odd grip on his cup, but
that he never staggered or stumbled,
he never slurred a word – and we all
thought ourselves deceived with what
we believed, until we'd heard he died;
but, imagine our surprise – and his too
likely – on learning it wasn't cirrhosis,
but cancer of the liver.

The Fifth and Last Winter
by J. R. Robert-Saavedara

I met him in my fourth winter
A cold and long winter it was
He slowly thawed off the ice from my branches
He made the sap run in my veins again.

In the spring, he pruned every branch
He made me flower, like a Sun
Every single bud, he opened
And to every flower, he gave a bee.

In the summer, he was the breeze
And together we danced, under a cloudless sky
My branches, he filled with birds
That sang to us, during the speeding hours.

But now it is autumn again
My flowers carpet my roots
My leaves dress me like a queen
But now the wind is getting chill, and the birds are gone.

It is the fifth and coldest winter yet
The snow is deep; the wind is deathly cold
Oh wind, why did you not uproot me in the fall
When will my winters cease to come?

Ballad of the D & L Diner
by Joe Metz

The line was long at Johnny's store,
the snow was ankle high,
but people came from miles around,
a claim to fame to buy.

This jackpot worth ten thousand bucks
brought out two long-time friends,
Dwayne a well-known, crafty merchant,
Lester, a cook of many trends.

"You put up five, I'll do the same,
"ten chances then to win."
Lester chattered his cold "O.K.,
"Hey, Dwayne, we're movin' in."

The day they won, they drank till dawn,
with vows to share it all.
Dwayne said, "We'll buy an eatin' place,
"don't matter if it's small."

Their diner had just seven stools,
two booths that seated four,
but people who had eaten there
kept coming back for more.

While Lester cooked, Dwayne bussed the plates,
served meals with talk and smiles,
kept track of what their diner earned,
which came, it seemed, in piles.

Lester sat next to Dwayne one night,
after they'd closed the door.
"I want my share. I'm pullin' out,
"Can't stand this work no more."

Riverside Writers

Dwayne got red, said, "You're a fool,"
afraid of what he'd done,
gambled nights, while Lester slept,
in games he seldom won.

"I ain't no fool. I want my share!
"Our safe's there at your place."
Dwayne shook with fear, grabbed up a knife,
slashed Lester in his face.

Lester flailed, caught Dwayne's flushed neck,
with calloused, greasy hands,
they thudded to the diner floor,
their lives now gasping strands.

Dwayne gurgled blood, then Lester too,
still punching as they bled,
Lester cursed once more at Dwayne,
then both of them were dead.

They buried them beneath the snow,
not knowing how these friends,
who always seemed to share their luck,
could meet such tragic ends.

The priest who laid them in the ground,
who prayed for their salvation,
said, "Men who play the game of luck
will feel its devastation,

"For luck is not a game of chance,
God holds the winning ticket,
And these who doubted that He did
rest deep beneath this thicket."

How Do Mermaids Mate?
by Larry Turner

How do mermaids mate?
Mate with men, I mean. The short answer is—
sorry to disappoint you—they don't.
They're merMAIDS, for mercy sake,
not mermadams or mermothers.

The mermaids we see are like the honeybees,
infertile females. It's easy to lift the lid
of a hive and see what's happening inside.
But to enter the marine mansions
of the merfolk is an endeavor few
have accomplished, fewer still survived.

All we know for certain is that just
as there are three genders of bees,
there are at least four of merfolk. Beyond that,
I don't want to tell you something that later
turns out to be untrue, and so I'll say no more.

There is a myth that mermaids mate with men
through their mouths, and give birth there too,
to little mermaids, never male. How this myth arose
you may imagine, but I'll say no more.

The hormones of the mermaids developed
from their piscine ancestors, not known
for fidelity. But mermaids do like to cuddle,
and if you comb a mermaid's hair
and treat her well, she'll stay with you
all day, perhaps as long as a week.

Riverside Writers

In her company your every sensation
will be heightened: colors more vivid
than any you've ever seen, every sound
a song of consummate sweetness,
and just so with smell, touch and taste.
Her departure will leave you with a longing
that will last your whole life long.

I know.

So if ever you meet a mermaid on the beach,
take care. Will a day of joy be worth
years of thinking on what can never be?

Chuckles
by Jennifer Anne Gregory

I was eleven when I acquired my first horse. His name was Chuckles and he lived quite happily for a number of years inside my head along with an assortment of other animals I was permitted to own. These included three English Mastiffs, several goats, a duck named Cactus Jack, and a couple of cows. Cheap to keep, they required no feeding, no grande mansion and no offshore bank account. My parents were happy. For a time at least.

Mature years have their advantage, in that one finally understands and gains something called perspective. For example, it is typically not normal for a thirteen year old pubescent child to gallop wildly around the field hockey pitch during an all important inter-schools county finals, arms stretched forward, hands clutching a pair of invisible reins, each straining against the airy head of an alarmingly absent horse as it prepared to jump the visiting team's hockey goal.

That the child was me, I would rather not say.

When the offspring in question, a.k.a. *me,* tripped over the ball, my parents were a bit troubled to hear the announcement from the referee via the loud speakers that "in the interest of good sportsmanship, both rider and animal should retire." Chuckles, I took pains to explain, appeared to be suffering from a nervous condition typical of thoroughbreds.

I understand now, at least from their point of view. The welfare of the transparent Chuckles was apparently far more important than the retrieval of a rather large pair of navy blue school knickers from off the pitch. It seemed the elastic snapped at the critical juncture between take off and approach to the five foot triple spread goal-jump. Likely, this might explain the fall, hurling the hockey sticks of several players from teams home and away to a premature demise. My back and even my head were littered with assorted arms, legs, feet and other body parts. From beneath the groans, moans and choice words, each knickered leg sat poised at the base of each grazed shin. One official game cancellation, two gym instructors and a school nurse later, I was at last upright. Stepping out of the offending underwear and head held high, I walked myself and the lame Chuckles off the field, hand tucked neatly beneath the bridle, under his chestnut chin. But not before the previously mentioned announcement unleashing the nuances of pure bred equines onto a stunned crowd.

In company, I neither recall, nor admit to any of the above. Nevertheless, other than my end laid bare to a wet Saturday afternoon in November, two other, very important discoveries were made that day. First, my parents, based innocently on the side lines and ready to serve a choice of orange juice or hot chocolate at half time, learned they could survive just about anything from here on out. Second, the mandatory wearing of that English school girl essential, the dark blue wrap around thigh high gym skirt that always flapped skyward during windy winters, ceased being mandatory. From here on out, it would be "leisure trousers of a sweatshirt-like material."

According to the letters sent home to parents the following week, it was a matter of public health.

The Structure of the Poop
by Dan Walker

Each pile of horse poop has a structure to it. The stuff comes out as individual rounded cubes, but they land in a pile, squashed and sort of wedge-shaped. The pile is a pyramid usually, but not always; there's no industry standard, and you have to respect that. Bill has learned this the hard way, like so much else. If you try to scoop a whole pile that's just a little too big, you won't just drop a couple of pieces, but maybe half of it. Then it's likely to separate and roll all over the place. So divide it into manageable halves. Also you have to look around the lot: where does it make the most sense to go first? Here's where: into the rough at the bottom. You want to go there first, with an empty cart, not when it's full and hard to maneuver and you have to push it all up hill. Avoid impulse: it's like building a forecast for week two: avoid impulse. Even if the models all agree, don't buy in all at once. Hedge your bets: "chance of," "occasional," "partly to mostly"... and use percentages. Even in a monotonous hot spell there's enough challenge to make it interesting.

Bill and Tally are down to three horses, but it still helps to clean the lot twice a day. Tally's off for the summer now, and she can do it in the morning. By late afternoon he's home and can do it. He *wants* to do it, you understand. He needs the exercise, for one. Also it's something he gets points for—they're *her* horses. He doesn't have to do this. But he knows this, that sooner or later he'll forget something that *is* his job. You can never have too many points.

When he's done with the barn area, he takes the wheelbarrow out to the end of the lot where there's a gravel riding ring, and empties the cart onto the manure pile at the other end of the ring. It's like a little range of mountains by now. Very much like. In fact, he likes to

Riverside Writers 63

think of it that way: each foot of elevation converts to five hundred feet of imaginary terrain. There's a valley in one place where he imagines a development—all over three thousand feet, so there's likely a lot of big hemlock, with good building sites near the stream. And further up there'll be great views and ski slopes. He's working on a peak at the north end that will top four thousand and—in his imagination—will really catch the snow since it faces north and west over the pasture.

All this depends on cleaning twice a day. Horses don't like stepping in their own excrement, but if you let it pile up, they trample it all around and ruin the structure, and you have to rake it up. Then it's just drudgery. At some point over the winter they'll have to bring out the Kubota and move most of the stuff to pasture or garden, and the whole range will have to be rebuilt—like after an eruption or a tsunami, some thousand-year event—and planned from scratch. A real challenge.

When he's dumped the wheelbarrow, he scoops up any pile left in the ring and tries to throw it, not onto the big pile, but beyond it, out over the fence into the pasture to feed the insurgency there. A tyrant rules the pasture, you see, and the freedom-fighters need re-supplying. Hard to make a game out of that. It's just something you have to do.

But the next part really matters. He puts down the pitchfork and shoves the wheelbarrow as far as he can out over the gravel back toward the barn. If the barrow goes three pitchfork lengths, he's pitched a scoreless inning. If it goes four, it's hitless. If the cart falls over, runs are scored, he's knocked out of the game, and he has to roll the die, which he keeps in his pocket, to see just how many runs come in. If it's less than three, the bullpen holds for him, and he wins. More than three, and he loses—he has a weak-hitting team. What happens if it's exactly three? Then he leaves in a tie ball-game, and there's no decision. So far, at about half-way through the year (June 30), he's 12-3 with a no-hitter and a 1.25 ERA. An all-star season is in progress. On this day, Tally is in the kitchen, cutting up zucchini. Tally is authentic about cooking, to the point of heroism. She will not use a Veg-0-Matic, even if its results are indistinguishable from her knife's. "In the first place," she would tell you, with the knife pointing at your throat, the "machine"—it's always called that, to avoid dignifying it with a name—"uses electricity." There is often not a "second place," because there doesn't need to be. Any reason of hers would be sufficient. Yes, the composite material in the knife would have taken much electricity to make, but he knows better than to say that. You can be right, his father had told him, or you can be happy.

By now, she has spent half the afternoon readying a particular combination of sprouts, greens, tubers, and other plants for stir-frying. He is allowed to do the stir-frying—a forgiving process that, unlike laundry, is hard to spoil. He happens to be good at seasoning. His secret is to not to do much of it. If he wants to really pile in the curry or the Old Bay or the Frank's, he waits till it's on his own plate.

She has also baked some zucchini bread, which took the rest of the afternoon. This has been a rough day, she tells him as she shakes water and oil into the pan, causing an explosion of steam.

"Trouble among your children?" he asks affably, meaning her animals.

"Hm!" She shakes her head grimly at the ironies in her pan. He realizes she has not actually looked at him since this morning, before dark, when she watched him leave for work and could see him only as a silhouette in the bedroom as she groggily reminded him to do something that she must have known even then he would forget to do.

"Did you put the new registration in the car?"

"No. Damn. And I was supposed to put the stickers on the plates, too, wasn't I?"

Riverside Writers 65

"I already did that while you were down at the barn, but you need to take the registration out there now while you're thinking about it." Then she smiles, as if she had meant to do that. Why? As a sort of apology for nagging? When he's back inside, she says: "There's a call for you on the machine. From Harold at your office." She always refers to CompuWeather as his "office," another example of the denial-by-generic-reference strategy. To Tally, weather forecasting seems not so much a real job as a kind of sport he is somehow getting paid for.

"Oh. Probably no big deal," he says. "I probably left something there that he thinks I'll need this weekend."

"I don't know." Still looking down. "He didn't sound as blasé as you guys usually do. Also he left his cell number."

"OK, I'll call him."

Now she looks at him. "Mono has cancer."

He has to think. He's not good on sudden implications.

"Oh…. Gee, that's bad. She's a great little dog. Is that what the lab said?"

"Call Harold. Then I'll tell you about it."

* * *

"You're doing *what?*" she says, after he's talked to Harold.

"It's nothing new. I've done weekend shifts before. Don hurt himself and I have to come in to do the weather video for the web site."

"What's wrong with Don?"

"He fell off his roof and broke his ass. Literally." *Change the subject!* "Listen, what's the deal with Mono?"

"She has a nasal tumor." She eats her salad, trying to get an olive on the end of her lettuce-choked fork, then eats it off the fork while she looks right at him. Under other circumstances it would have been very erotic.

"Can they treat it?"

"There's radiation and chemo, just like with people. If we want to pay three thousand dollars and drive to Raleigh and leave her, and then pick her up after a month."

"That's a lot—," he starts. She is looking down at her salad again. He continues: "But if that's what you want to do…"

Wrong thing to say, wrong thing!

"What *I* want to do?" she says quickly. "She's your dog, too. What do *you* want to do?"

"Well, you know the money better than I do. And what's the prognosis—if we do or don't?"

"A month if we don't. If we do—" (she sighs) "—maybe three months, maybe three years." She puts down her fork. "Why's *this* weekend so important? Why does there *have* to be a weather video."

"There's a storm. I'm going to be on TV. Just Bloomberg, but still—" He paused. "Look, we're going to Raleigh."

"What?"

"We'll both go. Or you can drop her off, and I'll go pick her up. She's our dog, she's family. That's it. I don't care what it costs. For the price of a used Camry, we have the greatest little dog in the world for at least three more months."

Recovery! Extra bases, at least.

She says nothing, looks at her fork, then looks up and smiles.

"Well, good for you." She gives his hand a squeeze. "I'll go. You stay here and do what you have to do."

And two RBIs. Back over .300, baby!

The World of Women and Men

Seed Planting
by Ummie

Passion pleasing and kneading
Harmony and unity
Is your treatment for me
Carefully planning
Placing one sensuous step
In front of the other
Making sure your formula is correct
Making sure your formula is working

The quintessential gardener
Tending me has become a researched
Sexually provocative garden scheme
I am provoked to a whisper scream to the sky
Ever wanting to return to you over and over
To be filled with your living water

Fulfilling my insatiable appetite
Takes precedence over your life's weight
Just to make it tight
You have probed, weeded and cultivated
To plant seeds of contentment and satisfaction
Allowing me to grow to completion
As an erotic, electric, lovely flower

Hit and Run
by Ummie

Are you the one
Who hits and runs
Are you the one?
Your days are numbered
They have come and gone
You didn't want to stay
For the life's fight
You do it on the hit and run plan
Oh sure you knew
Where your joy stick would land
The inside of me you didn't have a clue
That reed in your mouth
You began to blow
The tune of persuasive sound
Lyrical movements
You put it down

Still on the run huh?
Trying to beat the sun
Never mind nothing is tight
Because
You ain't going to do right
You will always be the one
Who just hits and runs

I Want to Kiss You
by J. R. Robert-Saavedra

I want to kiss you,
At the top
Of the spiral staircase,
Or the bottom!
It does not matter.
I just want to hold you in my arms,
And kiss you.

I want to walk
Behind you
To the top
Of the circular staircase,
And warmed by the Sun,
Hold you to my chest,
And kiss you.

I want to hold your hand,
And lead you down
The spiral staircase
To the bottom,
And among the wine barrels,
Hold you in my arms,
And kiss you.

To Claudia
by J. R. Robert-Saavedra

In mornings full
    Of moon shined dew
Of birds a flutter
    And full of song
Of coffee smell
    And flowers' bloom.

I see your eyes
    In the light blue sky
I sense you close
    And smell your smell
I reach across
    And touch your hand.

If storm
    Be blowing
If snow
    Be high
A sense of calm
    And warmth and love
Would hold my soul
    And hold my mind.

In Different Places
by Michelle O'Hearn

With mango in her eyes and plum on her lips
Powdering her face to perfection
She daydreams about the evening ahead.

Will he like this color?
What about his brother?
Is it too soon to start thinking of another
when he's only just passed last month?

Removing the hairstyle
She doesn't yet want to smile
Puts the dress back on the hanger
and closes the closet door tight....

###########

With love in his eyes and fire in his heart
Revving the truck and his nerve to ask the question
He plans for the evening ahead.

Will she like where I take her?
My brother would never blame her
For falling in love with me after a month.
Driving the quarter mile
He thinks about making her smile
Excited about a future with a love he can nurture
and holding the steering wheel tight....

Riverside Writers

Heels
by Ron Russis

She liked to say
her mother was a looker, but
I always thought she meant to say hooker.

Wherever she went
wolf whistles followed close
behind—and men's eyes—always, always

their eyes—drawn
to that sway, the provocative,
the suggestive way she moved her hips,

the flirtatious way
she licked her lips; and that last,
my god, how slowly that last got done

when she was sure
she had their eye; and it done
as if a taunt, a tease, a hint at pleasures

to come or maybe denied.
And without a backward glance
she led the sound of her stiletto heels,

as they staccato-tapped
down the walk, her motion driven
smoothly on by those curvy legs and thighs

that left each man's eyes
glued to her diminishing view; and you
could be sure every man she passed knew

what the other was thinking, and that she knew too.

Valentine's Day Surprise
by Donna H. Turner

Nina opened the door after the doorbell rang twice. Dom stood at the entrance smiling and holding a dozen red roses.

"Happy Valentine's Day," he said as he handed her the flowers.

Taking his hand, she led him into the apartment. Nina had the mixings for vodka martinis ready and went over to the counter to fix them.

"I could use one of those. I had a hell of a day. The Jackson account fell to pieces, and you-know-who had to fix it."

"Have a drink and relax. You don't have to fix anything else. Come on, let me massage your neck. You look so tense." She rubbed his forehead, then smoothed out the veins on his neck. "If you're hungry, I can call out for something. Otherwise, there is just me and thou. Alone. Together. Besides, I bought some satin sheets to love you on. Red, for Valentine's Day."

"You do know how to make me feel good," Dom cooed. "That feels great."

"How about it, then? Can we try out the new sheets all night?"

Dom didn't hesitate. "How can I resist? I'll tell Doreen I had to work late, and I'm spending the night at the company's apartment. By the way, you look fantastic."

"Thank you, kind sir, compliments of that photo shoot today. I spent my whole fee buying this negligee. You'll see it copied by everyone next winter, but you, my love, are seeing the original article."

"It looks wonderful. How did I ever get so lucky? A guy twice your age."

"So you keep telling me. You're certainly not old when we make love. And besides, I think experience counts. I will never want anyone else."

"Could I have another martini? My glass is empty."

Nina poured him another and sat beside him on the couch.

He looked at her glass. "Hey, babe, you're drinking water. No booze tonight? You on the wagon?"

She laughed and answered quietly, "Something like that."

Dom sipped his drink thoughtfully. "Are you okay? There's nothing wrong, is there?"

"Of course not," Nina reassured him. "Only, I do have something to tell you."

"Oh, Nina, if there is anything wrong, we can fix it. What did the doctor have to say yesterday? Did he find anything?" Dom appeared truly concerned. "I knew you weren't looking well. What's the matter?"

"Nothing is the matter. Everything is absolutely normal for a woman who will have a baby in seven months."

"Oh. I see," Dom managed to say. "How did it happen?"

"You know, Dom, it happens sometimes when people come together. This isn't exactly the reaction I was hoping you'd have. I thought you'd be happy. You said you wanted to be a father someday. Someday is here. What's the problem?"

"You know the problem, Nina. I'm married. Do you understand? I'm a hundred-percent married. For nine years."

"That can be taken care of. They do have such a thing as divorce." The color rose in Nina's face. She stood up and started pacing. "You son of a bitch! We've been together four years. This is a hell of a time to become the loving husband. I thought you loved me!"

"I do love you, babe, I really do," Dom pleaded.

Nina turned and faced him. "All right. You listen and listen good. I am going to have this baby, wife or no wife. You get on the phone and tell your wife you want a divorce now!"

"I will," Dom muttered, "but not tonight. It's Valentine's Day, for God's sake. It's our anniversary."

"And yet you are spending the evening here with me. I'm beginning to feel sorry for your wife."

"Nina, don't be like that. You know I love you—and only you." Dom added, "It hasn't been a marriage since I met you."

"Well then, get into the bedroom and call your wife. If you don't, you can kiss me and your new baby goodbye."

Out in Leesburg, Doreen picked up the phone. "Doreen, it's me. I know it's late, honey, but I wanted you to know that I'm too tired to drive home. I'm staying at the firm's apartment here in the city. Nobody else is using it, so I might as well."

"Dominick, what time is it? I was already in bed asleep. Are you in the apartment now? When did you get there?"

"About an hour ago. I just finished up the Jackson file. I'm exhausted."

"That's funny," Doreen replied. "When I talked to Maggie at six, she said you had gone for the day. Something's not right. What are you up to?"

"Nothing, sweetheart, nothing. Maggie must have got it mixed up."

"Your secretary does not get things mixed up. Dominick. I know you're not at the apartment because I called there just before I went to bed. So where the hell are you? Don't play games with me because you'll lose."

"Doreen, I'm sorry. I didn't want it to go like this."

"Who is she?"

"Her name is Nina. She's a model for Fleury-Rite Fashions. I'm sorry."

Riverside Writers 79

"You call me at eleven from your skinny model's apartment to tell me you're sorry? I ordered dinner from Andre's, had my hair highlighted, and bought a 600-thread set of white satin sheets. For the first time in years, I am lying on these expensive sheets in nothing but my birthday suit, waiting for you to crawl in beside me, and you tell me you have someone else? Do you have any sense of decency in you?"

"Doreen, you're overreacting. Nina told me tonight she's pregnant. I can't abandon her now."

"Oh, I see. I'm easy to abandon. Well, how does this sound, Mister Caught with Your Fly Open? You go back to your young skinny pregnant model. Or if you want to talk some more, feel free. I won't hear you.

"I'm turning over in my big brick house, in my large master suite, in my king-size bed with 600-count satin sheets, naked. Oh, and I forgot to add, half your retirement. Think about it, you jerk." With that, she dropped the phone with Dominick still on the line, turned out the light, smiled, and went back to sleep.

The Profane Egg
by Anne Heard Flythe

Dear Phillip, he would be remembered for his damned two minute soft boiled breakfast egg. Not one and a half, not two and a quarter minutes, but exactly two goddamned minutes. An indulgence she had granted in the beginning out of love and her perception of duty, then in the hope of peace, although it constituted perpetuation of one more small tyranny. She could not face asking Phillip to change nor did she have the temerity to tell him what a pompous ass he had become.

Their marriage never had been one of moonlight, sex and laughter as she had hoped, and it had grown onerous under the weight of twenty years. They had been young, naïve, ignorant, in love, their differences both critical and unperceived at the time.

This morning at breakfast she ate her cereal as quietly as its guaranteed crunch permitted, waiting patiently for the metallic "ting" of the small two minute timer beside her bowl. At the sound she scurried to the kitchen to retrieve the perfect egg which she rushed to Phillip in its English porcelain doubled ended eggcup. Then, ceremoniously, handed him the special scissors with which he snipped off the egg's top, shell and all, to permit the scooping out of its rich succulence with the tiny oval gilt silver spoon designed for that specific purpose.

She was comforted by the fact that chewing vigorously on her crisp, whole wheat toast would mask the wet sound of his enjoyment of the daily ritual, the ceremonial consumption of his goddamned egg.

She sat quietly, holding her coffee cup close to her lips like a shield, sipping cold coffee, avoiding conversation. Finally Phillip stood, untucked his napkin, coughed wetly, blotted his lips and placed the neatly folded napkin by his plate.

She averted her face to avoid his eggy breath as in passing he bestowed the customary air kiss above her hair.

She waited motionless until she heard the front door close behind him and the sound of his precious BMW pulling out of the garage. He was gone for the day until his return for his evening cocktail and dinner at six.

A bubbling up of wicked guilt and mischief curled her lips into an unfamiliar grin. She didn't clear away the crumbs or the dishes. She left the damned egg to coagulate in its special cup, the silver spoon to tarnish, the milky dregs to sour in coffee cups and bowls. She didn't touch the two soiled crumpled napkins, as close as their lips would ever come again. A thought that afforded her considerable satisfaction.

She abandoned the cluttered messy altar to habit. A liberated spirit, she light-footed it upstairs to her bedroom, and resumed packing a second, larger suitcase. For a moment she held her closed hand above a carefully folded silk dress then dropped the odious egg timer into the open suitcase. It would serve as a memoir should she ever question her decision.

Family and Other Creatures

Play Time
by Jim Gaines

My son's highway
Always a bridge to everywhere
Spans a quicksand
Boggy with old habit
His darting eyes bulldoze
Movie set walls
Reality incorporated
His war cry shatters
Conventions fragile as French crystal
Sweeps aside the hour
Others call failure
By the logic of puzzles
To the drafting of motor-like skills
To seats in which to keep one's place
To the register of weaker moments
My son pays
No toll to attention
Refusing to impale himself
On the purely obvious
His only clock reads
A mystery beyond time
A challenge to Einstein's theories
Emerald speed

Sunday Swimming
(That Summer of '62)
by Ron Russis

They couldn't keep themselves from watching me –
their eyes fixed on those brutal welts the belt
had branded on my skin, those C-shaped marks
of the buckle's end that ran wild across where
even my short-sleeved shirt couldn't keep them hid –
where I had failed to dodge when he had flailed – struck!

The other swimmers' mothers' eyes kept watching – struck
by the ugly sight and some fathers, too, had their eyes on me,
looking cold and long upon those welts that nothing hid,
as my old man, not 'father,' took another lengthy belt
from his bottle and noting their stares shouted, "Wear
your shirt, boy. No one here needs to see those marks.

Keep acting up. Keep it up and you can mark
my words, before it's over you'll sure be struck
by the errors of your ways and you'll know where
and when you're best off in believing me,
'cause if you don't, you'll find yourself wearing my belt
and there ain't no place I don't know where you can hide!

No, if you don't watch yourself I'll strap your hide.
You'll think back later on the merits of those marks,
no doubt give greater thought to the weight of the belt
and just how often, last and next, you might get struck.
A piece of good advice, you watch and mind me,
as I'll give you 'what for' at the drop of a hat where

and when it pleases me. I'll thump on you anywhere,
> *anywhere*

I take a mind! You ought know by now you can't stay hid,
you can't get safe away from me, boy, not from me!
Oh, sure, you could run-off now and hide, but that only
> marks

time – you'll get hungry and get home later – and struck –
and then you'll find yourself bit by my wide snake of a belt."

I knew he was right, at least about the bite of his belt,
though there were times, when I'd snuck in when and where
he was passed out on sofa or floor, mumbling or
silenced, struck
down by his bottle – and with no need for me to stay hid,
as it would be hours before he could think to mark
the passage of time and where he'd been, let alone me.

No, he'd be no threat to me, so long as I timed my visit right, where
and when his trousers still wore his belt, I wouldn't need a place to hide.
No, on those days I'd wear no new marks. On those days I'd be gone before he struck.

Go Fetch a Switch
by Ron Russis

He told me, "Go fetch a switch!"
and if I was unsure before,
I sure knew better now,
of what was coming on.

And I was slurred a reminder
as the porch screen slammed shut,
his words straining through the mesh,
"Don't you bring anything back
that won't *spring* and *sting*.
I want it to have some *snap*,
able to slice air and raise a welt,
to leave a mark, a deep impression
on seat and mind, enough to make
you mind! After a good cry
and a short nap you'll think better
on doing the likes of that again!"

I always wondered, just what "that" was,
but he never said…

A stand of hick'ry grew behind the sty
and it was there I went to fetch the thing,
where I found his whip, selected a switch,
but stiffer than the ones I used to bring.

I was slow to learn, but I was learning…
and so I made a hasty stop at the chopping block
and from the woodchip pile mounded there
I pulled out a pair of slim, wide, but not too tall,
cedar shakes and slipped them into my britches'
rear pockets to ward off some of the coming sting.

He wasn't apt to notice…
and if I shouted loud and played my part

today's whipping might go easy. But,
when I got back I could hear him still
ranting loudly along and going on about losing hands –
a straight that lost out to a flush,
of two pair beat by three of a kind
(the winner with a pair in the hole),
of spilled liquor and this month's rent
and the other bills still left to pay.

And for just a moment I thought,
as he paused for breath and balance,
that maybe he'd gone and forgot
what he'd sent me for, there were times
he did; but this time luck wasn't with me,
it was with him, though not in his cards.

And he surprised me again when he said,
"Time to drop your britches boy."
And while he switched me up good
the blood dribbled down off my chin,
as I bit my lip and tried to suppress my cries…

The Clay Girl
by Maxine Clark

Belle, my mama from rural Georgia, married my father in 1947. Mama was the girl in "You can take the girl out of the country but you can't take the country out of the girl." And, that is a direct quote from my daddy. To prove the point, Mama ate red Georgia clay.

Driving from Savannah on a sunny day to take school clothes to my cousins in Jacksonville, Georgia, Mama stopped the car along the roadside to visit a clay hole. A clay hole was a special place with both white and red clay exposed after a hard rain. Using a stick stripped of its bark, Mama dug deep into the earth to retrieve a chunk of moist clay. She removed the top layer to expose the clean layer underneath. Always, she shared the morsel with me and my two younger brothers. But, along the road to worldliness, Mama learned of parasites. She stopped eating clay. When Mama stopped eating clay, she ate dry, chunky, chalky Argo starch. The tell-tale signs of white starch sat in the corner of her mouth until someone brought it to her attention and then she hurriedly wiped it away. But before then—in those days of youth and sunshine—she ate clay.

Mama loved peaches. Driving to Jacksonville, Mama stopped whenever she saw peach trees tucked away from the main roadway. We would get out and look for fallen unblemished red and yellow peaches that had ripened in the warm sun. Sometimes, Mama hoisted me on her shoulder so that we could pluck fruit from higher up in the trees. Smacking our lips while savoring sweet juicy peaches, we continued our trip along bumpy and winding roads shaded by a canopy of trees. Mama maneuvered those roads carefully until we reached lots of blinding sunlight and Aunt Mattie's house. Presto! The old, weathered, plank house with its shimmering, glazed, tin roof seemed to magically appear before my eyes.

Mama slowly drove towards the house and stopped a short distance from the porch. Relatives rushed towards us.

"Lawdy Belle, we were worr'ed about you and those kids trav'lin by ya'self all way from Sa'vana. Child, you sumthin'!"

All of the aunts, uncles, and cousins would be there. Like joy on wings, laughter, hugs, and kisses flew from one to the other. Comments were made about me. "She's lookin' a littal po; needs some pork to fatten 'er up. How's 'er asthma?"

As the four of us climbed out of the car, outstretched hands reached around Mama and someone said, "Step aside, Belle, let me give you a hand with those boxes."

Mama laughed and talked as we walked towards the weathered wooden porch with its beaten-up straw laced chairs. A huge block of glistening ice sweated on top of a bed of sawdust that had been placed inside of a large aluminum tub.

Mama would say, "You all go and wash your hands so nothing gets on these clothes for school. I want all of you to try 'em on in case I need to take something back to the store."

Someone hollered, "Let those kids have them chars."

As if playing musical chairs, my brothers and I scrambled to grab a seat in three of the worn straw chairs that were unraveling in the center, but with still enough support for a small round bottom. Relatives sat on wooden crates, leaned on the porch railing, or stood while waiting for the cardboard boxes to be opened and the fashion show to begin.

Cousins pranced in tartan plaid skirts, dungarees, white socks, red and blue polo shirts, and long sleeved white shirts. The show ended with my mother's admonition: "Don't wear these things before school starts and change your clothes when you get home!"

After the fashion show, we kids ran off to play in an old rusting car from the '40's that smelled of oil, mildew, and old wet newspapers. Later in the day, as the sun

Riverside Writers

gradually receded from the sky, adults and children gathered on the porch sucking on chunks of ice that an uncle had chipped with an ice pick. Out of mason and jelly jars, we sipped cool lemonade made from well water. The sour sweet taste of sugar, lemon rind, and lemon pulp swirled together in well water. Well water whose essence conjured images of travel through layers of clay and rock deep within the earth.

Aunt Mattie would say to Mama, "I'm gonna git you a slice of poun' cake to go with that lemonade. Got up early this mornin' and whipped it up so that the house would be cool by the time y'all got heah."

My mama would take the cake, pinch off a piece, and she would swallow. Then, she would take a sip of the lemonade, smile, and inhale the earthiness, the pleasure of moist, rich clay.

Family Night
by S. Kelley Chambers

Quality time shared, bonds built, trust and communication foundations formed...SCREECH! Hormones brought it all to a halt.

One cold wintery Friday night, my husband, Darrin and I, decided to take our two younger sons, twelve-year-old Desmond and fourteen-year-old Travonté to the movies for our monthly family night. With four adult tickets in our hand, we headed for screen number three. Carrying two warm freshly popped and drowned-in-melted-butter tubs of popcorn, four large sodas, and an assortment of Junior Mints, Goobers, Twizzlers, Raisinettes and Mike & Ikes, we entered the theater.

Leaving one vacant seat between themselves, the boys sat in the row in front of us. Placing the popcorn on an empty chair, Travonté leaned back and propped his feet on the unfilled seat in front of him. He ripped open his candy, turned the box up to his mouth and drained the contents in a matter of minutes. Desmond placed the plastic wrapper of the Twizzlers in his mouth, tore it open and began stuffing the spiral red licorice sticks in his mouth, one after the other, until they were gone. To this day, I swear, I don't think either of them ever chewed.

After eating all the candy and drinking half of the sodas, all during the previews, they began reaching hands into the tub, grabbing and stuffing handfuls of popcorn into their mouths. It took every bit of my will-power to restrain myself from intervening and telling them to 'slow down.'

Ten minutes into the movie, they were pushing the tub of popcorn back and forth and exchanging words.

"You take it," Desmond whined. "You had it last."

"No I didn't," Travonté huffed, shoving the nearly empty tub back at Desmond.

Riverside Writers

"I'm not holding it." Desmond hissed and hit it back toward Travonté.

I watched the distracting scene for a few minutes before leaning forward and whispering to them, "Both of you ate the popcorn, so sit the tub in the middle so that whoever wants more can get it and whoever wants to go for a refill can take it to the concession stand."

"But he placed the popcorn closest to him so he could eat more." Desmond whined while reaching over and pushing the tub further away from him.

Travonté, in retaliation, thrust his hand out to stop the tub from coming close to him, causing popcorn to fly up like it was air popped. Desmond then grabbed a handful of popcorn and threw it at Travonté. Instantly they began shouting and throwing kernels at each other as movie-goers turned around and shushed us to be quiet.

Leaning forward, I snatched the tub from them, spilling what was left on the floor, the seats and on them, I angrily growled through clenched teeth, "You ungrateful little Neanderthals. You won't have to worry about this anymore, the next time, Dad and I will go to the movies alone."

They rolled their eyes at each other, settled down, and watched the movie. Darrin and I learned a quick lesson that day in letting-go, and even though it ended well, from that day forward, they were happy to go out with their friends, and we were happy to see them go.

Sink or Swim
by Greg Miller

Prelude

My wife and I both work, and have two daughters. This may not sound particularly noteworthy, except that my daughters, Anne and Colleen, are as different as the sun and moon. My older, Colleen, is mentally and physically challenged, requiring constant attention and monitoring. Since my wife's job leaves little leeway or flexibility for time off, I handled this chore and did so without question or complaint—just as I had been raised to treat every obligation and requirement. So, every day I woke, washed, dressed and fed my oldest, cleansed her messes and did what was expected of a parent and primary care provider. When our second child, Anne, was born we happily found her to be fully capable, but even so, because of her age I inherited additional burdens, which I—at least in theory anyway—thought I could handle. But just when I have life figured out, and set my eyes firmly on the horizon, things change. In my case, the storm clouds gathered quickly.

Act I—The Rain Falls

Exhausted from my usual morning routine of parental duties, I entered my office and immediately saw a note with the message "staff meeting at 9 am." A few minutes of foolish hope passed until the appointed hour. I sat in the staff meeting, staring at the faux-wood tabletop, quietly hoping and passively willing that the rumors weren't true. But alas, our funding had been cut. Starting next week we would go to sixty percent pay and time. That night, as I attempted to gain a few hours rest, my dreams poured forth.

Water stretched in every direction, disappearing into a gray haze, and lapped at the eaves of the house. I sat upon the peak of the first floor roof, my arms hooked around my daughters. Slowly, inexorably, the water crept up, submerging the first floor completely. I dragged the children up onto the second story. For the youngest, this was easy; she was small and fully capable. But for my oldest, in her twenties, her infirmities made doing so a challenge in terms of size, compliance and cognition. Yet, I managed to do it, only to watch as the water reached the second story, and crawled closer. As the water reached us, I clutched my ears, a painful buzzing echoing in them.

I awoke, sweating and breathing hard, my heart racing to the beep-beep of my alarm clock. With dull movements, I fought to clear my head of the cobwebs of sleep, and make sense of my dream, but a sudden rush of reality swept in with a checklist of duties and chores to perform.

The loss of pay necessitated painful cuts in our accustomed lifestyle, yet the changes resulted in more "free time," though much of it taken by chores, looking for work, and transitioning to work at home.

Act II—The Water Rises

Another staff meeting. Unsurprisingly, the axe fell. No funding—no work—no company. After mid-March everyone would be let go, with the office closing by end of May. Despite this news, I was offered the opportunity to help close the office, for which I would be paid on an hourly basis. As the whole IT department, my duty was to purge the company of the assets I labored to acquire and maintain for the last few years.

I spent days wrestling with my thoughts, from gathering inventory, counting assets to quantifying value. So, for a time, my unwanted dreams stayed away. Yet, they lurked behind the curtains waiting for a second act.

So inevitably, one fitful evening, as I struggled to sleep, the curtain rose again in my dreams.

We scrambled up as far onto the peak as we could, yet the water continued its inexorable march, until lapping against our feet. Though I could feel it touch my skin, it was neither warm nor cold. The girls did not cry as it lapped at their ankles. I pulled them to the chimney, the only part of the house still visible. Once the water reached my chest, I used my feet to gain a foothold on the brick sides. When it reached my chin, I slipped, my face plunging under the dark water.

With a gasp I popped up, the alarm resounding in my head, my lungs sucking in gobs of air. Brushing the sweat off my forehead, I swung my feet onto the floor. Though thankful to be awake, I shivered with uncertainty.

Colleen's case manager called; a group home spot had opened up. Would I be interested? I hesitated, and scheduled a visit on my free time, but by the time I did, the spot had been filled. Despite this, the case manager assured me she'd call if another opening became available.

Act III—Sink or Swim

I scrambled to determine what should stay, and what should go. Is it trash, or does it have value, and if so, how much? Decisions are made, corners are cut, and inevitably something gets lost in the process. Furniture and other assets disappear, some discarded, donated, or picked over by those with money, jobs, and a future. The list shortens as the deadline approaches; the nearly empty office echoed with silence. Staff slips out the door leaving their keys behind, the click of the door locking their only goodbye.

My office empties as the last of the inventory leaves, and what little assets remain lay stacked on remaining furniture in the common area, priced and ready to venture into the undiscovered country. I lay awake at night, ticking off what remains, as time, like grains of sand in the hourglass, is slipping past. Troubled by these thoughts, sleep does not come easily, but when it does, so do my dreams.

Water reached my chin, as I stood on the top of the chimney. All evidence of the house now lay beneath the surface. The girls hung listlessly from my arms as I kept their heads up, but still the water rose. I tipped my head back, catching breaths when I could, but soon, I was treading water. As I did so, the girls began taking in water; I kicked harder, but my legs grew tired. I lifted one child, then the other, until the pain numbed my limbs and my breath grew short. Anne began to cry, but this stopped quickly when she took in a mouthful of water.

The rational part of my mind spoke up, telling me I had to choose—one or the other—as there was no way to survive together. As I looked into Colleen's big beautiful blue eyes, full of unconditional love and trust, I slipped my arm from under her – her eyes widened, and with pursed lips she muttered, "Papa" and slipped beneath the water. My heart thudded, every beat sending waves of pain through my limbs. Closing my tear filled eyes to shut out the reality of what I had done, I grabbed hold of Anne, and kicked harder. She wrapped her little arms around my neck, as I nearly choked on the decision I'd made.

I lay awake—out of breath—drenched in sweat, my body aching as if I'd run a marathon. With leaden limbs I rolled upright, only to be startled by the alarm beeping. I slapped it off, wishing I could do the same with my dreams. Walking to their separate rooms, I look in at Colleen and Anne, as both sleep soundly, untroubled by the events surrounding our family. If only I could gain some closure.

Act IV—Endings

May ended quickly. My ex-boss left his now empty office, and I was the only one left. I gathered the last box of items and stood at the door. The bare white walls and dark blue carpet stared back at me. With some measure of regret, and relief, I flicked off the light switch and stepped out the door. It snapped shut with a click, locked. Goodbye.

When I reached home, the answering machine indicated I had a message. The case manager had called. An opening for Colleen had come available at a group home in our county. Did I want it? I desperately wanted someone else to answer the question, but then I thought of my dreams. Was it fear that kept me trapped? And what of the decision I had made in my dreams? Whose voice was that? Instinctively I knew the answer, and that the whispered grace I had been offered had given me what I needed. I called the case manager, and told her that I wanted the opening in the group home. The transition took some time, but within a few months Colleen was gone. But no, she was not gone. Instead, she had reached higher ground, as had I, and Anne too. Now I sleep untroubled by the dream. The water had fallen, gone back into the shadows of fear from whence it came.

Sisters
by Stanley B. Trice

Beth watched a cold drizzle streak across the car window and blur the passing farmland. The gray clouds hung low causing her reflection to look ghostly in the glass. Beside her, David drove in silence, his clean-shaven face losing its summer tan and, as usual, his blond hair needing a comb. Nevertheless, her husband was striking in his dark blue suit.

"This is going to be one dreary day," he said, "and I've got a lot of work to do at the office."

"We're going to my grandpa's funeral. Couldn't you be a little more considerate of my feelings?" Beth said clenching her teeth.

Beth thought how she used to tolerate David's workaholic attitude. Now, his overzealous desire for great achievements made her wish he was seeing another woman. *Then I'd know how to fight back*, she thought. Swelling tension narrowed her oval eyes and creased her forehead.

"I'm not being inconsiderate. I just made a statement I think both of us can agree on."

"You always have a lot of work to do and, yes, you are being inconsiderate. This isn't pleasant for me, either."

Beth turned again to watch the passing farmland. She recalled horseback rides with her Grandpa through the same rolling countryside. They'd ride under the arching reach of stout elms and follow whitewashed fence to gated ends. Back then, Grandpa's thick white hair tousled in the wind while her pigtails spiked the air attempting to keep up. He was always younger than his body, Beth thought.

Tears swelled in her eyes. Regret flooded Beth for the waning contact over the years. The laughter associated with the time of horseback rides was distant.

"We're leaving right after the funeral," ordered David. "I've got to get back to my office."

Beth knew too much about David and she could picture his thoughts racing about work. "You're obsessed with getting that director's position."

"If you would listen to me sometimes you'd know that selection is in two weeks and I'm not the only competitor for it." David clicked his tongue like he did when irritated. "I need to work on my marketing presentation. It could determine who gets the position."

"You already told me rumor has you in the lead. Can't you think about other things for a change?" Beth found herself challenging David's focused attitude toward his job.

"I don't have time to explain all this," he said. "Seems like all you're thinking about is this funeral. All I'm asking is that we not spend all day here."

"David, we can't just leave like that." Beth snapped her fingers releasing a small explosion of anger. "Your precious work can wait. This is my grandpa and my family. I know that doesn't mean much to you, but it does to me."

"Look." David paused. "I've never liked funerals and I'll feel awkward there. Besides, you haven't seen your grandfather in years."

"Yes, since we've been married." *Pacifying me won't work*, she thought. Besides, his last statement hurt. A card here and there over the years was not enough for Grandpa.

"I just don't see any need for me to be there. I hardly knew your grandfather. Besides, aren't you going to tell them today?"

"Don't be absurd. I can't tell them after my grandpa's funeral. Could you please not mention anything? I can't deal with more than one crisis at a time," Beth said. Their visits to separate lawyers and David's plans to move out in a few days tormented her.

"All right, all right. But you'll have to tell your family soon."

"I know, but not right now." Beth wanted the argument to end. She still didn't know how she was going to tell Mother that her marriage was failing.

Both turned their attention away and rode in silence with only the sound of the car slicing through the rain filling the inside of the car.

Arriving at the farmhouse, David maneuvered around several cars cluttered along the dirt driveway. On their way to the long wooden porch, Beth and David warded off misting rain with separate umbrellas. Inside, the well-lit house defied the shadowy weather outside.

Most of the men grouped in the living room near the wet bar where David went. Beth smiled at her dad who stood among the men, but his attention was elsewhere and he didn't notice her. With David already there, Beth kept walking.

Most of the women milled around the dining room table in an adjacent room. Beth didn't see her younger sister Annette, Mother, or Grandma among them. Respectfully, she chatted with her aunts and cousins before wandering into the kitchen.

"Beth, I'm glad you're here," Grandma greeted her from the kitchen table.

"Grandma, I'm so sorry," Beth said hugging the aged woman. Grandma had a youthful plumpness to her features and strength to her grip. Her long gray hair was pulled back into a bun like it had always been for as long as Beth could remember.

Mother sat at the head of the kitchen table commanding a presence in her authoritative pose with her dark blue dress pressed exactly. Seated next to her was Beth's younger sister Annette who matched Mother in facial features. Three years younger than Beth, Annette's long ashen hair was neatly combed and pinned back. Her burgundy dress had a slight print of flower petals along the collar and hem that accentuated her large brown eyes. Beth felt guilty about the plain dark, emerald green dress she wore. It felt sloppy and out of color.

"It's too bad you couldn't be at the viewing last night," Mother said. "Father looked wonderful. But, at least Annette made it."

"I'm sure Beth couldn't help it, Mom," said Annette. "I live a lot closer and Beth would have been there if she could."

"I did try to come, Mother," Beth said, angry at her mother's comments.

"Anyway, I'm glad you're here today," Grandma said. "It's good so many people came. John would have been pleased."

"Why don't we go in to the dining room," suggested Mother. "Other guests have probably arrived."

With Mother leading, Annette passed close to Beth and whispered, "Don't pay any attention to Mom. She's upset about Grandpa's death. Besides, you know Mom has to have everything perfect."

"Yeah, but she's right. I should have been at the viewing last night." Beth angrily remembered how David came home so late they missed the viewing. She didn't want to go alone and have to answer questions from Mother.

The two younger women followed the two older ones into the quiet conversations of the house. Gratefully, Beth allowed the swarm of relatives to envelop and hide her. That way they avoided any serious comments.

When the time came to leave, Beth pressed for her and David to ride alone despite Mother's insistence that fewer cars be used. Beth did not want to be trapped in a discussion about herself, David, and their future. Mostly, she wanted to be alone and she knew she would be with David.

The funeral home was in a converted house. Where it once had life, now it hosted the remains of life. Beth sat on a hard bench between Dad and David while in front of them Annette sat between her husband Rick and Mother. Annette sat closer to Mother than Rick. The two women held hands and clutched tissues together. Beth sat clutching her own tissues as the two men beside her talked about the quality of the casket.

A tall thin preacher in a black suit gave a cordial ceremony where his words made the audience quiet. He spoke of Grandpa's boyish enjoyment of life causing Beth to think of so many memories at one time that she couldn't focus on a single one. She tried to hold back tears, yet she ended up patting them away with a torn tissue. She sat alone between her two men who did not hold her hands.

From the funeral house, the cars formed a procession and drove through the small town toward open farmland. Five miles out, the line of vehicles passed through the tall wrought iron gates of the cemetery into a land of granite and marble monuments nestled beneath the spread of large hardwood trees. The rain had subsided, but gray clouds hung threateningly low. On a bright day, it could be peaceful here, Beth thought. More people arrived to crowd around the canopy and casket and listen to the final words.

As the preacher spoke, Beth could not repel the thought that this was the end of her Grandpa. Like curtains pulled closed across a stage when nothing more is to be seen, as the preacher had said earlier.

Beth let her thoughts drift away to when she was ten years old walking between Dad and Grandpa, each gently holding her hands. The three walked along a well-worn cow path, across pastured lands, and between rounded hillsides until a setting sun began to leave everything to darkness. The men she was descended from talked in deep tones with words that did not matter to her. It was their voices that were a comfort like the soft blow of wind high in the trees. That memory gave way to thoughts about her later wedding when she passed from one man's hands to another. Beth realized that this time when she passed out of marriage, no man would be there to hold her hand. She would get through this and be stronger.

Walking away after the funeral, Annette asked Beth, "You're coming back to the house, aren't you?"

"Yes, for a little while." Beth sensed urgency in her sister's voice and again David's wants irritated her. "If David wants to leave early I can stay and catch a ride back later."

"That'll be great. I'll see you at the house," Annette said as she quickly caught up to her husband Rick.

On the way back, Beth told David, "Annette wants me to stay awhile. So if you're in a hurry to leave, go ahead, and I'll find a way back."

"I hope you'll find time to tell them about our divorce."

"Funny, I thought it was a separation," Beth said. "Anyway, don't worry, I'll tell my family, but right after Grandpa's funeral is not the time." Beth felt tears swell in her eyes, yet she contained them.

"I'm sorry. Tell them whenever you want. They're your family."

Beth rolled down the window to let the coolness contain her emotions. The rain started again and she let the water dampen her hair and steal down her neckline and back. Still, her burdens did not lift and too soon she was back at the farm house.

Beth walked alone leaving David behind. He could have been like one of the trees nearby or a cloud passing overhead. Invisible to her consciousness. In the house, there was no opportunity to speak to Grandma because Mother flanked her protectively. Instead, Beth talked to her father, but it was not the same as she remembered. A hug from him made her feel like a little girl again, but now she was not sure she liked the fatherly protection. David came over and stole the respect Beth desired from her father. Beth could not stay in the presence of the two men.

Riverside Writers 105

She now realized how much she had drifted away from her tomboy self to a different person. Womanhood signified not only growing up, but moving strongly on. She would reacquaint herself with Dad at another time in another frame of mind, she thought, walking away.

Beth felt drawn to the women of the family that she had not known. Still, she eluded their condolences and instead found Annette alone in a back bedroom sitting on the bed and staring out a pane glass window.

"Annette, why are you sitting here alone?" Beth asked.

"I just got tired of the people," she replied. "It was a nice funeral, wasn't it?"

Beth sat on the bed beside her sister. "Yeah, Mom outdid herself. But, I wish I had seen Grandpa more these last few years."

"I was always jealous of you and Grandpa when we were kids. But, that was how it worked out. You with Grandpa and me with Grandma." The words came suddenly from Annette with a tone of resentment.

"I'm sorry you felt like that."

"I didn't mean it to sound hateful. I just don't want it to always be that way." Turning to Beth, Annette continued, "I need to tell you something."

"What is it?" Outside the room, Beth heard people leaving. She wondered if David was among them.

Annette turned her gaze back toward the window. "I'm afraid Rick is seeing another woman." A pause.

"How'd you know?"

"I was suspicious for a while because of strange perfume and when I called him at work he wouldn't be there. Then, I found a note in his pocket from someone named Suzie."

The tears came then, and Beth held her younger sister. After a few moments, Annette drew away saying, "I'm sorry. I really don't know what to do."

"You'll have to decide what's best for you. But, you have to at least tell him you know."

"What if he wants to be with her?"

"It's better to find out now than later." Beth wanted to instill hope in her sister. *How can I do that when my own marriage is over?*

"If Rick and I split, Mom will be angry. She's put so much pressure on me for my marriage to succeed and for me to have children."

Beth thought that Mother would accept my failed, childless marriage, but not Annette's. Dad would be my problem, she thought, yet he will not put the pressure on me that Mother will put on Annette.

"Forget Mom. She's not married to Rick and you are. Do you want Rick back?"

"I don't know."

It grew lighter outside as the clouds began to clear. Beth reached for her sister's hand unable to talk. They sat silently together on the bed waiting for the house to empty of parents, husbands, and family.

Dreadlocks and the Three Fishermen
by Fred Fanning

Once upon a time in a small village on the island of Guam lived a young surfer dude named Mario. His friends all called him Dreadlocks because of the way he wore his golden locks of hair. Near Dreadlock's village lived three Guamanian brothers called Rob, Bob, and Robert. These three brothers were great fisherman and spent all their days on their boat.

One warm day in May the brothers had just made a pot of Jambalaya. Bob poured a ladle full of the spicy dish into each brother's bowl and Rob added some Tabasco but as they tasted the Jambalaya it was way too hot (*temperature wise*). They decided to row ashore to take a Mother's Day card to their dearest mom thinking the Jambalaya would be cooled when they returned.

While the brothers were gone, Dreadlocks was boogie boarding a few miles away and was getting pretty hungry and tired. He decided to paddle his board home to eat and rest. He paddled for a while and became more tired and hungry than before. It was then that he noticed the lone fishing boat rocking on the mild ocean waves. He paddled his board toward the fishing boat and climbed aboard. Once on deck he noticed three chairs.

He sat in the first seat and exclaimed, "Dude" (*which meant this chair is like too hard*). He then sat in the next seat, and as he fell to the deck breaking the seat he yelled, "Dude" (*which meant ouch*). Finally in desperation he sat in the third seat and with a big smile on his face said, "Dude" (*which meant Ahh*). The mast and part of a rolled up sail blocked the sun and Dreadlocks rested in the shade.

About 15 minutes later his hunger took over and he went down to the galley of the boat to see if there were something to eat. He reached the second step when he noticed the smell of Jambalaya and his mouth watered. In the galley, he found three bowls of this spicy delicacy on the table. He took a big spoonful of the delicious food.

He screamed, "Dude" (*which meant ouch, that's like hot, spicy wise*). He tried the second bowl and said, "Dude" (*which meant this tastes like tuna casserole, yuck*). Finally, he tested the third bowl and with a big smile on his face said "Dude" (*which meant Ahh*). Dreadlocks ate the whole bowl and leaned back. Within a few minutes, he noticed how awfully dry his mouth was and got up and looked in the refrigerator where he found three bottles of grape soda pop. He opened a bottle and drank it down in one long gulp. Dreadlock was now full of food and drink and could hardly keep his eyes open. He wandered down the passageway of the boat and came to an open area with three hammocks. He climbed into the first hammock.

There he said, "Dude" (*which meant this is like way too hard*). He climbed into the next hammock, crashed to the deck where he yelled "Dude" (*which meant Ouch*). He picked himself up and carefully climbed into the third hammock and said "Dude" (*which meant Ahh*). There he fell fast asleep.

The three brothers Rob, Bob, and Robert were enjoying their short visit. Their mother asked them to stay for some coconut cream pie and sun tea. Each son ate a small piece so as not to spoil his supper, but to keep mom happy. They kissed their sweet mother goodbye, and rowed for home. As the brothers, rowed they began to imagine how wonderful the Jambalaya would taste. Finally, they reached the boat, and as they climbed aboard noticed the deck chairs were disturbed.

Rob said, "Someone has been sitting in my seat."

Bob said, "Someone has been sitting in my seat."

Robert sobbed, "Somebody has been sitting in my chair, and they broke it."

The brothers resolved then and there to make the perpetrator pay, after supper of course. The three went down to the galley. As soon as they arrived they noticed the bowls of Jambalaya had been disturbed.

Rob said, "Someone has been eating my Jambalaya."

Bob then said, "Someone has been eating my Jambalaya."

Robert cried, "Someone has been eating my Jambalaya and they ate it all up."

Rob the oldest brother comforted Robert and said, "We'll get to the bottom of this and when we do the sucker's gonna pay."

With Robert calm and the boat suddenly quiet, out of nowhere came a loud snore. All three brothers looked in the direction of the snore. In that direction hung the hammocks.

They quietly walked on tiptoes to the area and noticed that the hammocks had been disturbed.

Rob whispered to his brothers, "Someone has been sleeping in my hammock".

Robert responded in a whisper, "Someone has been sleeping in my hammock, and they broke it down."

Just then Bob yelled out, "Someone is still sleeping in my hammock."

The yelling woke Dreadlocks, and he jumped to his feet and tried to run. The brothers wrestled Dreadlocks to the floor and thumped him on the head.

Rob said, "Dreadlocks, what are you doing?"

Robert then said angrily, "Dreadlocks, you broke my chair and hammock. What's up with that? You also ate my Jambalaya."

Finally, Bob said, "Dreadlocks you've done it now."

The three brothers made Dreadlocks fix the deck chair and hammock, and made him cut bait for two hours to pay for a bowl of Jambalaya and soda pop. Then came the real punishment, the brothers took Dreadlock's home and told his parents what he did. His parents were mortified and grounded him for a week.

As he ran to his room in tears Dreadlocks heard his father say, "Son you know this hurts me more than it does you."

The In-Law
by Andrea Williams Reed

One 6 foot, 7 inch small-town young man,
entered a family.
A wedding in the spring,
made it official.

He fell in with the extended family,
with the care and tended the livestock.
Looked in on widowed aunts
Which endeared him to them.

Cooked, cleaned and cared for aging parents
Resourceful in times of bereavement and crisis,
while prepared with a dish and kind word.

Dealt with difficult people and situations,
with patience and an enduring presence of mind.
A natural arbitrator when conflicts arose,
and never complained of his role as the in-law.

Closing Days
by Ron Russis

Again this morning,
the same as every morning,
I listened close to hear my mother's broken breathing,
a sometimes noisy snore that fluttered,
a wheezing rasp that guttered,
coming out as muffled sound,
a thin whisper on my ear telling me
once more she'd made it through the night.

And later,
over coffee and toast,
the local news a hum of white-noise,
she'd tell me of her bouts from the night before,
of the futile struggles to find restful sleep
and of the long hours left lying awake,
left watching tv or of time spent idly staring
at those glo-stars I'd glued, one by one,
to the dark blue of her ceiling –
a means to give impression of sky;

and to enhance that perception,
that sense of infinite space,
of her nearness to heaven,
I'd hung a mechanical moon,
one that clung high on the wall
where it patiently progressed through its slivered phases,
that bright and changing moon
moving time ahead in crescent segments,
in halves of quarters at a time.

And as I listened to her story,
that shared prospect of finality became clearer to me,
my noting us each having grown older, grown poorly,
our ailing, failing selves slowly shutting down,
bringing us closer to each other
and nearer to our ends,
and a final
good-bye.

Interview with a Rabbit
by C.A. Rowland

"You came," said the rabbit thoughtfully as she ambled across the room towards the only window. Moonlight flooded the dirt hovel and the woman could see the sparse furnishings of the room more clearly now, the round cherry table, the chairs. She set her notepad and pen down and waited.

"You talked to my editor," the woman reporter said. "Something about having a story the world needs to hear."

"Yes. Why don't you sit down? I'm going to move closer to you," the rabbit said.

"Can we turn on a light?" the reporter asked.

The rabbit moved to a small corner table and flipped the lamp switch. A soft yellow light illuminated her.

"Dear God!" the reporter whispered.

The rabbit was not the pristine white, perky, soft Easter Bunny one would expect. In its place, this rabbit was disheveled with dirty dishwater fur. One ear hung listlessly down the side of her face and the other flopped backwards. Long furrows of wrinkles marked her face and a cigarette dangled from the side of her red costumed lips.

The rabbit belched an ugly laugh. "Not exactly what you expected, I see. But I wasn't always this way. That's what I wanted to tell you about. And the role of Santa's head elf in all this."

The reporter drew a deep breath and forced her shoulders to relax. "I'm ready when you are," she said.

The crimson lips curled into a smile, at once genuine, cruel and sad. "I was born four years ago. My father was the current Easter Bunny. I was the runt of the litter but my mother always had a soft place in her heart for me. She made sure I got plenty to eat. As a result, I soon gained enough weight to hold my own with my siblings. But I was a late bloomer and they had all moved away to start their own families when the tragedy happened."

The rabbit stopped and stared at the reporter. She finished her notes and looked up. "What tragedy?" the reporter prompted.

"Do you know how long rabbits live?" the rabbit asked.

"A few years," the reporter said. "But you've lived longer than that."

"Wild rabbits live about two to three years. My family is protected since we are the Easter Bunnies but even so, we only live about ten years. My father was seven years old. He was expected to be the Easter Bunny for several more years. He had what would be a mid-life crisis in human terms."

The reporter rolled her eyes.

"Yes, I know," sighed the rabbit. "He must have thought he was some kind of Peter Rabbit incarnate. He succumbed to his natural instincts. He began running vegetable patches. Stealing from a human farmer at his age is dangerous business. Especially for a rabbit that's lived a pampered life. "

The rabbit paused. "I can relate. Working in an enclosed office everyday and dealing with candy and sugar sweets all these years –it's not a natural rabbit's life. But we do what we must. "

"What office? What happened? I'm confused," the reporter said.

"A bullet to the head. He'd been warned. It was a clean shot from a farmer's gun. I know he didn't suffer," the rabbit said. "Imagine. I was less than a year old thrust into the world of being the Easter Bunny with no training whatsoever."

The rabbit watched the reporter choose her words carefully.

"You've lost me. And you haven't answered my questions. I understand you had no training, but Easter is once a year, right? You have to deal with the weeks running up to Easter, the whole whoopla and all. The hiding of Easter eggs. Didn't you have others to help you?" the woman reporter asked.

"Of course," the rabbit said frowning. "It's big business. We have a main office, several subsidiaries, and staff to rival other large conglomerates. Who do you think comes up with the ideas, the chocolate, the plastic eggs, the baskets? The responsibility I had was mindboggling."

"That's all corporate businesses, isn't it?" The reporter paused, realization dawning across her face. "You had? Don't you still?"

A sly smile crept over the rabbit's face. She crushed her lipstick stained cigarette in the ashtray, one ear flopping further forward and lit another. "You're supposed to think it's just business. Do you really think the idea for Cadbury came from a human? But I see I've jumped ahead. To answer your questions, I should begin at the beginning of where I left off, and then continue to the end," the rabbit said.

"That sounds familiar. I think I've heard that somewhere before," the reporter said.

The rabbit ignored her comment. "Now, where was I? Oh yes, my father was tragically taken. I was the only single bunny at home, so naturally, I was being groomed to take over. Only not that quickly. I was thrust into the

Riverside Writers

world of manufacturing plastic eggs, recipes for chocolate and all the varieties of baskets."

"Weren't there others to help and advise you?" the reporter asked.

"Of course, but who do you trust? I was too inexperienced and my mother was no help. She pined away for my father and died shortly after him. It was sad but she'd never been part of the business so she didn't know what to do either. Then the recession hit. Then the stock market tanked. So much pressure to keep profits up. I mean, what's a rabbit to do?"

The reporter studiously took notes. "Really? So what did you do?" the woman asked, uncertainty reflecting in her face.

"Alas, I bowed to those who did not have my best interest at heart. My uncle and cousin who had been in the business much longer suggested outsourcing the chocolate processing and packaging to China. It all sounded so easy. I was sucked in."

"Isn't China where they banned things being brought into the US? Contaminated food products with melamine?" the reporter asked.

"Yes. It was our specialty candies that were affected. But that's not the issue. If we had known about them or if someone had simply told us about them, we would have changed our practices. Unfortunately, that's not what happened," the rabbit said.

"Then what did?" asked the reporter.

"Santa's head elf. He's always thought the Easter Bunny bringing toys to children infringed upon Santa's role," the rabbit huffed. "It's a totally different time of year. I never saw a real conflict."

"I don't understand," the reporter said shaking her head. "What does that have to do with China?"

"It was the elf who notified the Food and Drug Administration. Did he come and talk to us like civilized animals? Oh no, he set out to ruin us. The problems were in our Kinder eggs, melamine in the milk and chocolate."

The rabbit rung her paws and shook her head. "I had no idea the elf had it in for us. I would have tried to maintain better relations but I listened to my uncle. He said not to worry."

"Couldn't you just use a different facility? Stop outsourcing to China?" the reporter asked.

"Yes, but not before the stockholders demanded my head. I was too inexperienced they said. No matter that it was my uncle's idea. I should have researched this better. I was ultimately responsible," the rabbit said. "And now look at me. I am a wreck of a bunny. Four years old and my life is over."

The reporter stared at the rabbit. "Why am I here?" she asked. "It doesn't sound like much of a story."

"Ahh," the rabbit said. "There's more. It was a conspiracy between my cousin and the elf."

The reporter dropped her pen and began to close her notepad.

"No, wait," cried the rabbit. "I can prove it."

The rabbit paused to let her words sink in.

"Don't you think the world has a right to know the truth?"

"Sure," the reporter said, "but I'd need hard evidence. Assuming I believe any of this, I don't see how your cousin and the elf could control products in China. Why would your cousin want to hurt the company?"

"They didn't need to control the products. Only when the problems were discovered, did they take advantage of the situation. My cousin wanted power - my position," the rabbit said.

"Let's see your proof," the reporter said.

"Everything is in here," said the rabbit reaching for a binder from the other chair. She opened it as the woman reporter leaned in. "I have pictures, dates of meetings and a recordings of conversations. I tried to show it to the stockholders but no one will meet with me."

The rabbit smiled her wily smile. "Plus they embarrassed me publicly. Seems I should return the

Riverside Writers 117

favor, don't you think? It might be the story of the century. Are you interested?"

The reporter considered the rabbit's words. "If you've really got proof, I'd love to see it. I'm not promising anything but if you have what you say you do, it's a great story."

The rabbit smiled. "I realize it's a lot to digest. It's like a nightmare I wish I could wake up from."

"This is all so unbelievable," the reporter said, shaking her head.

"Perhaps a cup of tea would help," the rabbit said. "Sugar or cream, Alice?"

Icicle Days
by Michelle O'Hearn

Steaming icicles refracting the light
In splendid rainbow delight
To the eyes of people and animal alike
Gazing in wonder at the visions before them.
Drip, drip, drip
They thaw and slip
Down from the bark of a tree branch so slight
It creaks and a squirrel shrieks
Scattering prints across sparkling white fields of snow.

A Labrador is spending restful pleasures
Rolling around in frozen treasures
The cat watching in careful measure
A common comfort in the company of each other.
Nip, nip, nip
They play and skip
Flipping powder behind flailing paws
And dashing to the call of the birds.

Now That You Ask...
by Ron Russis

Why yes, I'd once had a herd of outdoor cats,
but I'd often found them staining the road, chewed up
and spat out by the cars that sometimes came in a rush,
speeding past too fast down our quiet country lane,
with the cats either too slow at crossing the road
or having failed, first, at having looked both ways.

I've lost more than twice a dozen cats to that road;
each one pasted somewhere between its two yellow lines
and left to lie, until the rising warmth of noon-time
day caused them to bloat and reek, their pungent smell
leading the way for my nose and that over-ripe stench
making them easy for the scavengers and me to find.

My sign to seek – a circling of crows – an omen
showing me exactly where to look, as certain-sure
as a compass needle, pointing me to see where
it was they'd met their unexpected fates and so I
bring their broken bodies back home, rag-wrapped,
in brown paper bags for burying beside the shed.

Although, truth be told, there were some I never did find.
They simply disappeared, went AWOL and over the hill.
I'd adjudged them missing-in-action, caught up by some
    hawk
or owl or fisher cat – and that last no long-lost next of kin.
I've just two cats, now; and these seem to have learned their
    lessons
from all the rest, that to survive this world, they'd best be
    wary.

These last two are leery of fleeting shadows overhead,
are fearful of streaking cars, their noisy roar – the road's
 grim edge.
Their only interest in the out-of-doors is in watching our
 feeders,
our feathered-friends – the cardinals and jays, the juncos and
 wrens –
and that they only do from behind the bay windows' double-
 panes
of glass or sometimes the mesh of the kitchen's porch screen
 door.

Acorns as Vocabulary
by Anne Heard Flythe

A hard winter, heavy snow
judging by the white oak mast.
Myriad gray squirrels glide
up and down the trees'
rough bark, highways
for small sharp claws.

Flicking tails exchange
urgent semaphore—
food, sex, danger,
a sparse language
but sufficient
for their needs.

Signs
by Ron Russis

I watched as two dozen birds winged past, went by
in a broken vee, one leg four birds short and so low
I could hear their wing-beats, could see their eyes;
close enough to shoot, were it still season and had
I brought the gun. And as I watched them flap past
I thought, the first sign of spring, that last of winter.
Small buds would soon follow these flights of birds.
First crocus, then tulip would break free their bulbs,
erupt to replace the winter's sullen drab with bright
flags of color waving wild in breeze, like small kites
tethered tight to short strings of green. Ah, spring!
Spring! Yes, let the days lengthen long, let the sun
grow from cold to warm and let time pass by slow,
let the days drag along – and me enjoy their leisure.

Triceratops:
A Dinosaur Mystery Solved
by Larry Turner

The devotees of dinosaurs adore
Triceratops. His jagged neck frill, like
Some Elizabethan dandy, or

His three thick horns, each one a massive pike.
A Torosaurus' horns have lesser weight.
He sports a smoother, rounder frill than Trike.

Two professors at Montana State
Have scanned the fossils of each dinosaur,
looking at all fifty. Just how late

In life did each one die? They learned for sure
That each Triceratops had through some fault
Expired while still a youngster, and what's more

That every Torosaurus was adult.
Was that coincidence? They don't think so.
Although to us the thought is difficult,

Each Triceratops was, they now know,
A Torosaurus, but a juvenile!
How could it be that as a Trike should grow,

The skull and horns and frill all changed in style
Until Triceratops that we had known
Became a Torosaurus? Think a while.

These features never grew as stiff as stone,
But pliable and plastic cartilage,
They never changed to hard, unyielding bone.

Triceratops adapted to each stage
of life. I too should greet the turning page
and never grow bone-headed as I age.

The Goose
by Jill Austin Deming

I saw your broken body
lying in the highway

Silently I blessed you

Your life ended
violently and abruptly

I wanted to stop to
cradle
your
soft
crumpled
body
carefully lifting
you out of the road

I could imagine sinking my fingers
through your chalky feathers
into a cloud of down

I wanted to become part of you

But I didn't stop
I was too afraid.

City, Town, Country, Nature

City

A Moment to Own it
by Michelle O'Hearn

A car driving through the dark morning
    a daily ritual
    a commitment
    moment
To rest the vehicle on heated pavement
    to sleep for the day
    to wait for action
    own it
The driver checking the clock
    on his wrist and one
    on his phone
    time
He holds high hopes
    for this day
    for a positive start
    atonement
Grabbing the bags and your guts and the books
    for the crunch
    for a punch
    your opponent
No more time to discuss.

Boxcars
by Stanley B. Trice

We stood on the concrete platform made for people like ourselves who climb into commuter trains the way zombies move across graveyards. On the far track passed a hotshot freight train, one with priority over other train traffic. It had a long consist of cars that seemed endless and made the wind windier and the cold colder. I know it was a hotshot freighter because the conductor of our commuter train told me two days ago on Tuesday when one made our train late, again. She said hotshot trains are the primary reason for other train movement. That reason announced through the overhead speakers in a futile attempt to appease cold and waiting commuters.

The line of rattling and squealing cars moved slowly enough that any writing along the sides could be easily read. I guess because it was a hotshot it could go as slow as it wanted. I could even read the small warnings of hazardous material on the tanker cars; things we never wanted to know that moved past us just feet away. Liquid petroleum gas, molten sulfur, phosphoric acid, acrylamide (whatever that is), and creosol girders. I got the distinct indication we should not stick around in a derailment.

But, we were strong. We could stand against these threats from passing tankers. After all, standing in the open and exposing our bodies to the cold wind couldn't put us in any more peril in these short winter days that kept us coming and going in the dark. What was that doing to our psyches?

Maybe it might make us commuters edge a little closer to the yellow caution strip trimming the edge of the concrete platform that attempted to warn us of peril. I was thankful for the bright platform lights hanging from the blue awnings or perched on tall black poles and keeping back the impending dark of a winter commute. I just wished that instead of reading tanker car warnings that the light gave off more heat.

I looked at the waiting crowd and spotted this man I recognized from many previous commuter trips. He stood beside a woman who stood beside me. I noticed this man because anxious commuters waiting for a late train always made me nervous when I'm standing so close to the yellow caution strip.

This other man looked anxious. Unnaturally so. More so than the rest of us who wanted to get out of the cold and onto a crowded commuter train so we could breathe each other's breath. How could anyone miss this guy on my right?

He stood tall and thin with a long unshaven face and the visage of a sad clown. All other times I remembered him always dressed impeccably with a starched shirt, expensive tie pulled into the folds of his neck, and pressed suit pants nestled against polished dress shoes. Yet, today he wore a brown cardigan sweater too big for him, soiled jeans, and sneakers that weren't white anymore. I got to thinking he didn't have a good day.

Boxcars, flats, tankers, and something with a mesh of girders sprouting upward to hold something that was not there went by in a steady, slow procession. I kept a side view of Cardigan Man, but I didn't say anything to anybody. I didn't want to start something that could make our train even later. I wondered if it'll rain tomorrow. Cold enough for snow. I'd notice a snowflake, despite the darkness.

A boxcar rumbled by with its side door open. It was empty. Maybe everything in it fell out. I looked at Cardigan Man and saw his eyes get big and his face open up with a drop of his chin. He puckered his lips as if kissing someone he remembered while focusing on another boxcar with an open door drifting by. A lot of these cars coming past us empty. What's up with all these empty train cars? A downward trend in the economy? Man, I hope I don't get laid off or moved to

Riverside Writers 129

some other department. I can't take any more changes in my life.

As this next empty boxcar approached us with its door opened, Cardigan Man made his move. He slid around the woman, crossed in front of me, and jumped from the yellow warning strip. Right off the platform where it was safe. Away from us who were no threat. And, onto shiny steel tracks where big heavy trains rolled past like the one on the far track. Man, I hope he didn't do something stupid and cause our train to be late like getting run over.

I looked around for some would-be hero to jump down and rescue him, but maybe we were all taken by surprise or too cold to move or didn't care. In any case, he didn't stand still long enough to be greeted by some hero.

At least no one attempted to be one as Cardigan Man started running after the open boxcar door that was about to pass us. Good thing he wore tennis shoes instead of his dress shoes. He ran like a gazelle bounding up and down over the steel tracks until he met the open door almost perfectly. Almost. Right in front of me.

His foot slipped on the steel railing. A gasp from the commuters who hadn't turned their heads to avoid something gory. I wondered who was this man we were watching about to be cut into pieces by heavy wheels of the boxcar and make our commuter train late. I watched as he jumped again and this time slammed both his hands into the metal edge of the open boxcar door. He struggled for balance grabbing again for the metal edge. He had one last chance.

One good leap and Cardigan Man pulled his torso across the lip of the open boxcar door. Clawing and crawling to get his legs inside, he scrambled all the way in and rolled onto his back. He just laid there on the wooden floor and staring at who knows what as he passed by me on his way to wherever the freight train was going.

Rappahannock Voices

He made it. Everyone seemed to say this at once. I didn't. I didn't think he'd make it. I watched the open boxcar slide past me and down the steel tracks following the rest of the slow, hotshot freighter.

"I took graduate classes with that guy," someone on my left said. I didn't look, hoping he wasn't talking to me. "We even presented our theses together."

All right, so here we are watching Cardigan Man becoming Boxcar Willie and now this guy next to me I won't look at was talking to me. We never talked to each other before. I hope this talking was not a trend. I didn't predict this trend.

"He thought with a master's degree he'd get a promotion. He told me they promoted someone else who had no degree. The person had connections, I guess."

"I used to work with that guy," said some other man coming up on my right on the other side of the woman. Everyone filled in naturally as if it was natural for someone to jump into a moving boxcar and leave an open space in the crowd.

I looked past the woman's thin brown hair and was met by the man's comb-over. The elongated strands didn't help keep his bald scalp from looking blue. His jowl became his neck somewhere along his Windsor knotted yellow tie.

"I don't think I'd want to work with a guy who just risked his life climbing into an empty boxcar still moving." What was I doing responding to Comb-over?

"He was a good worker, but always a little strange," said Comb-over. "He told me he had two teenage daughters and a wife who called him every day. They wouldn't let him alone. He told me he grew up with a mother and two sisters and no father or brothers. I guess all that estrogen just got to him. Courageous guy. He lasted longer than me." I wondered what Boxcar Willie's real name was.

"Women nag and criticize and push you. Sometimes the sex just ain't worth it," said a guy behind me. How close was he standing? Personal space, personal space. He sounded like a smoker. This was a non-smoking section.

"I bet he lost his job," said the man on my left I wouldn't look at. I wished people would stop talking to me.

"Probably did," said Comb-over. "His company didn't do well in quarterly earnings. I heard that the woman who got promoted over him botched a contract bid. She kept her job, but that guy was blamed unfairly. His family, I heard, blamed him, too. No one took his side. Man had a lot of courage to put up with those women that long."

"All right. This is what we're going to stop doing. That's blaming everything on the women," said the lady on my right. She looked up and I wondered how she could talk through the purple scarf wrapped around her neck like a noose. She had thick eyebrows that looked attractive. "We need to tell the authorities what this guy did."

She started punching numbers on her cell phone. Each time it made cute little beeping sounds. I watched her long, dark red finger nails cut across her cell and I could not figure out how she managed to hit those little buttons so perfectly. I decided not to mess with her. She punched those buttons like it was our fault Boxcar Willie escaped.

In front of us, the train cars started to slow even more. Man, that woman was fast. But, wait. That means our commuter train will be even later. How did she manage to stop a freight train with her cute, beeping cellular? I wonder how Boxcar Willie would stay warm.

"They call it a catch out, what he did." The man who sounded too close behind me said with a voice that arrived at my ears deep and scorched sounding.

I turned and saw him standing right behind me. He looked right at me. I didn't retreat, mostly because the yellow strip was at my heels.

"It means someone who hops on a freight train." He had a gray, trimmed beard, thin hair on his head swept straight back like he was in a wind storm, and blue eyes. His breath smelled minty.

"What's it called when he hops off?" I had to say something. We were looking right at each other an instance apart. I hope I didn't have bad breath, but why do I care?

"Stupid, if the train's moving. Arrested, if he gets caught."

"I guess we won't know either way," I said. I gotta stop talking to these commuters. I turned back to look for my commuter train. I needed a ride home quick.

"Well, the emergency dispatcher was going to try and call someone. I don't know if he'll do anything." Purple Scarf Woman had a pitch of voice like nails across chalkboard.

As she continued to tell us something we weren't listening to, the consist of cars jumped. Each coupler, where the knuckle joints joined the cars to make the train a train, let out a sequence of bangs. The line of train cars started picking up speed and the commuting crowd muttered quiet hoorays. I'm glad the guy got away clean.

"Excuse me," said the gravelly voice man behind me. I stepped to the right; he moved to my left. I looked up ahead of me on the train tracks and saw another empty boxcar coming down the line with the sliding door open. Gravelly Voice didn't hesitate to step in front of me on top of the yellow warning strip and jump.

Seriously? Another commuter running away? Like a sprinter, only slower and older, he ran toward that opened boxcar door as the train picked up speed. I and everyone else watched the man take a looping route to intercept the door of the open boxcar. He had long legs and I had an open mouth that didn't say anything.

Someone yelled for him to stop. I wished I didn't have such a good view being in front of the waiting commuter crowd. I was still recovering from the previous fellow. The train picked up speed along with my heart and breathing. I didn't want to maintain memories of

Riverside Writers   133

amputated and crushed body parts. I needed the memory space to remind me not to wear the same tie every day.

He met the open boxcar door and latched one hand on the edge of the doorway effortlessly. Keeping in time with the train's movement, he swung his body out and up like an acrobat. He had such fluid motion that he was up into the door and in a standing position before any of us could close our eyes. He waved to us as he passed by.

"What did you say to him?" Purple Scarf asked me.

"Nothing. Hey, those people obviously didn't see the tanker cars labeled with molten sulfur and phosphoric acid."

"What'd he say to you?" asked a man on my left. He seemed like he was accusing me of being a renegade leader. He had a wide brim, green felt hat and a long drooping nose that looked like it wanted to escape the pudgy face.

"I don't know. Nothing." Short term memory was always my problem. "The guy's nuts like the other man."

Great, I thought. Now, I'm the one giving conversation. People are talking to me. I'm going to end up frozen here like a sausage in a freezer. All I wanted was to stand here quietly until my train arrived. Where's my commuter train? I looked at the second Boxcar Willie fading into the distance and he still stood in the open boxcar door waving goodbye to everyone. Now, he was gone and I was still waiting for my train in the cold.

"I'm going to call again. Someone should know about all this," said Purple Scarf. Her long brown hair danced in her face from the train's gust of wind. She was not quite my height. She did not pull her hair away and I wanted to cut it off and feed it into her cellular.

"No one got hurt. No harm done." I wonder if anyone else is going for another boxcar. It looked pretty cold riding in an open boxcar. It'll be darker further down the line. I wonder if either of the men thought about that.

"I wonder who else is going for it," said the green-hatted man.

"One of you men should have done something. I'm gonna tell our conductor," said Purple Scarf.

"I'll hold my breath," said the green-hatted man.

I could be that strong and impress the women by saving people from doing risky things. I proved it almost forty years ago when my high school friend Donald and I walked across a railroad bridge high over a river because neither of us could get girls. Girls were always looking for boys of adventure. Donald and I didn't meet anymore after our bridge walk, but some girl let me kiss her. Maybe Donald went back to the bridge alone. Anyway, after high school I never heard from him. He disappeared like the men on the boxcars. I hope they don't get caught because some people deserve freedom and adventure.

I'm not a hero and I don't do adventure. I can't get girls anymore. Even the wife I had left me for some other man because I was too boring. I'm not crazy enough to jump on a boxcar when it's moving. I'll just stay here waiting for my commuter train. I'll stand here with these other people getting colder. We'll wait together like every evening and morning standing in silence.

The hotshot freight train picked up more speed, maybe never meaning to slow down again while passing a pile of cold commuters. With the train went my opportunity to leave on it. Just like the Boxcar Willies left me. I wonder if the priority for the hotshot train had been those commuters. One more empty boxcar flew by. No chance anyone would jump on it, or at least no one sane. These boxcar experiences I just witnessed made me remember my grandfather who died when his heart exploded in his chest.

I was about ten when Grandpa told me about when he was a ten year old kid and lived in a clapboard house with a roofless back porch facing railroad tracks. He said that on hot summer days he'd sit on the edge of the porch and chew on a piece of watermelon rind. Few scraps made it into their trash after the Panic of 1907. When a freight train went by, he'd see the white and black faces of men flash past staring out of open boxcar doors.

He told me about how these men's eyes followed him, beckoning to trade places, maybe wishing for a piece of his watermelon rind. None got off near his house because of the downhill grade. Clayborne, Grandpa's friend from grade school, knew the boxcar riders. He lived on the other side on the uphill grade where the trains went slower and there was time to get off.

"I could have gone with them, if I wanted," he told me as his short term memory failed, leaving only his most far off memories to be relived. "I could have had an adventure. Instead, I never visited Clayborne. He came to my place and told me about the hoboes. He told me the traveling stories they'd tell and how their sour, burning smell of liquor made him feel good. I never went there. I stayed put. Clayborne left before high school ended. He went on a westbound freight train with the hoboes. People who ride the rails have more purpose and drive than those of us who stay put forever in the same place. Sometimes it gets them killed. I'm not afraid to die." He died a week later.

In my fifties, I've finally decided to disagree. I don't have any purpose or drive as I move between point A and B five days a week. Maybe because I won't change at this point. There's something to be said about sameness. It may be long and painful, but it's inevitable and purposeful, like death.

Sometimes it's better to relax than always being on the go. Like the two men who leaped onto the boxcars. They're in hobo land and nothing will be the same again for any of us commuters, at least for me. Where they go doesn't matter. The concrete platform seeped cold up through my ankles as I waited for a commuter train that's late because of slow moving hotshot freight train.

It's best to stay away from too many adventures. It's bad enough having grown children who don't respect you because your job is not exciting or a wife who complained that you don't make enough money and who left for someone who does. It's bad enough not having the courage to jump on an empty boxcar and get away. Worry can drive a person to an early grave and maybe that would be better.

I don't need adventure. It's the cold I need. It lets me know I'm still alive and not some dead wood zombie shuffling back and forth to work five days a week. I feel the cold. The cold is here enveloping me like a wet blanket, siphoning off my body heat. It keeps me awake and prepares me for sleep when I get on my warm train. Even with all that breath. That's the best sleep.

It's best to stay away from what makes me feel nervous, lest someone else is lured away on steel tracks like those men now in hobo land. It's best I stop thinking about things. I'm here and they're where I'm not. I could be adventurous if I wanted. I could make the girls like me. I know, I know, I got to do something. Not just thinking about things. Not keep hitting my head with regrets.

This weekend, I'll have dinner with my kids at their house. That's an adventure. Looking at immortality and enjoying it. Like Puff the Magic Dragon, in a puff of diesel my commuter train is here and not too, too late.

Town

You Call That a Massage?
by Juanita Dyer Roush

My sister Judy and I don't often get away together so the weekend was anticipated with great joy. We had no plans; just get in the car and go. I straightened up the house and took my shower. My hair looked exceptionally good. Washed, dried, the curling iron did its job, it fell right into place...perfect.

We drove to Winchester, Virginia with only a minimum of stops, once to get Judy a passport and once to do some shopping. No, Winchester doesn't require a passport, but we just might take a trip someday to visit my son when he returns to Germany from Iraq. One more stop to have lunch and then we were on our way. As usual when we are together, there was lots to laugh about, events happening in our family, things we had done that we found humorous.

Our first stop in Winchester was the Apple Blossom Mall. It's not a large mall, and there are much more impressive places we could have gone ... but we chose Winchester. Judy and I got out of the car, already laughing and talking about our plans once we hit the stores.

We opened the large glass doors and walked into a quaint mall that appeared to be under construction. We turned the first corner and saw the office of Chinese massage therapists. Being more adventurous about those kinds of things, and having had a couple of Reiki massages, I talked Judy into going in with me. She had her doubts about getting a massage. "I don't know about removing my clothes in a mall," Judy stated.

"Well it didn't stop you from spending two hours in the dressing room at Belk," I reminded her.

I walked around the cubicle style wall and saw two people getting massages with clothes on. After that, Judy was a pushover. We picked up a copy of the brochure lying on the desk and read the prices. We saw they offered a 20 minute massage and a 30 minute massage. The word that we had skimmed over was acupressure. Judy, having never had a massage said, "uuuuhhhh, I don't know... I think I will just have a 20 minute one." As I stated earlier, being the more adventurous of the two, I was all for a 30 minute massage. I tried to convince Judy by telling her how wonderful the Reiki massage had been. I told her that it was so relaxing I almost oozed to the car when it was done. Oh yes! I was looking forward to this!

The Chinese masseuse tried to help convince Judy. "Thirty minute? Thirty minute?"

Judy said, "Twenty minute, ummm minutes."

"Thirty minute?"

Finally Judy stated in her most exasperated voice, "Twenty minute!" I knew better than to persist at that point and apparently so did the masseuse.

Judy and I walked around the wall and watched the last two current patients' ... errr, patrons' massages. The women got up and left. Judy said, "I want that one!" and laid on the massage couch closer to her. I took the remaining couch, lay on my stomach, and put my face in a little round hole on the padded pillow. It reminded me of the one time when I was 18 and drank too much. I ended up with my face hanging over the commode.

The masseuse gently brushed my hair (remember it's my good hair day!) up off my neck and then brushed the wisps of hair away. I thought to myself, *"Oh yes! This is just what I need."* It felt so good. Go ahead, brush your hair gently up off your neck and see how great it felt. I had high hopes for this massage.

Riverside Writers

The next moment, I felt pain so intense it brought tears to my eyes.... Did I tell you that my make-up also was having a good day? Well, it was. Luckily, with my face down like that, it couldn't run down my cheeks. The next few moments were agony. The masseuse dug into the muscles around my shoulders with such intensity I could hardly breathe. He worked and pushed and gouged with such force I began to try to imagine I was elsewhere. I tried thinking of pleasures but there was only pain. The entire time the masseuse said under his breath, "OOOH, muscles tight... oooooh, muscles tight!.." Being a big proponent of prayer, I began to pray, "Oh God, please, let me relax so this guy doesn't kill me!"

His hands were on my shoulders, down my back, up to my shoulders again–but not a light relaxing rub using his palms! No, this man used his fingertips and his knuckles. At one point, I swear he was digging into my muscles with a rock. He was determined to massage my muscles from the inside out! "OOOh, muscles tight!"

About 10 minutes into this Chinese torture, I had a thought that sent me into a spasm of giggles. "Judy is going to be out of this pain 10 minutes before I am!" I was trying not to laugh at that thought, holding back with all that was in me. Holding back made my entire body begin to shake with pent up laughter. I believe my masseuse thought I was having convulsions. He stopped his torment long enough to ask, "You awight? You awight?"

"Yes, I'm awight...ummm... alright; thank you... sorry, so sorry!" Giggle, Giggle...

Later, Judy told me that she could only think, "What does she have to laugh about over there? This guy is killing me!" Apparently her masseuse wasn't a lot easier on her.

The hard knuckles again began to grind into my back working their way down my buttocks and to my thighs where he seemed to concentrate a little longer than I thought was necessary. "Okay, Buddy, move away from the Monkey." He must have heard my thoughts for he proceeded to knead my muscles from my butt to my feet and then spent a moment grinding his knuckles into the bottoms of my feet before going back to the shoulders.

It had felt so good to have him in an area of the body other than my shoulders. But now he was back with a vengeance. "Oooh, muscles tight!" I could hear him speaking as he jabbed, pushed, pulled, kneaded and punched. Again, the pain was almost more than I could stand... I began to think to myself, "Go back to the Monkey!! Go back to the Monkey!" You could tell I was getting desperate. I'm even uncomfortable with my gynecologist being too near the Monkey.

Twenty minutes into my suffering, I heard the alarm sound. Judy's massage was over. That lucky duck was finished. I heard her masseuse say something to her but I couldn't make out her response. My masseuse plagued me with a few minutes more of massage and then he told me to turn over ... in Chinese. This took a few minutes to convey to me since my Chinese is a little rusty. I even use number 6 or number 8 on the Chinese restaurant menu rather than try to pronounce Chow Mein. When I finally realized what he wanted, fear struck me. If it hurt my back that badly, what was he going to do to my front? The thought of Judy whacking him with her purse if she thought I was being manhandled sent me into another spasm of laughter.

The laughter came to an abrupt halt when he put one arm under my head and one across my shoulders in a head lock that would have made Hulk Hogan envious. Somehow, he held me like this and rolled my head back and forth, back and forth. Then he took hold of my feet, bent my knees and rolled me into a little ball. Next, my feet went behind my ears and back down. I began to wish I had not dropped out of my yoga class since having a little elasticity in my joints and muscles would have helped at that moment.

Remember my good hair day? He placed his hands in my hair at the temples and pulled them upwards, up, down, up, down, up, down...all over my head, up, down, up, down...with hands greasy from the lotion. By that time, tears were rolling down my cheeks. I could no longer control the laughter and even though I felt like an idiot, I couldn't stop. I think I was hysterical.

By now, every inch of my body was in pain. Or at least, I thought every inch was ... then he discovered my cheekbones. Pressure, pressure, push, push! *"Oh no, I thought! Please don't let him break my cheekbones!"* A few more minutes and my alarm sounded. What ordinarily would have sounded harsh and tinny sounded to me like the music of angels. I readied myself to jump off the table and, oh my! My body doesn't want to work! Every inch of me hurts. I know why people love massages now. It feels so good when they quit.

"Restroom? Restroom?" He asked.

"No, I don't need to go."

"Restroom! Restroom!" He emphatically pointed me to the restroom so I decided that perhaps I should at least freshen up. One look in the mirror startled me. My lovely hair was hanging in limp spaghetti strings. My perfect makeup was making black trails down my cheeks. The worst part was, I was so sore I didn't care. Not wanting to subject mall patrons to the horror in the mirror, I did much needed repairs and hobbled to the front where my sister waited.

The masseuses offered us "tea" which consisted of water from the cooler beside the desk as we paid. We quickly made our way out the door where we both collapsed with laughter. Judy said, "Didn't yours hurt? Why were you laughing?" Then she proceeded to tell me how dignified I looked rolled into a ball with my buttocks in the air. I wanted so badly to tell her that my massage had not hurt at all but my inability to walk without limping paired with the fact I asked her to carry my purse gave me away.

I assured her that my massage most assuredly hurt like H-E-double hockey sticks! She told me that she could only think, "What is so funny over there? This guy is killing me and her masseuse is making her laugh!" That is when she confessed that she had watched them as they massaged the other women and chose the one she thought didn't look as rough. So that's why she pushed me out of the way getting to her table.

I asked what her masseuse had asked her when her alarm rang and she said he asked if she wanted 10 more minutes, but my little 5'2", size 6 sister had balled up her fist and told him if he came near her again she was going to deck him. The rest of the evening we went into fits of giggles whenever we thought of our massage. The waitress at the restaurant told us that the masseuse where we went gives "deep muscle" acupressure massage.

Now, I probably should add, you don't go to the mall to get a massage. Perhaps you already knew that ... but that little bit of knowledge had escaped me so we walked into the office, giggling like two teenagers and limped out no longer having knowledge; but having wisdom.

The Five and Dime Fork
by Madalin Bickel

The house was clean thanks to two ladies and $250.00. No way was she going to cook and mess up her sparkling kitchen. She would grab a bite at a local eatery and read excerpts from the "hot off the press anthology" that her writing group had published. She chagrinly pulled into the parking lot of a "chain" restaurant and sincerely hoped no one who knew her, saw her.

She was shown to a table beside a window. It was Thursday night so a single woman was actually given a decent table albeit for two, but not bad. She ordered a glass of wine, the best on the list which wasn't saying much, and looked at the menu. Her good intentions of a salad left when the menu "pictured" a shrimp and steak combo. She settled for a peppercorn steak, vegetables, and a baked potato. That was a special request. What was it with these places serving "garlic" mashed potatoes lately! It was difficult to ruin a baked potato, but what some places did when they "mashed" them was criminal.

Ok. She wasn't a food critic tonight, but seeing the closed hamburger joint next door didn't help. Who in their right mind would name any restaurant "Fuddruckers" and expect it to succeed! Just looking at the sign made her lose her appetite. Time to read.

She read several short stories and poems before her food arrived. There were some great stories in the collection. She made a mental note to contact some of the authors of the better selections and let them know their efforts did not go unnoticed.

She was cutting her first bite of steak when a voice said, "Hello." She looked up and tried not to act startled. It was her recent ex-significant-other who had turned out to be not so "significant."

"Hello to you." She saw it in his eyes; knew it was coming...

"Eating alone? Mind if I join you?" He asked not even waiting for her to say "yes" or "no."

Awkwardly but with grace (she hoped) she quietly answered "Of course. Good to see you. It's been awhile."

He took the seat opposite and with slight embarrassment he whispered "Are you secretly critiquing this place tonight."

She laughed and said no and commented that it was probably a good thing too. She held up her fork. It was a cheap ugly aluminum fork with a bent tine. They both laughed. "It matches the paper napkin quite well, but doesn't do the steak justice."

"Should I warn the staff who you are?" He asked with a conspiratorial twinkle in his eye.

"No, we'll let it pass tonight."

"So what are you reading?" He was trying to make polite noncommittal small talk.

"It's an anthology. The writing group to which I belong just published it."

"Really. Could I see it?" He seemed genuinely impressed. Surprise!

The waitress appeared at his left elbow. He gave her one of his famous flirtatious smiles and ordered his favorite whisky and a thick steak with fries. "As you can see, I still like my whisky even if it isn't always Dewars. So, let me see your book."

She handed it to him and proceeded to eat her dinner. The potato was growing cold and the steak had lost some of its flavor. Typical.

"Wow! You wrote the preface. I'm not surprised. Those poems you sent me were really good - not that I'm an expert, but I really think you can write."

"You better hold your comments until you read some of the excerpts. Some are quite good, others could use some editing." They both laughed. He unrolled his flatware and made a production of checking the fork and testing the tines for sturdiness by biting them. The waitress appeared with his drink.

"Your steak will be right out. How is the peppercorn steak?" She replied it was fine and the waitress left.

A little more small talk and his steak arrived. He talked about his son and grandson, and that work was getting him down. He didn't talk about where he was living or with whom and she didn't ask.

"So, if *you* were writing about tonight's meal, what would you say?" she asked him as she sipped the last of her wine.

He motioned for another whisky and said in a reporter-like voice, "The steak was cooked as ordered, the vegetables were crisp tender, and the fries had just the right amount of seasoning. The best part of the meal, however, was sitting with my dining partner and sharing quiet conversation. No dessert was needed."

"Always the comedian, aren't you," she laughed. "You're right about the vegetables. Finally, even a restaurant with bent forks has learned not to overcook the broccoli."

The waitress brought two checks. She picked up her own. She didn't offer to pay for his and he didn't offer to pay for hers. Those days were over. He'd need to go somewhere else for *apple pie alamode*.

"Nice seeing you again, Hal. Hope your son finishes college soon. Tell him I said hello." He had the sense to stand as she left, but sat down to finish his drink and probably another.

"Bye Maggie. It was good seeing you."

She said good night to the wait staff and went out the door. She didn't look back. She didn't want to know if he were watching. She unlocked the car door, and slid into the cool leather seat. Maybe she *should* write about tonight's eating experience and title it "Eating a Steak with a Five and Dime Fork." Yes, that would just about describe the evening."

House on Route 17
by Andrea Williams Reed

along the county's long, curvy main route,
stood a single family house, with three bedrooms,
one and half bath, on less than an acre.

it sheltered humans, an occasional dog or fish
with cats in constant residence.
the stork came twice and each time left a baby girl.
extended family members brought connections
and friends called with conversation and news.

twisters passed over and took a fence.
lightning demonstrating its powers came more than once.
the cost: a TV, furnace and tree.
illness stayed and stayed, took health as its prize.
a lay- off settled among us and claimed wealth.
the bank foreclosed, ran off with the house.

commercial endeavors occupy
the walls and spaces now.
signage and asphalt where trees and grass once
graced the landscape.

previously residents now Route 17 travelers,
with memories, connections, and affections for a
single family house, with three bedrooms,
one and half bath on less than an acre.

Country

In the End, I Couldn't Sell
by Ron Russis

Eight generations had owned the family farm,
had persevered against all kinds of times,
sharing in each success and failure, every struggle
whether one overcome or partly overcome by. Ours were
    relentless
efforts, across all the seasons and decades of work,
and by every measure it was near always hard.

No there wasn't much that was easy. Hard
times was more the norm – all days long on a farm…
And always more to do than you knew, with work
from first light 'til last, even in the best of times.
The only word to carry a sense of it all was 'relentless.'
It seemed every day contained its own unique struggle.

Struggle, that was a kind word, generous even. *Struggle* –
yes, that is what we did. The simplest of labors, hard,
if only because of a lack of hands to do. We were
    unrelenting,
like ants, each of us contributing all we could to the farm;
to make it work, all devoted all their time – *all their time*.
It seemed work was all we knew, never an end to the work.

And yet there were short, infrequent breaks to the work,
between the plowing, planting, reaping – a continuous
    struggle
to fit it all into the day, month, season – making time
and stealing time – from chores that needed doing. Hard
choices and often no choice at all on a working farm,
to permit the doing of leisure – weather and life relentless.

Few options for us back then, this way of life relentless
in its demands. In each generation someone ran from the
    work,
ran to the city or out to sea, ran anywhere to escape the farm,
to break away from the cycle of the seasons, the endless
    struggle
to put food by – crops stored in cellar bins or canned in jars,
    and hard-
salted or smoke-cured meats hung from butcher hooks for
    the leaner times.

I knew good times came with the bad, as in all times,
and always the labor waited its doing, relentless
in its patience, knowing whether easily done or hard
it *still* needed doing and the work would wait, the work
would wait, but that struggle to find willing hands, that
    struggle
to keep the farm afloat was harder now that none wanted to
    farm.

Once more times had changed. My children's children
    relentless
in their avoidance of hard work, wishing the farm and work
    sold off…
In deciding to sell I struggled; instead I gave the farm
    away…

Midwestern Corn
by Norma Redfern

Flowing in the breeze, sunshine covers
Far miles of dark emerald green.
Graceful silken heads rising strong and tall
Glossy strands of bright golden tassels.
The wind carries seeds flying high.
In air a golden mist covers dark green leaves
A haze of heat in summer afternoon.
Months of drying, secreting all moisture
Tall withered stalks remain in stiff summer heat
Until the cool days of fall.
Machines crush and grind the bounty
To be bagged, used to feed cattle and hogs
In the Heartland.

Father and Son
by Rod Vanderhoof

The ancient river is clear and cold. Spruce,
    alder and abandoned apple orchards
        line its banks.

The song of wind stirring through trees
    and the tangy scent of conifers create
        a sacred, comfort-wellness.

Indian paintbrush and Oregon grape
    flourish in bright reds, yellows and purples
        while orange salmon berries are ripe.

At daybreak, Dad kneels at river's edge
    and hand-scoops water to drink,
        just like Indians of old.

He places beer and soda pop in shallows
    among rocks that keep bottles from
        sweeping away in brisk current.

We begin fishing. I step on
    a slippery boulder and am
        splash-swallowed by the river.

I swim-clamber to shore and remove
    my soggy sweatshirt,
        hanging it on a branch.

I keep my wet tee shirt but
    shiver with cold. No matter, I'll be
        warmer as we work downriver.

The best cutthroats hide where rapids
    roar into calm pools bordered by
        branch overhangs.

A trout ambushes morsels rushing along
    the boil. Dad floats a grasshopper and
        the water explodes.

A fish doubles the pole, leaping
    high in the morning air, shaking
        its head, trying to throw the hook.

Skittering on tip-tail, it crosses the pool and dives,
    gains speed, then goes airborne.
        Dad keeps steady pressure and

coaxes it closer. His
    net flashes out and
        the battle is over.

He lays his cutthroat on sword ferns to show me the
    black spots on its green top and sides, while crimson
        knife-slashes brand both sides of its lower jaw.

At the next riffle, I go first. My hopper drifts near
    an underwater log. My pole snaps downward
        with the strain of a heavy

fish making deep runs.
    I keep the line taut, but not
        so taut as to break the leader.

The cutthroat tires and draws
    near. Dad nets him for me,
        a full-bodied prize.

We fish till afternoon and catch many.
    Some escape by entangling
        in branches that drape

the river like museum tapestries,
    creating shadowy hideaways for
        cutthroats when sun is bright.

Leaving the river, we push through heavy
    undergrowth toward the logging railroad,
        then stumble-walk on uneven ties back to the car.

At our starting point, we clean the fish.
    My hands are covered with bloody guts.
        "What now, Dad?"

"Wipe your hands on your pants, that's what pants are for."
    "They are?"
        "Sure, but don't tell Mom I said so."

He builds a fire and cuts two filets,
    covering them with flour, sprinkling them with
        spices. He fries bacon for flavoring, placing

the filets in the pan with diced potatoes
    and carrots — a gobble-down meal. Dad
        savors his beer and I, my soda.

Meanwhile, I retrieve my sweatshirt. We are exhausted from
    the morning trek. Dad fetches blankets from the trunk and
        flat-stretches them on green grass.

Using jackets as pillows,
    we float in billowy sleep, then
        pack the car and, with regret,

turn onto the highway.
    "I'd rather stay, Dad!"
        "Me, too."

Sunlight dims and the river remains
    clear and cold. Spruce, alder and abandoned
        apple orchards line its banks.

*Wind stirring through trees
 and the scent of conifers create
  a sacred, comfort-wellness.*

*Indian paintbrush and Oregon grape border the
 stream in bright reds, saffron shades and purples.
  Orange salmon berries are ready for eating.*

Cold January
by Madalin Bickel

Cold January entered wild and new
as blowing snow began to drift and bank
around each tree and bush that quaintly grew
and turned each one into a ghostly flank.

Like soldiers caught in frozen timeless war
each marching forth to break the chilling spell
that hung from tree limbs, eves, and roofs afar
to silhouette old stories yet to tell.

A tale of farms abandoned to the wind
as wood no longer kindled sparks and burn.
Each family left to starve and freeze in kind
and left the comfort of past times to turn.

Surviving life to live again in peace
and knowing cold and death at last had ceased.

Night Chase
by Kelly Patterson

The midnight curtain falls again
On our mountain-bottom grounds
Deep hollows find a bushy tail
Fleeing from the hounds

Corn whiskey warms our gullets
Kinfolk from my clan
Reflecting from the lightwood fire
A fox horn in my hand

I bugle for the pack to stop
My hounds of Black & Tan
When in a graceful voice he barks
From the hole in which he ran

It entertains us mountain men
To listen to them run
So not to kill a cherished friend
We hunt without a gun

Nature

Old Rag Cottonwood Stag
by Michelle O'Hearn

Smiling faces of the flowers
A happy audience to my awe
Flaunting fragrances
as daunting as the claws,
or some may say, mandibles,
of the beetle grabbing my toe.

Flicking and flailing the Cottonwood Stag
I fling it on the fern.
The sunflowers dancing in laughter at me
I chuckle back in turn.

Smelling the scent of impending showers
The farm is active with clawing paws
Longing for the magnificent taste
of satisfying water in the jaws,
very well understandable,
after the drought the year has known.

Portrait
by Ummie

The trees have not budded
What happened to the green leaves
That used to grow so beautifully
Now lifeless, listless, dead, still
The branches are so thin and withered
Bending with the wind
Luster gone, producing no song
Branches dark and twisted
Electrical wires dominate and restrict
An out of control spark
might hit its mark

Branches down on a wet muddy ground
Every other space full of holes
The black furry one digs
Leaving imprints of my soles
Ground bare, stripped of the grass
That was there once but didn't last
Rose bushes no longer bloom
Thorns are all it gives
Everywhere you look gloom
Forsythias used to grow yellow leaves
Now the color brown exists
Laughter laughing the word resist

Should the branches be stripped away
Should the trees be cut down
Because
My song no longer makes a sound
Should the yard be paved
Or with rich brown soil be saved
Should the rose and forsythia bushes be pruned
Pulled up and thrown away
Or left to stand come what may
To begin the soft, sultry sound of a crown

The Quickening
by Jill Austin Deming

Soft and pliable newborn leaves
transform sunlight into a chartreuse glow

Slipping soundlessly into this leafy cathedral
I know I am touching
holy ground

Goodness, life, and breath
emanate from each leaf
I inhale deeply
this earthy fragrance of the gods

Warm, soft air
envelops me like a cocoon

This is the smell of possibility.
The quickening isn't just in the earth
But also in me

The Tree
by J. R. Robert-Saavedra

High above the canyon floor
But underneath where eagles soar
Struggling up from a crack
Among droppings and refuse
A seed gave root.

A seed sunk its fingers
Grabbing for a hold
Into the stern face
Of the fiery red rock
Defied gravity
It challenged the wind.

Roots went
Deep into the rock
It grew
High-up and over the canyon's floor
so far below
It spread its branches to the sun

Sunrise
by J. R. Robert-Saavedra

A sharp, cold, dagger
Silently strikes
Puncturing
The soft, black, velvet skin
And a red drop falls.

Staining
Slowly at first
And then
Completely covering the horizon
In a sea of crimson red.

The trees, like giant, black ribs
Silently stand
Mute witness
To the death of night
Afraid, to break the silence.

The ambers flicker
Awakened by a stealthy breath
And in the distance
A cock, gives the alarm
Sending the stars on flight.

And the stained veil
Of the soft black night
Is rent
By a probing finger of light
The day is born.

Ignored
by J. R. Robert-Saavedra

The sea
Gathered all of itself
Into a wave
And gave all of his self to the beach.

Drenched in the gold
From a harvest moon
On a warm summer night
Underneath the diamonds of the night

The sea
Caressed lovingly
The curves
Of the sandy beach.

Every strand of hair
Every turn of her body
It lovingly touched
Revering it.

Beneath the starry sky
Bathed by the golden moon
The beach stayed mute
Impassive.

Slowly the sea
Gathered himself up
And sank back
Into its fathomless darkness.

Camping in the Woods of Wisconsin
by Julie Phend

In the mornings
    We wake to the sound of birds,
    sun filtering through the top of our tent,
    sweating in sleeping bags that now seem too warm.
    We rise and feel the breeze on our backs,
    wash our faces in cold lake water,
        and cook.
    Soon the scents of coffee, bacon and wood smoke
    waft through the trees,
    and we eat
    together in the open air.

In the afternoons
    We hike through woodlands flecked with
        wildflowers,
    clamber over rocks and
    shiver in shady valleys,
    the children strapped to our backs.
        Then we swim,
    long strokes in cool water.
    Lying on warm sand,
    we relax tired muscles,
    build castles with moats and turrets,
    wet sand slipping through small fingers
    while the sun creeps across a sapphire sky.

In the evenings
    We build a big bonfire,
    roast hotdogs and marshmallows,
    lick gooey juices from sticky fingers.
    We watch forest creatures crawl
    close to our campsite,
    hoping for a handout:
    Ground squirrels, chipmunks, raccoons,

even a skunk.
We play games,
   sing songs,
      laugh and tell stories.
Lying on our backs, we snuggle together,
gaze into the sky and
watch the stars come out,
one
   by
      one.

The Pond
by Jill Austin Deming

On the bank of the pond
surrounded by stately trees
I find refuge
from the hectic
rhythm of life

tensions roll away
as I crunch through the thick carpet
of fallen leaves
their sweet fragrance
envelops me

I spy a doe as
she sounds her barking alarm call
then flicks her white flag
and bounds away

Around me is the busy,
   constant peeping of
cardinals as they flit from
   branch to branch.
I pause to drink in
   Their song

Above me, a hawk closely
observes my approach and
waits a beat before
sliding smoothly off his perch
into flight

Before me, translucent
dust motes float lazily in
the slanting sunlight of afternoon

A tiny woodpecker circles the
base of two trees, moving
onto a third before setting to work
and drumming out a beat

A gaggle of geese is silently swimming
I hear their laughter
as their contentment rolls out in waves

In some imperceptible way
all this becomes part of me

Matters of Gravity
by Anne Heard Flythe

A rumble of dry thunder in the west
like the swallowing of day by a great throat.
An easy hike became onerous as the weight of August
slowed each heel-jolting downward stride;
air almost too dense to breathe, the constant crawl
of sweat beneath damp clothing maddening
as the whining, stinging, pestering of gnats and flies.
And then the lake, a flat silver mirror of the woods
filling a great hollow in the land.

No way could I resist its cool seduction, I stripped
and waded into the warm shallow surface water,
pushed deeper to gain the cold marbling of springs.
Spread-eagled I floated among reflected trees and sunset fire.
The cool division of air and water sides a thermal Plimsoll.
The world muffled as I sank to fill my ears with silence,
the rush and thump of blood and heart confirmed
I lay suspended between two elements.

The evening hatch arose around me, lifting into air,
drawing hungers from the depths to dimple
the silver plane, pout-kissing the mirrors' underside.
My hair fanned Medusa-like, alive as waterweed,
when lazily I raised my head to hear the lustful groan
of bullfrogs, the lunge and splash of feeding bass
among the narrow reeds that fringe the shore,
a brief metallic flash of green and silver.
Overhead the twittering of swallows and the almost
subliminal squeaks of early bats.

Myriad minnows, their lips like effervescence explored
my skin. Embracing the present, still as a floating log,
inert, I remained irrelevant to fish, frog, turtle,
and to a great blue heron, immobile as a metal
garden sculpture frozen in hunting mode nearby,
spear like beak poised, one yellow eye as focused
as a camera lens on the clear water around its legs.

A lucent moon floated ghostly in a sky gone dusky lavender
turning tree tops to black lace silhouettes.
The heron now standing at water's edge, explosively
unfurled all seven feet of wingspread, leaped high
and with giant strokes was airborne so violently
I entertained the fantasy that earth spun faster on its axis.

Neck still sinuously curved, long legs trailing,
it flew slowly across the lake and out of sight.
Still I hesitated, hanging weightless as an astronaut,
until centered as the heron, I stood and walked ashore,
growing heavier with each upward step,
but prepared to deal with gravity in all its aspects.

Frisky
by Kelly Patterson

Cabin walls repel the cold
Birch wood burns hot and bright
Reindeer steaks atop my stove
Same thing every night

One dirty book . . . a dirty glass
Filled with homemade whiskey
Pot-bread laced with honey sweets
Can make a hermit frisky

Always knocking at my door
When meat is hot and sizzly
"Come in, Boo-Boo, and warm yourself"
Says the hermit to the grizzly

Pastime
by Jim Gaines

My brother liked to visit Penny Brook
It begins in a swamp back in the maple grove
Cattail tussocks and peevish red-winged birds
A smell of green things turning into earth

My little brother fished in Penny Brook
So narrow second graders straddled it
In spring alewives struggled up to die
Too bony so they fed the Pilgrims' corn

My brother fished in the brook for eels
He saw them writhing on the mud below
At first he tried to grab them with his hands
No one hereabouts was quick enough

My brother caught no eels with my old rod
Watching borrowed red and white plastic bob
He daydreamed in the long June afternoons
Till finally he got a cautious nibble

My brother caught a frog in Penny Brook
He delicately reeled it and unhooked the jaw
A minute drop of brownish blood remained
From his hand it sprang into a glass-green swirl

*Far Away
and Long Ago*

Only in America
by Rod Vanderhoof

From the sands of Kitty Hawk to
the towering Hawaiian surf,

from the Arctic mists of Point Barrow to
the coral reefs of Florida,

from colonial sailing ships to
the frontiers of space,

our forefathers entered the wilderness
and built this land.

We became
    sawyers and lawyers,
    sellers and tellers,
    miners, explorers and loggers,

    preachers and teachers,
    farmers and charmers,
    salesmen, inventors and joggers,

    breeders and seeders,
    chandlers and handlers,
    brewers and bankers and buyers,

    musicians, beauticians,
    millers, distillers,
    soldiers and sailors and flyers,

    policemen and firemen,
    electricians, technicians,
    tutors, tailors, magicians,

foresters, choristers,
mothers and others,
poets, writers, physicians,

and . . .

we created a great nation because

in America we are free!

Long Distance
by Jim Gaines

John calls me from Australia's fields.
Where today is already tomorrow.
The people are so open there,
Refuse to harbor sorrow.
The kangaroos and cockatiels
Have hardly any fear.
I ask if he's kept his razor blades and wallet.
He tells me of the dream time,
As the aborigines there call it,
And how forgotten crime
No longer phases Aussies of this age,
Who unlike us have learned to turn the page.
I ask about the meals he's being fed.
Instead, he talks of art -- a Judas stippled red,
Apostles dark folks draw like unfilled urns
Of dotted swirls without a single stroke,
And Christ a whopping chalice of a bloke,
God-blessing them as holy sun returns.

Beachcombers
by Jim Gaines

Men on the margins swing metal
detector arms out in crisp arcs
over softer sway of guts as rigid
polished metal contrasts with organic flab.
The bulging beachcombers' legs
bear up surprisingly to end in tight plastic
galoshes admitting no sand between toes.
Incongruously their tee shirts advertise
martial arts and linebackers.
They've finished upper reaches where less
efficient four-wheeled sweepers pass and leave
little wracks of cigarette butts.
Now the combers work the edge of ebbing
tide and shove beeping disks down
into wet sand and dig with hinged scoops
that seem designed to sift up
turds from giant hounds but most of the time
treasure's just a bottle cap, a twisted hinge
from sunglasses, or a scrap of fishing rig
to drop into incongruous aprons
just to avoid a second useless dig tomorrow.
Every hundredth time a real coin goes
into the purse and every thousandth a ring
to take to pawnbrokers strictly under the table
to be liquidated in the Sand Dollar Bar
after 10 A.M. when moms and kiddies
take over the beach as swells promise to return.

Hawaiian Surfer
by Rod Vanderhoof

I steer my longboard
forever on toward
the shores of Waikiki,
riding waves in the sun,
cutting turns on each run,
surfing's my life, you see.

I have endless reasons
for spending my seasons
in striking, beguiling Hawaii,
with weather so nice
in a posh paradise
where folks bid aloha to me.

Where hula girls wriggle,
waheenees giggle
and palm trees bend in the breeze,
where the northeast trades
bring keen escapades
and surf booms in from the seas.

Hear the slap of the sails,
see black pilot whales
from a catamaran skimming through spray,
feel tropical heat,
a rousing heartbeat
as flying fish scatter away.

I steer my longboard
forever on toward
the shores of Waikiki,
riding waves in the sun,
cutting turns on each run,
surf's in my blood, you see.

Route Sixty-Six
by Madalin Bickel

August nineteen sixty-eight stretched
hot and humid wings before
the green Oldsmobile
traveling west, beckoned by
black-top lanes and
hypnotic adventures.
Only the young and brave
could follow its yellow lines.

With precious presents packed,
everything they owned
stowed in carrier and trunk
they waved good-bye to family,
safety, and security to see
the west and California; their
dream since Walt first mesmerized
their childhood eyes with
siren's sights of Mickey's Disneyland.

The west was welcomed with the
murky muddy waters where the
ominous Ohio merged into the
Mississippi - golden in the setting sun.
When morning dawned, route
sixty-six enticed the pair to wind and
wend into Oklahoma.
Bronze cowboys rode their bucking broncs.
The concrete path crossed the state line
marked by towering tepee signs.

Tucumcari's tribal dancers,
Albuquerque's Old Town,
with silver turquoise and
cool nights in azure blue adobe huts
with wooden floors and musty smells.
Craggy brown mountains and scrubby pines,
topaz painted deserts, tumble weed,
dry land and dancing heat waves
stretched everywhere but home.
Mojave wasn't Disneyland -

The water bag flopped against the grimy car.
Where were the orange groves and movie stars'
the surf and beach of song?
Cool green Appalachians left far behind,
the dream dried up and yet
beyond the knoll, freeways
awaited excited eyes.
Concrete became four lanes of magic.
The Pacific a welcome mat,
Mother Road at an end -
A continent of tomorrows ahead.

My Man in Pamplona
by Rod Vanderhoof

In the morning sun,
a rocket booms and the
corral gate opens onto a
narrow Pamplona street.

From a shady balcony,
my grandson looks for the
mystique and glamour and glitz of a Hemingway novel

but sees only bulls galloping,
chasing smart alecks and fools and buffoons
trying to outrun behemoths poised to
rip and trample those who
stagger
stumble
fall.

Amid the white noise of the crowd
and the clatter-clank of cowbells,
he feels the throb of cloven hooves on
cobblestones and

smells
street odors from
all-night frolics.

In the bullring that evening,
he sees
a strutting, golden-garbed matador
skewer a tormented bull
with a single thrust.

Blood-red torrents gush from the bull's mouth
as it tries a feeble charge,
collapses to its knees
and dies

while the crowd cheers.

The Thorny Branch
by Steven P. Pody

Neanderthal, you silly man,
how is it that you guttered out?
When Cro the Ho was sapient,
you were the tougher, and had smarts:
      Surviving as some chunky skulls,
the scientists measure, in our time,
a larger brain than modern heads:
      A hominid, ...but Oh You Kid...!
Your timing wasn't quite the best
to be a European.
But a big, robustus corpus
   would have been
      advantageous, per diem.
The rage of the age was ice,
but ice reflects thee not today.
I look for heroes on my cereal boxes,
     and you're not there. Nowhere.
You're not in my shirt or shoe size,
and you're not in my acid-washed genes.
W h e r e v e r   d i d   y o u   g o ?

It is said that you were a lesser competitor
because you weren't very social.
Cooperation deters not the rugged individualist!
Unless it does. No names on your dance card...
Pushed into the margin lands, perhaps
you answered evolution's ad for a job
as a race of Yeti or Sasquatch.
Maybe you intermingled a bit, after all,
and survive as part of the very intelligent,
hairier people of the Earth.
Maybe some passing extraterrestrials
took pity on you, and you colonized
a fairer planet, producing trinkets and selling
Mammoth burgers for intergalactic space-ways.
What a mystery! What a tragedy!
Bad times, bad neighbors,
        and bad karmageddon.
Extinction sucks. Whisper to me
your echoes. Tell me you are hiding
in the deep roots of the Himalayas. Tell me
you ran into a god of your own, who cared.
Tell me of the greatness you could have been!
Together, eventually, we might have been awesome.
As it was, Cro-Magnon talent manifested thusly:
Brother,
over eons, savage conquest or slavery wasn't
our cruelest gift.
That would be
        oblivion.

Birth of a Nation
by Ummie

Storm coming, screeching and howling
Thunder clouds breaking and bowing
Streaks of lightning brought cry moans
Thrashing and crashing pushing out a red bone
She came amidst the pain
She came wide eyed with no name
To forever carry Mama's blame
First generation wondering about the gain
She came in the dead of the night
To set upside down and crooked, straight up right
She came, birth of a nation
To prepare her generations
Her generations, to stand on her shoulders
As the flames she extinguishes smolders

Betsy and George
by Greg Miller

    George dipped with practiced precision under the low lintel of the door frame. At six-foot four, he was quite accustomed to doing this, but of course, since he was wearing a tricorn hat, he had to simultaneously doff his chapeau, slip into the room and look regal and dignified. All of this was quite an annoyance that almost set him to grinding the few real teeth he had left. Nevertheless, when he spied a lady in a blue hooped dress, sitting in a rocking chair, hands fully engaged with a pair of knitting needles, he quickly affected a deep bow, hat in hand. "Madam Ross, I am at your service."

    Betsy Ross looked up from her work. Her face reddened as she hastily put down her knitting. "Oh, General Washington! I apologize, I forgot that you meant to call on me today."

He looked at her with kindness, "Quite all right, Mrs. Ross; I did not mean to startle you." Stepping forward, he took her extended hand and gave it a courteous peck. "Do you have time to go over the designs for the new flag?"

"Oh yes!" she said. She stood up, quickly straightening the ruffles in her dress, and walked over to a large cabinet. With a wide smile, she turned to look at him. "I have a few for you to look at."

"Excellent news!" He strode over to the cabinet, careful to avoid catching his boot spurs on piles of cloth laying on the floor.

With a flourish, she pulled the cabinet open, and on the shelf lay three folded bundles. She grabbed the first one. "This design I came up with as I went to church." With care, she gently unfolded it, until the entire flag hung from her extended fingertips.

His face froze. The main part of the flag was pink, with yellow and white daisies on it, a multicolored rainbow, and a sun in the corner. "Interesting," he replied dryly.

"Yes, last Sunday, on my way to church, as the sun came up, and mist lay in the air, I passed a field of daisies surrounded by flowering pink phlox. A beautiful rainbow graced the sky, and I thought to myself—isn't that just like our country, a rainbow emerging after the storm of revolution."

"And the daisies?" he asked with a crinkled brow.

She quickly pointed a daisy and drew her finger toward the corner of the flag. "Oh see? Daisies turn to face the sun, and there are thirteen of them, just like the states."

Struggling to maintain his Roman-like bearing, he replied as calmly as he could. "Yes, well. Very pretty, but I was hoping for something with more of a martial flair." He smiled gamely, and slapped a gloved fist into his palm for emphasis. "Perhaps something that might inspire the troops toward bravery and steadfastness."

"Oh..." she replied, a bit hesitantly. But then, with a smile she set aside her first flag and quickly grabbed the second. "I understand. Let's see what you think of this one." She unfurled it.

Sweat broke out on his brow. On a field of yellow, thirteen kittens ran and tumbled about, and in the corner stood a giant rectangular piece of wood in a bucket. His eyebrows shot up, as he glanced at her.

"The kitties are the states, which are cute and cuddly. Especially that little one, Rhode Island. But, you see..." she pointed at one of the kitten's paws ... "they all have very sharp claws that can scratch." At that she clawed the air with her fingers and meowed loudly.

Wide eyed, he stared for a moment before catching himself. "Okay." His eyes darted to the flag. "What about the stick in the bucket?"

"Oh that," she quickly replied. "That's a ruler in an ash can."

He looked at her with confusion.

"Get it? We are getting rid of our old ruler!" She giggled loudly.

With a small nod, and sick smile, he pointed to the last bundle on the shelf. "What about that?"

She looked at the bundle. "Oh, that is not a flag; it's a saddle blanket for your horse." She put down the second flag and grabbed the last bundle. Unfurling it, there were thirteen red and white stripes on the right two-thirds of the blanket, and blue field with thirteen stars arranged in a circle on the left third of the blanket. In the middle of the circle of stars was a large round hole.

He tapped his fingers against his chin. "Very nice. But what is the hole for?"

She stuck her fingers through the hole. "Oh, that's for your horse's tail of course, and so he can ... "

"I understand," he interjected. "Actually, I like this design for the flag, just move the blue field into the upper left corner." He cleared his throat. "Oh, and sew up the hole."

She pursed her lips, "Well, if that is what you want. Are you sure you wouldn't like something in the middle of the circle of stars?"

Looking warily at her, he replied, "Like what?"

"Maybe a fierce creature," her face brightened, "Like a badger, or an angry beaver!"

"Uh, no." He dug out his pocket watch and gave it a cursory glance. "Oh my, look at the time, my horse is double-parked."

Taking no notice, she continued, "Or better yet, a possum carrying its babies on its back. You know they get quite cross when you try to chase them out of your attic."

Trying desperately to scrub out the image of his soldiers marching into battle with probably the ugliest animal in North America on his war banner, he backed out of the house, bumping his head on the door-frame. Nearly choking on the cloud of powder from his wig, he shouted, "I'll be back next week to pick up the new flag!"

Following him to the doorway, she replied, "All right, but if you think of something, let me know in a couple of days!"

She swung the door almost shut, before suddenly whipping it open again. "Woodchucks can be mean too you know." After staring out the door for a few moments, she shook her head. "My lord, he moves quickly for such a big man."

At Home with Mrs. Madison
by Michelle O'Hearn

Hard-edged heels clicking against wood
polished to a sheen
is she
Draped in tapestries now used
as bedspreads
Miss Dolly of the child wore cotton
southern summer cool
Her golden bosomed dress
in velvet
the Mrs. Madison of honor
at home.

Soft feminine fingers caress wall panels
crafted by the finest
is he
Her husband to hire her desire
for beauty
Artisans at work and blindly aware
of a presidential mission
Yet how trim can humble live
in her eyes
from windows of honor
Many eyes will see.

Ceilings high enough for the acoustical ring
of debate to be echoed
the wit and intellect of wise guests
are they
To argue the politics
of science
and God-driven inventions,
the thoughts of idle instincts.

Burlap-wrapped hoofs warming against snow
pampered equine divine

were we
Enamored and pursued
born and bred
The mistress leaving nothing rotten
Summer hands left to soothe
Kind to harvest no distress
one moment alone
entertained by Mrs. Madison
at home.

Ain't Nothin' Left
by Madalin Bickel

The heavy drops of rain relentlessly
were soaked into impoundment dams along
the Middle Fork of Buffalo's dark creek.
The sludge built dam held while black water rose.
One hundred million gallons poised behind
eight hundred thousand tons of waste—the gob—
the remnants of the miners lives, spare change
from Pittson's purse. The souls downstream awoke.
Cold stillness filled the air, no barking dogs,
no singing birds, just nothingness until
the ominous black wave of sludge, water,
and clay careened from side to side to sweep
away the homes and lives of gentle minds
and hearts from Saunders, Amherstdale, and Stowe
to Mann. The Guyandotte absorbed the wrath
and carried it downstream. The path was clear
to any eye. Survivors hung from limbs
protruding from the mountainside above
the mud, debris, and chill. "Ain't nothin' left
no church, no house—a holler runs not down
but up." So looking back the wall of black
erased it all. Now time has passed and still
I see no road, no homes, just faces blank
with hollow eyes and nightmares for their dreams.

Collapse of the Silver Bridge
by Madalin Bickel

She sparkled in the early morning sun
A jewel that spanned the ochred liquid way,
The hazardous Ohio's muddy flow,
Aluminum and steel suspended high.
Above the concrete pillars, traffic passed
The busy life along route thirty-five.
Her soul was in the bedrock deep; her life
Held in the chains; an artery of trade,
A sign of things to come. A day for crowds
To shop then gaily head for home across
The silver span upon the fifteenth day,
A cold December nineteen sixty-seven.

No one imagined in the pouring rain
Of Cornstalk's hand upon the eye bar's pin.
A crack, a slip, and then a sonic boom.
The western deck began to fold and bend.
It shuttered, dipped, released its heavy load
That tumbled down toward an icy grave.
The twisting towers crumpled soaring down
While bodies mixed with Christmas gifts and bobbed
Like ghostly heads. A curse or flawed design?
That met with fate to meld within our minds
The memories of superstitious times.

Passages of *Josephus*, from Liverpool to Boston, 2 May to 7 June, 1853
by D.P. Tolan

The construction, outfitting and 1853 voyage of the ship **Josephus** from Liverpool to Boston in many ways embodied the passage from the Old to the New World. Among her 308 passengers were my great grandparents, and my grandfather was born at sea on the journey.

Josephus was constructed at Kennebunk, Maine and launched 1 August 1850 at the Lord family yard at Kennebunk Landing. Lord family interests in local banks and businesses eased financing. Shipbuilders used half-models, not drawings, to pick offset distances and craft each frame, stringer, and gusset to the desired contour. Local materials from Lord family forests, mills and yard were used by Master Carpenter Ira Grant. **Josephus'** documents list construction trades as carpenters, smiths, joiners, painters, caulkers, fasteners, riggers, boat builders, iron founders, and makers of sail and spars, brass, pumps and blocks, and tin ware.

Contemporary practice was to begin framing amidships, then work towards stern and stem. There naturally curved pieces termed "compass" added strength to the hull. Great care was exercised in locating and cutting these, which as hand crafted "knees" stiffened deck supports and other critical components. Master carpenters were always on the lookout for this curved hardwood, sending talented assistants far afield with "moulds" of the required size and shape to obtain what was needed. These "compass" pieces cost many times what other timber cost, though defects could make them unusable. Hand hewing with adzes was required, as their value did not allow automated milling. The Lord shipyard was "marked principally by a carpet of wood chips strewn with raw timber." American shipyards early on used mill cut timber, whereas British yards used hand-hewn pieces.

Hardwoods—birch, soft and hard ash and maple, or red oak—were combined with stocks of white and gray oak to fabricate the great keel and keelsons, stem and stern-works, frames, shelves, clamps, stringers and deck framing. Oak contained tannic acids and could weaken metal bolts holding planking; consequently treenails were used to preclude rapid corrosion of the expensive metal fasteners. Treenails were wooden nails cut from white oak or locust wood which fastened both planking and ceiling through the frames. After being driven, their ends were sawed flush. Treenails were the acknowledged equal of metal fasteners and were cheaper, and thus remained standard.

To reduce wastage, keels or frame components were often scarphed or laminated together. After the ship's frame was in place, it was covered with two separate layers of planking; the inner thicker than exterior planking and usually of southern hard pine. Hard pine was not soft as British insurers thought but "exceedingly hard, durable, and compact." Wherever strength was unimportant, soft woods were incorporated; if available, spruce or even cedar ceiling was used.

Selection and careful cutting of curved timbers followed by seasoning substantially extended the life of ship's timber. Seasoning compass pieces could take up to three years. It was unnecessary to season softwoods—firs, spruces and pine—which had internal resin. Standard practice called for hulls to be copper sheathed below the water line to protect against marine borers. Sheathing replaced tarred hulls for protection from borers, but neither method reduced marine growth on hulls which diminished ship speed and profit. Wooden ships with sheathing had an economic advantage over unsheathed metal hulled ships, an advantage for years until the "working" of a wooden ship neutralized this advantage.

Months passed during construction as the weight increased on the keel blocks and side shores below. Here spaces were left open to promote air circulation and aid in seasoning. Under the hull were long heavy frames—ways—to guide the ship into the water. Atop these ways and under the hull were cradles onto which the ship's weight would be transferred. The weight of the hull, less masts, rigging and stores—added later—were transferred onto cradle and ways, greased before launch. At the right moment and with the proper tide, William Lord Jr.'s wife broke a bottle of champagne, restraining timbers were cut, and *Josephus* slid into the river. Area dignitaries listened to speeches recalling Lord family participation in the recent War of 1812, watched the launch and then attended a reception.

Josephus was launched into the Kennebunk River stern first and upstream, to avoid hitting the other riverbank. Controlled in mid-stream by lines restricting her motion, she was turned around in the river bend and towed to a dock for outfitting. Outfitting, the process of completing construction, was a busy period. While first Master Alden B. Day signed on a crew, Oliver and Horace Davis installed and tested bilge and fresh water pumps on deck. Joshua and Daniel Emery put finishing touches to installation of her three masts, riggings, and cargo stowage. As completed she drew nineteen feet, had a length overall of 175 feet, masts of 90 to 125 feet, a beam of 35 to 40 feet, was of two decks and carried twelve major sails. She had twin boats aft by the ship's wheel, rigged outboard on davits.

Her three masts were from trees of substantial height, cut straight and clear of "visible branch growth" before use. Ship masts were built in three segments from the keel up, lower, top, and top gallant. Each was topped by mast caps, frequently of iron. Sailing ships required stone ballast to offset the weight of masts and rigging when not carrying cargo. Ballast was required even to move among docks, a factor that eventually made sailing ships unprofitable. As with most three masters, *Josephus* carried square rigged sails.

Few wooden ships lasted beyond 10 years, after constant use and the stress of winds, waves and motion. The risks of the seas were offset with insurance. *Josephus'* records show her owners hedged losses through multiple coverage. Accounting records reveal the owners insured both the ship and her cargoes quarterly. Her owners were William Lord Jr.; George C. Lord and Ivory Lord; Charles H. Lord; George C. Lord Jr.; and Alden B. Day, her first Master. Records for 31 July 1852 reflect *Josephus* as profitable; each of the quarter shareowners was paid $754.04 as their share.

Josephus was painted by English artist W.E.D. Stuart in 1856. That painting of *Josephus* under sail off Ramsgate, England is held by The Mariners' Museum in Newport News, Virginia. Stuart's marine works were on display at the Royal Academy, and being a noted artist he would have little reason to paint a foreign merchant ship. The relatively intermediate size of *Josephus* suggests the painting was done on commission by proud owners.

Thomas Wroe, my great grandfather, was born in Lancaster, a small industrial town on England's coast. Thomas' parents were shop owners according to oral tradition, and weavers according to his death certificate. The *London Times* and Boston papers stressed international trade and featured daily articles on stock markets and goods from around the world. These articles informed young Thomas of the world, especially America. Urban crowding and competition for jobs in Lancaster and the promise of America combined to persuade Thomas and his wife Mary Meagher, who fled Ireland, to emigrate.

Liverpool was England's principal port. "Assisted emigration" of Irish after the 1821 Potato Famine came through Liverpool, and records in 1854 alone show 42,000 left for Australia, 200,000 for America, all from Liverpool. Liverpool's growing mercantile trade dominance rested on port organization, excellent rail and canal connections, expanded demand, and increasing industrial capacity. Dock expansion and upgrade provided the city with an economic boom, for her merchants not only traded, they bought ships, thus requiring more docks. Most ship imports in May were of American or Canadian construction, reflecting their better quality and prices. The port saw wide tidal fluctuations, and ships berthed at docks with locks controlling water level. Prince's Dock, completed in 1821, incorporated eleven acres of water area and two locks of forty-five foot width. *Josephus* probably loaded there for this voyage, having arrived April 1 from New Orleans.

Stores of hardtack, salt pork and beef, the best that chandlers, butchers, and other Liverpool merchants could provide, were loaded and secured for sea. Master Paine wanted everything shipshape and seaman-like. The Lord's company agents Pilkington and Wilson were competent and aggressive, and American business was aided by a branch of the American Chamber of Commerce established in 1801. Master Paine contended with ship chandlers, butchers, stevedores, dry-dock people, agents, customs officials, shipping master and port officials. Casks and barrels of rum and wine, firkins of butter, barrels of meat, cooking oil and water, pallets and slings of cargo were loaded. There was dockside congestion caused by hundreds of carts on the docks. *Josephus'* cargo reflected product availability yet profitable transportation to distant markets. The cargo, stowed low in the hull, served as ballast. *Boston Post* editions of 8 and 9 June noted Liverpool Stock market reports, and the *London Times* carried more coverage of Liverpool stocks and business than accounts within London itself. The anchors and anchor chain reflect the cheaper availability of these products abroad, testifying to America's fledgling Industrial Revolution. "Yellow metal," an alloy of copper/zinc applied over a layer of tar and paper, resisted borers and marine growth, but was not used on metal hulls due to corrosion.

Letters of credit on Liverpool firms at varying rates of interest appear regularly in *Josephus'* records, all bills processed after the fact. This method of making payment several months after delivery, with promissory notes as payment, suggests the market's transatlantic breadth and stability. Accounting records show that upon return to the States, English Pounds were invariably exchanged for American currency.

Josephus departed Liverpool 2 May. She cleared the Mersey River channel 4 May, arriving in Boston 7 June. The passage took thirty-six days averaging over six knots. Master Paine had exhaustive dealings with Captain C. Patey, the Emigration Officer at Liverpool, clearing his passengers before leaving port. Ships designed to transport passengers were not in vogue. "No passenger ships worthy of that name existed until the middle of the nineteenth century."

A popular guidebook noted that Irish passengers preferred American ships, "Let the ship be American, remember he is going home, and the captain probably will never pull off his clothes to go to bed during the whole voyage." Europeans often traveled through Liverpool, preferring it to southern ports, which were less organized, had irregular schedules, and were more costly. Passage in 1816 cost £10 per person, but competition and efficiencies lowered this to £2, 2s in the 1830s.

The passengers ate salted meat, hard bread or hardtack, and had fresh water, perhaps some beer. Meals were eaten on deck, weather permitting, otherwise below decks holding on as the ship moved. Hammocks were three to four high in rows. Lighting was primitive within the ship where passengers slept; danger existed from use of whale oil lighting. Undoubtedly many prayed for deliverance from disorientation and nausea at sea during this stormy season. The ship continually rolled, pitched, and yawed with the waves, and heeled with the wind, making real rest difficult, with fatigue finally facilitating sleep.

In better seas and winds she ran before the wind, the sails pulling for all they were worth. The crew continually worked the sails, reefing, furling and unfurling sails. As the wind picked up or slackened, the amount of canvas a ship carried was changed, and a captain always tried to keep as much sail as prudent. Each day's task was to endure until the New World was in sight.

A total of 308 passengers were aboard, suggesting crowding for a ship designed for cargo. They boarded after cargo was stowed. They faced many hazards, including the seas, dangerous whale oil lamps, the cold, dampness, poor food, lack of ventilation, and overcrowding. Living conditions were primitive; of the crew of nineteen, thirteen slept aft, and six forward, passengers in between.

Legislation began to appear in mid-century to protect shipboard passengers from greedy ship owners, who skimped on food, sanitation, space, or all the above. Some ships were so dangerous as to be called "coffins." Parliament established a Board of Trade to regulate transportation, inspect ships, standardize construction, and protect merchant seamen, and increasingly emigrants.

The passenger list of the ***Josephus*** was written in a single hand, suggesting a ship's officer or customs agent wrote all names. One passenger's name was crossed out, and an entry made, "Did not ship," suggesting the list was made on departure from Liverpool. Of the 308, two were Americans, John Walsh age 24 and Michael Wheelan age 17. Three were English, Thomas and Mary Wroe (both listed as 25 and Thomas carried as an iron founder) and Jonathan Butterworth a 30-year-old shoemaker. The remaining 303 were Irish, emigrating as a result of the 1840s Potato Famine. No profession or job was listed for any of the women passengers. The list showed Thomas Wroe, with Mary on the last sheet, probably because she boarded last, being very pregnant. Crewmembers' names were listed in her log, held in the National Archives in Washington, DC. Her crew were all "Americans," though their surnames suggested Italian, French and Irish ancestries.

Josephus and its passengers probably encountered few other ships except as they departed Liverpool or entered Boston. Mary Wroe, unable to move easily because of her pregnancy and the confines of the spacious women's area aft, had an uneasy though fulfilling passage. One day out of Boston on 6 June 1853 William Joseph, my grandfather, was born. Several of the older women, all Irish, probably assisted with his delivery. Among these were Mary Dolan, age 30 and with three of her children onboard, and Mary Sanders, age 40, with a 21-year old daughter onboard.

The passage ended in Boston 7 June 1853. Boston records usually held by the Regional Office of the National Archives—Customs, Registry, Entry and Departure, etc.—burned in 1875. Charts of Boston Harbor and its approaches allowed reconstruction of *Josephus*' entry. No doubt Master Paine entered at first light to ensure safety in the congested waterway, Boston then known as "a dangerous port to enter." His approach left Queen's Island to starboard, Winthrop Head on the beam, and then he tacked past Governor's Island to port.

On arrival at Boston, the ship was quarantined for two days, one of only two vessels so restricted. Records indicate two of her Irish passengers died enroute, passing on at the end of the passage and occasioning the quarantine. Boston papers fail to note their deaths, suggesting they were not among those one could term "well off." British law focused attention on better health conditions on ships, and American laws echoed English laws, which from 1826 required a "surgeon" onboard "every emigrant vessel." Few ships actually had medical personnel of any kind.

Riverside Writers

Josephus moored 9 June 1853 at Long Wharf. The passengers left to get their land legs, clear immigration, and to make way for cargo removal. Thomas, Mary, and baby William went to the Custom House at the wharf's end. Built just seven years before, it served as clearing house, immigrant detention center, and office space. *Josephus*' launch in Kennebunk and her voyage in May/June 1853 marked a passage from Liverpool to Boston, from an Old to a New World, and a great family story.

*Composing
Dancing
Acting
Writing*

When I Get to be a Composer
by Julie Phend
(with a nod to Langston Hughes)

When I Get to be a Composer
I'll sing a song about a summer breeze
As it winds its way through the whispering trees
And the lonely night wind when it sings along,
I'll capture all of them in my song.

When I Get to be a Composer
I'll croon a tune about time in its flight
And the way the day turns into night.
How the young become old, and the old move on,
I'll muse about all of it in my song.

When I Get to be a Composer
I'll tell a tale of teenage tears
How sometimes they're wise beyond their years,
But other times they're young and frail.
I'll try to tell it in my tale.

When I Get to be a Composer
I'll sing my song about the beauty of life
The wonder, the joy, and even the strife.
I'll shout it, flout it; it won't be wrong
'Cause I'm the composer, and this is *my* song.

My Evening with Igor Stravinsky
by Rod Vanderhoof
*(Royal Festival Hall — London, England
Tuesday, 14 September 1965)*

At Royal Festival Hall,
the aging composer,
Igor Stravinsky,
enters house-left to
golden applause.

He wears a tuxedo,
uses a cane
and totters
to the podium.

Ted Heath,
future prime minister,
sits near the back,
dapper with
his white lapel carnation,
anticipating a
musical adventure.

The orchestra is
poised for
the maestro who
starts with

Fireworks,
a short opener of
musical color flashes,
followed by

his old friend,
Robert Craft, directing
The Rite of Spring,
a ballet piece

of pagan sounds
from
mythic,
tribal Russia.

After the mid-evening interval,
Stravinsky again
leads

Variations in Memory of Aldous Huxley,
that resonate as
avant-garde wind chimes in a
gasping breeze
and

The Firebird Suite,
with heavy rhythms,
harmonies, and disharmonies
enhancing
a prince's journey to
overcome evil and
win his lady.

Stravinsky pushes the players to an
emotional fervor.

When *Firebird* ends,
giddy listeners
applaud,
shouting, "Bravo! Bravo! Bravo . . ."

Now sweating from
exertion and passion,
he bows,
smiles and
exits,
but the audience calls him back.

He returns.

The musicians stand,
put aside instruments
and join the
thunderclaps.

Waving adieu
and visibly exhausted,
Stravinsky departs,
but the crowd demands his return
again.

Finally, he reappears in
winter overcoat,
waves his hat,
and is
gone.

A silence enshrouds the hall.
The throng remains in place,
not wanting to leave,
still savoring this coda to
his
brilliant life of music.

Way Back
by Ummie

Do you understand why I dance?
Way back when my ancestors
Heard music, they pranced
Rocked, jumped, shuffled
To the sounds of the drums
Moving, swaying, twirling in a frenzy
Entering a trance
Do you understand why I dance?
Way back when my ancestors
Heard music, they pranced

Her Flowering Audience
by Michelle O'Hearn

Smiling faces of the flowers
Project a happy audience to her awe
Flaunting tart fragrances
as daunting as the dark
with a backlit proscenium,
to the intangible flaws of the grand drape.

The sunflowers dance in laughter
as the script plays out a scene to climax
She reacts to the gasps and the wilting limbs
Some rising actions and collapse.

Smelling the scent of impending showers
they all cower and applaud to prevent
a new casting of fasting and magnificent waste
of a talented, uninhibited crew.

Yet all hesitation is a cause for hydration
Whither a relentless pursuit to conclusion
Engorged and inhaling the air
from laughter, encores, and asides
She stumbles to the wings and drips in persistent sweat,
the indicator of exhaustion.

The blooms soak it up and squall for them all
Waving and swaying for the gentle curtain call
before she hides away in the fly loft -
A monologue to the sun-setting fade
Into a quiet ad lib in honor of her devotees.

The Actress
by Kelly Patterson

TAKE "21" . . . ACTION!
SITTING IN MY DRESSING ROOM
A STAR UPON MY DOOR
DIRECTOR SCREAMING . . . "WHERE IS SHE"
HE ASKS FOR MORE AND MORE

THEY TEASE MY HAIR AND LINE MY EYES
FACE PAINTED TO A TEE
MY FEATURES CHANGE MOST EVERY HOUR
I HARDLY KNOW IT'S ME

DRESSES ALL BROUGHT IN FROM FRANCE
HATS FROM GAY PAREE
JEWELS SPARKLE FROM NEW YORK
WHERE MONEY FLOWS SO FREE

MY SHOES ARE CUSTOM WALKERS
BOUGHT IN LONDON TOWN
I'D RATHER BE IN TENNESSEE
FEET UPON THE GROUND

MY MIND IT WANDERS WAY BACK HOME
WHERE ARE MOM AND DAD TODAY
I BET SHE'S CHURNING BUTTER UP
WHILE DAD BRINGS IN THE HAY

LIFE HAS CHANGED SO VERY FAST
I DIDN'T KNOW IT COULD
TAKE "21" ONE'S THE ACTION NOW
HERE IN HOLLYWOOD

COSMETICS RUN UPON MY CHEEKS
DOWN ONTO MY FACE
IT SEEMS SO QUEER TO BE OUT HERE
I FEEL SO OUT OF PLACE

"MAKEUP MAN" COME FIX MY FACE
SPRAY GLITTER FAT AND THICK
PAINT A SMILE WITH HAPPY LIPS
ANOTHER MOVIE TRICK

Casey's Part: A Fantasy
by Joe Metz

I'm still not sure who got me the part. When I read over the lines, I knew immediately how significant it was for the play's meaning. It was "Casey's" part. He would be a central character, one of the major leading roles.

I got the call just before we left on our trip. The part was mine. There'd be lots of mental preparation but I felt confident I could handle it. And I was intrigued by the play's setting—a huge field, lighted by overhead floodlights, surrounded by tiered, wooden bleachers. No curtains. No props. Just a team of actors, in designated positions, skillfully reciting our parts. We'd receive no compensation. Only the honor of having been individually selected for the cast. Admission to the field and bleachers would be by invitation only.

The script was complex, with rapid, powerful dialogue. Each part thrived on the others. For the trip, I took two copies with me. I needed to memorize, rehearse. Once we got back, there'd be time for only a quick review before the presentation date.

I don't know exactly why I never learned "Casey's" part. As soon as we got to the beach, I'd remember the script lying back in our condo. The days we stayed in our room, relaxing with cheap rum, I'd read a line or two, telling myself there was plenty of time left. My reflection in shop windows reminded me I'd been honored with a part other actors could only wish to have. Then we'd keep on walking, shopping.

The day before the night of the play, we arrived home exhausted. I unpacked the script and laid it by my nightstand. "Casey's" lines were there to be memorized. "Casey's" essence, painstakingly crafted by the author, was there to be captured. I barely made it through my first three speeches before falling asleep.

When I got to the field, I never felt there would be a problem. The other actors were already walking around, finding their assigned positions. Each one carried a copy of the script. Seeing that, I expected that once the play started each of us would read our part. Surely the audience would know that "Casey's" words, memorized or read, still molded the character created by his author. It was just a matter of experienced portrayal.

When the bleachers were full, we started. I was the fourth to appear, so I spent the time looking over my lines. Just before my entrance, I noticed that other actors were not reading their parts. Projecting just the subtleties of character intended by the author, whispering in this moment, shouting the next, they breathed the life of the script onto the field. They had prepared.

Members of the audience who had seen this same play presented in different fields, waited expectantly for my entrance. They knew that "Casey" was the author's created catalyst. That a skilled actor with "Casey's" words honed to a fine emotional edge gave the story its impact, its memorable significance.

I walked onto the field, carrying the script at my side. The words of my first speech were nearly perfect. Just the right intonation; just the right amount of reserved authority. I could sense the audience's appreciation. The other actors responded to "Casey's" part. One revealed the intense hatred the author felt must be "Casey's" due. Another expressed love; another doubt; another repentance. The play's Narrator structured those emotions for the audience, unraveling our personal territories and boundaries. Our separate roles, with the author's deliberate disparities, were fused by the Narrator's timely interventions.

It was time for my second speech. I started, hesitated, then stopped. These were lines I had not taken time to fully memorize. The other actors stared at me, waiting for their cues. I lifted the script and started to read: "For the first time in my life, there is some difference, although small, to which I have given too little . . ." Pretending his action was rehearsed, the Narrator grabbed my copy of the script, folded it in half, and placed it in my rear pocket. Some people in the audience applauded softly. Here was a new intervention, one never included before in this author's play.

I couldn't speak. This was "Casey's" major monologue. This was the speech bringing "Casey" to his full expression, giving him the enduring complexity that justified another actor's venting his hate, another's statement of love, another's doubtful meanderings. And there I stood, silent.

There was no alternative. I grabbed the script out of my pocket, trying to turn the pages to "Casey'" part. But there was some light wind now. It was difficult to keep the right page. I couldn't remember whether "Casey's" monologue came before or after the Narrator's next comments. The other actors stood in their assigned positions, waiting for my cue.

It was the silence from the audience I heard now. They knew I hadn't learned my lines. I had accepted "Casey's" part with no personal compulsion. No commitment to making it vibrant, real. How could I now portray the emotions, feelings, expectations the author intended for "Casey"? Feeling their disappointment, I grabbed at the folded pages of the script. Was that "Casey's" part or another actor's speech? Where were my next lines?? Was this the right page? Or the next one?

The wind blew stronger across the field. Dust swirled around the pages. I couldn't read; I couldn't think. One of the other actors started to walk toward me, smiling. Then another started in my direction. And still another. The Narrator made an announcement to the audience, but the wind was too strong for me to hear it. Then I noticed more movement. The audience was walking off the bleachers and onto the field. They were coming toward me, just in back of the other actors. Everyone was smiling.

Riverside Writers

Couldn't they see I'd tried? Didn't they know I really wanted to take "Casey's" part and give it the spirited voice the author had intended? Wouldn't they have taken the trip too? Enjoyed the beach, the rum, the reflections? What was it they wanted?

Suddenly everyone stopped. I turned in a circle, trying to face all of them. Grasping the creased, dusty script, I read from "Casey's" monologue. "I cannot stifle the hatred that some bring to my life. I sometimes cannot return all the love that is offered. When I face the doubt that others feel, I may not be able to provide enough assurance. And, when some of you feel repentant, I can do no more than to acknowledge your regret. So there is more that makes us like one another than makes us different."

One of the other actors, now given his appropriate cue, replied. "That's true, Casey. We do feel the likeness you describe. But have you thought about other feelings not yet expressed here? Have you given any consideration to what it means when there is nothing to feel? Do you know, Casey, for all the insights you seem to express so easily, what it feels like when . . . "

I looked desperately for my part, for "Casey's" reply. The wind was louder, the dust thicker. All the words I was cued to say were muddled, indistinguishable. There was no way now to find "Casey's" part. I dropped the script, turning to walk toward the other actors, the audience. They were gone. The field and bleachers were empty.

I stood there alone. A small yellow paper blew up from the ground, whirled around my feet. I picked it up and held it close to my eyes. The dust was thicker. It was the Narrator's announcement to the audience. "It is unfortunate that "Casey's" part has been so poorly prepared. There can be no refund for this performance. A new presentation will be scheduled as soon as a replacement actor can be found. You are invited to come onto the field now. Along with the actors, you will see firsthand the person to whom "Casey's" part was given and who, for his lack of . . ."

I crumbled the note and threw it at the bleachers, into the wind. It blew back, past my ear. Somewhere in the dust, in this field where I had hoped to bring "Casey's" part to life, to share my own experienced portrayal with an invited audience, there was something like the sound of weak applause. I strained to hear. It was there again. But the wind roared, driving the dust against my body, into my senses. I needed to feel that comforting sound, however weak. But now there was only silence. A caretaker somewhere shut down the floodlights. I walked off the field in darkness.

A Whimper and a Bang
by Jim Gaines

Are these few poets England? There were more
When Norsemen beached their drakkars on the shore
And drank from grinning skulls to Odin's wrath,
That drew them over Ocean's dire grey path.

Are these rare blossoms, civilized and wan,
All that remain of courtly gardens gone
To seed? A blight that stretches sea to sea
Spews from the ceaseless maw of BBC.

Oh, England! Sidney hurried to embrace
Mortality with lovers to his taste,
Unlike this flaccid Larkin, dogged by death,
Who withers juicy wenches with foul breath.

Perhaps the answer to this peeked ramble
Lies in a madness desperate to gamble
On rasta rappers bleeding love and hate,
Bards unafraid to meet the bitch of fate.

Shape Up, Sylvia!
by Larry Turner
Meditation on Sylvia Plath
The italicized lines are adapted from her villanelle
"Mad Girl's Love Song."

I shut my eyes and all the world drops dead.
Avoid such thoughts! Two children need your care.
I think I made you up inside my head.

Forget the pram! Your kids should ride a sled
In this December's frigid slush and air.
I shut my eyes and all the world drops dead.

You need some faithful friends who have not fled,
Who know you split with Ted and are aware.
I think you made them up inside your head!

Listen to them; note what they have said—
But not how Ted and his new love will fare!
I shut my eyes and all the world drops dead.

Truth to say, you should return to Ted,
Although you were a most contentious pair.
I think I made him up inside my head.

Alone you cannot put aside your dread.
He'll help you with the things you need to bear.
I'll shut my eyes, and soon I shall be dead,
Escaping all the turmoil in my head.

Michael McDonald's Reading
by R. L. Russis
North Hall, Huntington, Mass., Sunday, July 31, 2011

As he read I could imagine him *back in the day,*
reading with that same magic of beat, that same rhythmic
echo of sound drawing or dragging the audience along.
He could have been another Kerouac or Ginsberg,
given what he wrote, given the way he read,
spieling his own version of *Howl* –
one more graying member of those classical beats.

I could imagine him seated on some three-legged stool,
beneath a shallow stab of light, his pointed goatee jabbing
in emphasis, keeping rhythm with the words,
with the thoughts he drove home like ten-penny nails,
while he ranted, raging on against politicians,
against their support for the war, against the way
Government stifled much-needed change…

I could imagine him sitting on a slightly-raised stage,
one built to put the poets up into public view
from the far back of the room, so they could be seen,
as well as heard, through that late 2:00 A.M. blue film
    of smoky haze,
while in the background the beat of the bongos lifted up,
back-filling the spans of silence that sat between his words –
and that soft, finger-tapped beat coming from off the heads,
the taut skins of the drums, the muted tones coaxed
from off the rims – those sounds folding, melding amid
the subdued moaning of an alto sax that climbed,
    then dropped,
as it ran through its scales, that wailed its pure notes between
what seemed to be those perfectly laid out pauses.

And all the while his veins *popping and pulsing,*
those thin blue lines *bulging and thumping,*
    tracing his temples,
telling us he was into it and had found his groove,
    was cra-a-a-zy cool.

And now with him but slightly mellowed
from the last five decades of fast-passing time,
I listened close to his words and wondered,
although I was slow to solve, to resolve the issue before me,
of whether the question I asked of myself, had raised of him,
were those perfect pauses accidentally read?

They could have been the result of emphysema,
of his desperate lungs' collapsing,
gasping in their frantic grasping to get more air.
They could have been due to the heart's own failure,
it worn fat and waiting its full and final stop –
his uneasy breathing made ragged and coarse
by the lifestyle he'd led, by the countless packs of Camels,
by the constant plumes of smoke he drank in,
by all that hard-drink, the bottles of bourbon and whiskey
he'd swallowed. And was this, his slow suffocation,
the price to be paid, their ultimate toll?
Or were those pauses deliberately penned and aired
    for effect,
a conscious and cunning effort he employed
to force a contemplation, a serious consideration
    of the issues
he raised – and the objections he thoughtfully made?

And as I listened and weighed the phrases he formed
against those pauses he let sit mid-air, to tensely hang,
as I watched his lips utter those tight writ lines
that forced me into giving their subjects a greater depth
    of thought,

Riverside Writers

I heard none that were hung just to let him stall,
to let him catch his breath; I heard and saw them all
as having been cleverly strung and smartly played out,
as cunningly laid to ensnare our ears, to lay capture
of our minds, and to instigate, as provocation,
a means for instilling in us the want for a more inquisitive
and demanding line of socially conscious thought.

How I Became a Poet
by Rod Vanderhoof

Once, I was a poetry outsider.
A sestina, to me, was an afternoon nap in Mexico.
The difference between iambic pentameter
    and a limerick was a mystery.
My favorite poem was, "The Cremation of Sam McGee,"
a song of the Klondike for the ordinary guy.
Poetry was far beyond the likes of me.

But I mingled
with the effete literary elite,
being critical,
asking the wrong questions,
a pest infesting arcane, bibliophilistic circles
with snide remarks.

I read the poetry of Tomas Tranströmer,
    Nobel winner from Sweden,
who created notions
anchored in abstruse and barely fathomable enigmas
and memories
from a vantage of grey misty lands and cold northern seas.
Brrrr!

Then I wrote a poem
of the fiery Arabian desert.
A poet laureate deemed it concise and powerful.
It won a golden award.

How can I now be dismissive of poets?
Alas, I cannot. I have become one of them.

Lines on the Iowa Writers Workshop
by James Gaines

The editor was very plain
I did not have the writer's stuff
I did not have the sign and seal
I had not been past Council Bluffs

My verse reveals a dearth of craft
That justifies his stern rebuke
I lack exposure to the world
I have not slummed in old Dubuque

My metaphors run all amok
And some of my ideas are vapid
My awkward stanzas surely crave
The expert touch of Cedar Rapids

A workshop would be just the thing
I'd learn the faces and the names
But if I must put up the cash
Perhaps I'll spend a week at Ames

Breaking Good
by Elizabeth Talbot

My girlfriend left me. It wasn't like the neighbors had to call the cops. But the end of the relationship had been a long time in coming. Still, I was surprised when she announced, "This is going nowhere. I'm leaving." And then I was furloughed. All in the space of a week.

We were civil about it. Not having kids or pets helped, so she and I spent the last week before the shutdown going through stuff, the dishes, some paperbacks and DVDs neither of us had touched in years. As she was picking up the last overstuffed duffel bag before leaving, I asked, "Can I at least friend you on Facebook?"

She put down the bag as if to give my request some thought. "Not right now. Maybe later." Then she left.

What had been going on in the outside world really hit me when I saw a Senator reading from a children's book on C-Span late at night. I knew then they had gone over the edge.

There had been speculation at the office as to whether we would be deemed essential and allowed to stay, or sent home. The last shutdown took place 17 years ago and I had not been working for my agency then. One old timer thought maybe our work group had been deemed essential, but she couldn't remember for sure since she had left the country for several weeks.

My supervisor wasn't around in the days before the furlough. He was always in meetings with other supervisors, not letting on as to what had been discussed. They behaved like parents at Christmas except I knew we wouldn't be getting any presents.

On Tuesday morning, we were informed we had been deemed nonessential and advised that we would be sent home shortly. "Do we get paid?" asked one of the clerical workers. Her husband was on dialysis and she brought home the paycheck.

"You'll be paid for the last week in September," replied my supervisor, "minus all the usual deductions." We called him the Sphinx. He didn't get mad but I could never tell if he liked or disliked anything. Not the reassuring type we needed in this situation.

"And after that?"

"I don't know."

I later found her crying in the breakroom. One of the older women was patting her on the back, "It'll be ok, someone up there will come to their senses." I wanted to tell her the same thing, but I wasn't sure myself and I didn't want to get her hopes up.

So we cleaned out the refrigerator, which was good, because we had let things slide. The cleaners turned up long forgotten lunches now congealed into a gooey mess. Turning in our Blackberries was far more traumatic. Without my phone, I was disconnected, alone, almost as bad as when my girlfriend left.

The next few days, I felt trapped in my apartment, idly switching from MSNBC to CNN to Fox to CNBC to C-Span. Stuart Varney was shouting on TV that he was mad at federal workers and they shouldn't be paid at all. I had no idea what I had done to make Stuart Varney so mad at me.

I shut off the TV and left the apartment. I was paid up for the month but my ex- girlfriend would not be around next month to split the rent. I realized that I might have to move out if I couldn't find a roommate. I didn't know how many landlords would want to deal with a renter without a paycheck. Should I move out of the city?

I wandered through Adams Morgan. I skipped the Ethiopian restaurant where my girlfriend and I used to eat. Then I passed a bar. A hand lettered sign announced half-price drinks for federal employees during the shutdown. I stopped inside and found a bartender wiping glasses and putting them away. There were posters from the expected teams on the walls, worn booths, and Christmas lights wrapped around the bar, as if it had been too much trouble to take them down.

"I saw your sign," I said.

The bartender looked up. "Got your ID?"

"I think I do." I was still carrying my ID even though the building was closed. I must have been a total Fed to still carry this thing with me.

"Good," he nodded, "I just wanted to make sure you weren't a member of Congress. Although I might make an exception for one of their long suffering staffers. What's your pleasure?"

"Whiskey and coke."

The bartender squirted some soda into a glass. "You really should take advantage of this special and try something new. A martini? Sex on the Beach? Orgasm? How about a Screaming Orgasm?"

"I just broke up with my girlfriend," I deadpanned.

The bartender put down the glass he had been wiping and looked at me with pity. "If you want to talk, I'm here. I've listened to a lot of break-up stories." He pushed a tumbler in my direction.

I looked up at the TV to see two legislators reassuring each other they were "winning." Charlie Sheen had also announced he was "winning" during his big crack-up. The legislators were also involved in a big crack-up they had helped cause, but of which they were similarly unaware.

"Can you mute that?" I asked the bartender.

"Sure." He found the remote behind an array of liquor bottles.

Though I had expected more furloughed workers taking advantage of the special, I saw few customers. In the corner, a heavyset man was staring into his drink, or what was left of it. He noticed me, turned, and saluted in my direction. "Are you one of those in the service of your country to find themselves suddenly cast off?"

I nodded. He waved for me to join him in his booth.

"I used to be on that path myself. But then I realized my true calling."

"What do you do now?"

He straightened up and tugged at his tie. "I am a writer. Or an aspiring one. I am trying to sell a pilot for a TV show."

"Really, what about?"

"I'll tell you, but you have to buy me a drink first. After all, you are the one eligible for the special."

"OK, what would you like?"

"Scotch on the rocks." The bartender brought around another tumbler and took the used glass away.

"It is about a lowly government worker. He was an idealist in his younger years, but no more. He's stuck in the same pay grade, he hasn't had a pay raise in three years, and his boss doesn't appreciate him."

"We can all relate to that."

"He reads many stories about people hurt by budget cuts. He reads about a young widow who cannot get her child in Head Start because of funding cuts. Then there's the combat veteran with the brain injury who's having his pay garnished by the Army because he received hazard pay while he was in a coma."

"That's pretty bad. The little guy always gets screwed."

"The hero, the lowly government employee, gets a call from his doctor. He finds out that he is dying from terminal cancer."

"Bummer." I reached for a bowl of pretzels.

"He wants to help all these people before he dies. He'd always wanted to help people, but he never had the money."

"What is he going to do next?"

"He has one thing going for him, he is a master of the arcane and complex world of government contracting. He carries out a complex scheme to defraud the government out of millions and transfer the money to the people who need help. He doesn't take the money for himself, see? Still drives the same car, lives in the same house. No one suspects anything."

He sipped his Scotch and waited for my reaction.

"Well, I can tell you're going to have some problems with that story. For one thing, it doesn't have enough conflict. Is he married? What does his wife think of this? He's dying and he wants to do something that could send him to jail for whatever's left of his life? Wouldn't she want some of the money? He can't be traipsing through the country giving away this money without taking care of his family."

The writer took out a pad and began scribbling. He nodded in agreement. I recognized the pad, they were found in about every government supply cabinet. He must have made off with a lot of them before he left federal service.

"Maybe he doesn't tell her anything, but she finds money in the laundry room!"

He scribbled my comments on another page. He reminded me of one of those homeless people in libraries and near courthouses with large legal pads filled with undecipherable scribble. I wondered if he was homeless, but his clothes appeared to be freshly laundered.

"You need some obvious villains. It's too bad your protagonist wasn't involved in the drug trade. You'd have a lot of made to order bad guys, the Mexican drug cartel, the Russian mafia, strung out punks. "

Riverside Writers

"I could throw in a shady Oliver North character." He scribbled again.

"Oliver who?"

"That Marine who was caught selling weapons to the Iranians back in the eighties."

"Be careful with that because the public likes the military nowadays. Some of his co-workers might make good antagonists. I don't think he would be able to pull off this scheme without help from a few of them. But they are not as altruistic as he is. And that could be a problem for him."

The writer rubbed his hands. "Excellent!"

"Maybe you also need to add someone on the right side of the law, preferably in the same agency. Better yet, someone related to the hero. Their families tailgate at football games every Sunday, they play a few rounds of golf. This relative senses something is wrong but he can't put his finger on it."

The writer put down his pen. "You are a genius! We could make a great team. I have so many ideas I don't know what to do with them. A mall security cop wakes up from a coma and finds out that the world has been taken over by zombies. Yeah, zombies."

"Well the zombie theme has been used a lot . . ."

"How about this?" He half rose out of his seat, "Women endure sexist behavior in a male-dominated advertising agency run by an erratic genius in 1960s New York City."

I hold up my hand. "Whoa there! One idea at a time. What do you plan to do with the first story?"

"First I have to find a producer." He sips his Scotch. "And the producer has to find an investor. You always need money."

"Just like the government."

"Once the producers get the money, the producers will change things and dozens of people will get their hands into it. Maybe I'll recognize the final product, but it's likely I won't."

I knew the shouting in Congress would subside and someone would eventually miss the government. They would appropriate the funds, and I would be back at my desk, as though nothing happened. This poor guy will be waiting for years to see if anything comes to fruition. I wished him the greatest luck and left.

Crime and Crime Fighters

Black Mask
by John M. Wills

Bill's wife hung up the phone and walked into the bedroom.

"Who was it?"

"Your sister, Helen . . . again. That's the third time she's called looking for you, Bill. Why don't you just tell her no?"

He put on his vest, then pulled on his dark blue sweatshirt over it. "Listen, Mary, I am not lending her any more money. Hell, she hasn't paid back the $250 I gave her last month."

Mary watched as her husband fastened his gun belt and then hung the chain around his neck holding his police badge. For the past several months, she had seen this ritual repeated daily as her husband prepared for his plain-clothes assignment. She walked over to the dresser and picked up the towel her husband had dropped on the floor.

Bill glanced over as she walked toward the bathroom. "Thanks, Hon."

"Yeah. I guess I'm your secretary *and* your maid," she said, sighing heavily.

"C'mon . . ." He pleaded.

"I'll be glad when this assignment is over," she complained. "How close is your team to grabbing the guy wanted for the rapes?"

"Gettin' there," he answered. "We're sitting on an apartment over on Third Street this afternoon. We had some info that the suspect is supposed to have a girlfriend living there. Probably be a long day."

Mary followed him out of the room and into the kitchen. Bill grabbed his jacket, wallet and car keys. He turned to his wife and kissed her goodbye. "Don't know what time I'll be home tonight," he said, while opening the side door leading to the driveway.

"Honey, do me a favor?"

"What kind of favor?"

"Please call Helen; she sounds desperate. The job Dave applied for didn't happen. They hired someone else."

Bill shook his head. "No wonder. Dave's a felon—he'll be lucky to get a job washing dishes and bussing tables. I told her she was making a big mistake letting that guy move in with her. Anyway, I don't have time for Helen right now. This stakeout is draining all my energy."

His wife held the door open as Bill walked to his car. Her tight-lipped frown conveyed her disappointment. "She's at her wit's end, Bill," she shouted, as her husband opened the car door. "She's your sister."

Crap. "Okay, I'll call her tomorrow."

"Thanks, Hon. Love you."

~~~~

"Three o'clock," Bill said, as he glanced at the dashboard clock.

His partner, Rod, took his last sip of coffee and then tossed the empty cup over the seat and on the floor. "I know what time it is, but thanks for the update."

"You're welcome."

"I wish we were sitting in the alley instead of out front," said Rod, squirming in his seat. "I gotta take a leak."

Chuckling, Bill shot back: "We've only been here three hours. You've got the bladder of a one-year-old."

All units, we have a robbery in progress at the First State Bank, Fourth and Main.

Any units close by to respond?

Bill looked at his partner, eyebrows raised. "We're right around the corner—let's go!"

"What about the stakeout?"

"Hell, it looks like we're sittin' on a dry hole," Bill replied, yanking down the gearshift lever. "We'll come back after we see what's going on at the bank."

A minute later, the partners quietly pulled their unmarked car into the far corner of the bank parking lot.

All units, bank manager advises suspect is headed toward the exit.

He's carrying a bag and wearing a black mask.

"I go left, you go right," Bill barked, as they exited their vehicle. Hunching down as he crept along the few cars in the lot, Bill secreted himself at the corner of the bank and saw that his partner had taken up a position behind a van on the opposite side.

Suddenly a lone figure, wearing a dark ski mask, emerged from the door carrying a black duffle bag. The suspect began to run toward Bill's partner.

"POLICE! STOP!" shouted the plainclothes officer, as he pointed his pistol at the robber.

Startled, the bank robber reached into his waistband and displayed a handgun before he quickly turned and ran in the opposite direction—towards Bill.

"GUN!" The cop yelled, alerting his partner.

Seeing the suspect coming his way, Bill stepped partially away from the edge of the building. "POLICE!"

Trapped, the robber began to raise the gun. At that instant, Bill's .40 caliber pistol exploded twice. The figure dropped both the duffle bag and the weapon before collapsing in a heap on the sidewalk.

"Cover me, partner!" Bill shouted, as he slowly approached the figure lying motionless on the ground. The officer retrieved the robber's revolver and put it in his pants pocket. He searched the inert body for any additional weapons. "Clean."

Rod stood over the apparently dead suspect. "Turn him over, Bill, and take off his mask. Let's see what this guy looks like."

"Wow, this guy's a lightweight," Bill remarked, as he easily turned the body over.

"Yeah, the money bag probably weighs more than he does," his partner added.

Riverside Writers

Bill grabbed the ski mask at the top and slowly removed it. "No! he screamed. "It can't be . . ."

Tears trickled down his cheeks as he struggled to his feet. He braced himself against the nearest parked car as sobs wracked his body. "Why, Helen? Why?"

First Damned Day
by Darrin E. Chambers

Is this how it ends?
Is my life over?
...the door slowly closes with a thunderous click

Four walls
Restricted
No looking in or out
...what is that smell?

"Lockdown,"
An irate officer yells
...angry shouts and painful screams fill the air

Damn, I'm a wretched man
I fell in love with
A beautiful woman
...how I miss her so

Who will be there for her?
Will she be disappointed in me?
...a tear runs down my face

No phone
One-hour visits
Time is my enemy
...what is that awful smell?

I'm so hungry
It rocks my core
Declining that cheese sandwich
Another mistake
...cannot breathe, hyperventilating

God please don't turn
Your back on me
I feel so alone
... is that foul odor coming from my body?

I may never see
The light of day again
...calm down, compose yourself
So no one sees you or hears you
...I scream inside
...this is just the first damn day

Second Chances
by Elizabeth Talbot

One of the things Zach loved best about this gig was the days spent hanging out in the open bar next to the beach. His glass never went empty. The waitress knew his favorite drink, a shot of tequila with a splash of orange syrup and pineapple juice, not unlike the tropical sunsets of St. Kitts. He also enjoyed the view of Nevis Peak across the narrows. Zach had never seen the summit, obscured by clouds, giving the illusion of a snow covered peak in the tropics.

He opened his cell phone to check the time and then snapped it shut. St. Kitts was in a time zone ahead of Eastern Standard Time, and so the calls would begin at 10:00 am. After taking so many of these calls, he could imagine what his callers looked like.

He could hear a baby crying in the background during one call. A harried young father pleaded. "Look, I had a bad break-up with a girlfriend years ago. They charged me with assault after I threw a beer bottle. But I've changed. I'm married with two kids, another on the way."

Zach had answered so many of these calls that he already knew what would come next. It did not require any premonition or any psychic ability. "I'm trying to find a job," the caller continued, "I send in my resume, I get scheduled for an interview, and suddenly, the interview's canceled. It's the damn picture."

"The mugshot?"

"How did you get it?" asked the caller.

"It's public information. And everything's available on the Internet, don't you know that?" He lifted the sweating glass to his lips. He knew how the caller's picture had been obtained, but he would not divulge the information. When Zach was in his first year of college, a roommate of his had designed a web-scraping program for police websites and created a website,

Seeurownmugshot.com. His friend needed help with the customer service end, and so they dropped out of school and relocated to St. Kitts. Zach already knew the caller's next question.

"How can I get it removed?"

"For $399 we can make it disappear." Zach never knew why his friend didn't charge $400. It was an old psychological trick from the retail trade.

There was an audible sigh on the other end. "Why would it cost so much to remove a picture?"

"To cover the costs, legal, administrative, whatever," Zach explained.

"That's way too much!"

"Take it or leave it," said Zach. "If you don't want to pay, you must not want the job."

Zach hesitated to answer the next call. The clouds were suddenly unfurling from the peak, and he thought he might actually see the summit. Then the clouds swirled around the top again, as if the mountain had been teasing anyone in the vicinity.

They'll beg, plead, even cry, his friend had told him. Everyone pays. It didn't matter if the caller were Mother Theresa, or Pope Francis. We don't care. Just get the money, credit card or PayPal. Zach thought long and hard when a sultry voice offered to fly out instead to St. Kitts for a "good time" if he took down her mugshot. Her offer tempted him until he clicked on her picture. Zach was repulsed by her decayed teeth and the sores on her face. She had been picked up for meth. He told her to pay the $399.

A former tough guy broke down during one call. "If my employer sees my picture, I'll be fired. My wife has cancer! All of our health insurance is tied up with my job!"

"Sorry about your wife." Zach rested his feet on the table as the waitress rushed by with a round of shots. "But I have my instructions. Do you have a credit card?"

Riverside Writers

"Credit cards! They're maxed out from co-pays. We're being eaten alive!" Zach referred him to a friend in the States, a payday lender. Callers caught in a lender's clutches never escaped, but this was of no concern to Zach as long as the $399 appeared.

"I haven't the faintest idea why my picture is up there," another caller explained. "The judge told me my record would be expunged! I'd have a second chance!"

"Well, I guess it wasn't," replied Zach, "Pay up."

One caller argued, "What you're doing is extortion, pure and simple! The legislature even passed a law against you guys!"

Zach laughed and hung up. The authorities in St. Kitts could have cared less about anything passed by some state legislature. He could have explained that his website was protected by the First Amendment and how they performed a public service by informing the public about the dangerous criminals in their midst, but he had so many tequila sunrises by that time he didn't want to go into the niceties of constitutional law.

In the late afternoon, Zach left the bar and rode his motorbike back into Basseterre to pick up a rich tourist at a bar. When she asked him what he did, he mumbled something about "the Internet." In the morning, she remarked how he liked to talk in his sleep. "What do you really do?" she asked in a concerned tone. He'd dodge the question and suggest breakfast or a visit to a beach, but she would decline. At first, he couldn't figure out why his relationships amounted to no more than a string of one-night stands but then he stopped thinking. He sometimes dreamed of making love to a faceless woman. Her features would come into focus, then fade again. It was like looking at Nevis Peak; he could almost see the summit, then the clouds would swirl again.

Lately, Zach noticed that his dissatisfaction was beginning to leak from his love life to life in general. He had dropped out of college in time to avoid the college debt trap, but he tired of faceless and desperate callers.

He entertained vague plans of going into a scuba diving business. Still, he could never save enough for equipment. The money would come in, and then roll out like the tide, through endless rounds of tequila sunrises, rum punches, dinners of lobster and prawns, and dime bags of weed. Why were they called dime bags anyway? When the calls slowed, he would stare in the direction of Nevis Peak, obscured by clouds, but no answers came to mind.

One morning, as Zach ordered his first round of sunrises, he noticed an incoming message from his business partner, Steve. "That's odd." Working late into the night and early morning, Steve added fresh mugshots and handled technical issues. If he wanted to reach Zach, he would call at noon at the earliest.

He was about to return the call when a paramilitary burst through the door, brandishing a semiautomatic. "Down on the floor," he ordered, "if you don't want to be shot." A waitress began shrieking while the cook emerged from the kitchen, protesting. Soon the waitstaff had forgotten English and began pleading in Creole, as men in black uniforms fanned across the room, pointing weapons at surprised patrons. In the back, Zach heard a stack of plates cascading to the floor.

"Hey, what's going on?" demanded Zach, "I'm an American!"

Swiveling in his direction, the paramilitary aimed his weapon at him. "That's him," shouted the paramilitary. "On the floor!"

Zach complied. Rough hands jerked his arms behind his back, and he could feel a plastic tie cut into his wrists. "What the hell's going on?" Zach asked, "You can't treat me this way. I'm calling the embassy." He almost tripped as another raider pulled him upwards and shoved him towards the back seat of a waiting patrol car, a dented Toyota with rusting hubcaps.

"I can't leave my laptop behind," Zach whined. Anxious moments passed until an officer emerged with

Riverside Writers

Zach's laptop. But instead of handing it to Zach, he opened the trunk and let it drop, as though he was handling something disgusting or foul.

"You can't do that!"

The driver turned back and grinned through tobacco stained teeth. "Evidence." Another policeman climbed into the passenger seat, and the patrol car sped into Basseterre. Zach couldn't figure out why he was being arrested. Had the supplier of dime bags turned them in? He couldn't imagine the seller, a slight youth, as a police informant. Images of Locked Up Abroad ran through his mind. Zach had been scornful at the naiveté of the westerners who tried to smuggle drugs abroad and were caught. But neither he nor his partner had sold or smuggled drugs. The Swat team was overkill for buying a few dime bags. He would find out soon enough.

The patrol car stopped at a nondescript barracks, and Zach was pulled out of the car and escorted by a uniformed man at each side. They stopped momentarily in front of a desk sergeant who was almost protected from view by piles of overstuffed manila folders. "I demand to call my embassy," Zach pleaded one more time, "Or a lawyer."

"Oh, you'll get to talk to one of your countrymen soon enough." Zach did not find the desk sergeant's tone reassuring.

They undid the plastic tie and shoved him into a chair in a windowless room before slamming the door. The air was stifling. He was grateful for the slight breeze when an officer opened the door. This one was dressed in a black uniform with the exception of a cap with the letters "FBI" embroidered on top. From his bearing and the crispness of his uniform, he was clearly from the States.

"Am I glad to see you," exclaimed Zach, "We smoked a couple of joints, but we never sold drugs. Please tell them. There must have been a mistake."

"You'll wish it had been about drugs!"

Zach was surprised at the interrogator's hostility. "If this is about our business, we have a perfect First Amendment right to do what we do!"

"That line isn't going to work here!" Zach found himself pinned against the wall. "There is no First Amendment right to download kiddie porn!" The FBI agent was so near his face that Zach could have identified the cologne and mouthwash.

"Kiddie porn! What the hell!"

The agent lifted Zach off the floor and allowed him to sag back into the chair. "We traced everything, no mistake! Sick, horrible stuff. Enough to make a judge cry. Now you can cooperate and tell us everything or you can make it harder on yourself."

"I don't know anything," Zach replied, "I want a lawyer." The FBI agent left. After an eternity, a local officer jerked Zach from the chair, and half-led, half-shoved him to a bench where his partner was waiting.

"You're a mess!" Zach exclaimed. Steve's t-shirt was torn. He must have been nabbed early that morning. A five o'clock shadow hung on his face, and he was still wearing his sleep shorts. His frames barely hung on his bruised face; a lens had fallen out.

"I tried to call you," Steve whispered, "Why didn't you pick up?"

Zach ignored the question. "You weren't downloading child porn, were you?"

"No!" His partner's breath smelled like rotted fruit. Zach saw some of the agents at the water cooler, joking about the raid and how hilarious the guy in the glasses looked when he jumped over the sofa in an attempt to evade capture.

"There has to be a mistake," Steve whispered. "Some FBI agent back in the states may have traced the source to the wrong physical address."

"How are we going to prove that?"

"I don't know!" Steve's head sagged between his shoulders, and he fell silent. Then he revived as though

Riverside Writers

he had been stricken with an idea. "Maybe it was the open router. Someone else may have downloaded the porn using our router."

Zach despaired at the thought of contacting his father for bail, the same man who had never wanted him to leave school in the first place. What would he tell him now? If only he had been busted for buying dime bags of pot. He would have to use every last bit of his money to get a real lawyer, not the overworked Court-appointed kind. He didn't want to go to jail because he couldn't afford a good lawyer.

Zach looked out the window, unwashed and wrapped in wire. Through a film of dirt, he could see Nevis Peak, still sheathed in clouds. Then unexpectedly, the clouds broke, and he could see the peak for the first time. There was no snow, as he had imagined.

His attention drew to the FBI agent, who was speaking to a local policeman, sitting hunched over an electric typewriter. "We might as well take their mugshots now. Leave the glasses off of that one over there. We don't want more evidence if there's a police brutality complaint."

Now Zach would have his own mugshot. Then one of their competitors would scrape it off the police site and display it for anyone to find. Zach Brandon, arrested for possession of child pornography. Now he would be doing the calling. It was all a mistake, some computer glitch. Couldn't someone take it off? And someone on the other line would laugh. "And how would you like to pay, VISA or PayPal?"

Why I Became a Cop
by John M. Wills

Shots fired. We're the first car on the scene. My partner and I bail out and explode through the front door of the corner bar. Bullets, blood and beer make the floor slicker than Lake Michigan in the winter. Nevertheless, we throw ourselves into the middle of a melee that is escalating quickly and threatens to be totally out of control if we don't try and stop it. Out of the corner of my eye, I spot a glint of silver as one combatant furtively conceals a gun in a jacket pocket. I immediately grab him and the fight is on. We wrestle for the nickel-plated pistol that at any second could end my career before it's hardly begun.

It's 1971 and I'm a rookie Chicago cop fresh out of the Army. I completed my thirteen weeks of police academy training two months earlier, but can't recall any class that covered what to do in a bar fight, particularly one that involves a gun. Life experience kicks in and I deliver a well-placed knee to the man's groin. We wind up where most fights do—on the floor. Luckily, I'm on top and I pin the man's arms. After what seems like an eternity, help arrives and several patrons are cuffed and stuffed into the back of a paddy wagon.

I quickly replay the incident in my head, but I don't begin to shake from the fear until I'm safely in the car with my partner. He turns to me and says, "Good job, kid, that a**hole coulda killed us. I never saw the piece he had." I take a quick inventory of myself as we drive to the station to complete the paperwork—ripped pants and a bump on my head that's going to make it difficult to wear my uniform hat. "That guy wanted to kill me," I thought. "But he didn't." Then I smile.

Why would anyone want to be a cop, particularly when one stops to realize the dangers involved? What causes someone to rush toward gunfire, while others flee from it? Who wants to subject themselves to ridicule, taunts, name-calling and oversight by local, state and federal entities? If you answered, "me," you are probably a cop.

My first thoughts about the profession began to surface in grammar school. My friends and I used to play cops and robbers on the playground. (Yeah, I know, kids aren't allowed to play that game anymore . . . or tackle football, tag, it, or dodge ball—all too violent and politically incorrect). However, back then it was acceptable and popular. I never wanted to be one of the bad guys; I always wanted to be a copper—the euphemism used for police officers during that era. My classmates and I chased each other around the school while we made believe we were driving cop cars. When we caught the crooks, we'd pretend to handcuff them and haul them off to jail.

In high school, the make believe games morphed into more serious ones—football and hockey—but the theme remained the same. I was one of the good guys. I represented my school and played as hard as I could to uphold the honor of the school colors.

I grew up and learned that being a cop was not a game, and that there really are good guys *and* bad guys. As a kid, I never realized how horrible the bad guys were, but I quickly found out. After high school, I joined the Army. I wanted to serve, wanted to do something worthwhile for my country. Afterward, I became a member of the Chicago Police Department because I still had the desire to help, to serve, to be one of the good guys. More than twelve years later, I left the CPD to become an FBI agent. In that capacity, I continued to serve and help others, but on a much broader scale. I travelled around the world and learned that criminals are the same, regardless of nationality. Nevertheless, the theme remained the same throughout my tenure with the Army, police department and FBI: stop the bad guys from hurting the innocents.

I don't think I'm unique in my career choice. Nor do I think I am special. Most cops feel the same way; they choose law enforcement because they truly believe they can make a difference. Whether it's saving someone's life, finding a missing child, or settling a domestic dispute, they put themselves out there to help others. They run toward danger, not from it. As we recently observed in Boston, the smoke had not even cleared before the cops were there helping the innocent victims. Courage.

Sadly, some of our men and women don't make it home at the end of their shift. Families say goodbye in the morning and never see their loved ones again. Those brave individuals killed in the line of duty, sacrificed their lives so that others may live. Each year in the month of May we honor our heroes during National Police Week. If you have never attended this sacrosanct event, prepare yourself for a flood of emotions. The enormity of what police officers and their families endure to ensure everyone's safety is painfully apparent during the weeklong event.

Watch as spouses, sons and daughters, mothers and fathers, brothers and sisters gently touch their hands to their loved one's inscribed name on the low-slung wall of the Police Memorial in Washington, D.C. The pained expressions and silent cries are heartbreaking.

Try to hold back tears during the Candlelight Vigil, as the names of the departed officers are read aloud solemnly. I guarantee it will not be easy. Each time I visit the Memorial and brush my fingers over the half dozen names of officers I've known, I say a silent prayer of remembrance and thanks. Heroes.

Why did I become a cop? For the same reason many of my colleagues did—because we were called. It's not a job, it's a vocation. We don't become cops for the money. We serve because we want to make a difference. Most times we love what we do. Sometimes it's almost more than we can bear. There is no other calling that

Riverside Writers

compares to that of a cop, nor are there any finer men and women.

Now, my law enforcement days are behind me, but I look back at the years I served and thank God for watching over me. Why did I become a cop? Because, thankfully, that's what I was born to do.

War's Legacy

Private First Class Michio Kobiashi
(Late Summer 1944)
by Rod Vanderhoof
Dedicated to the Nisei soldiers of World War II

At the abandoned Kobiashi place
I looked but saw only darkness,
I listened but heard only silence,
I sought solace but felt only the anguish of loss.

I entered the greenhouse,
its panes smashed by hoodlums,
the air reeking
of regret and moist, rotting wood.

"Michio!" I cried.

His apparition loomed through the murk
of huge tomato plants,
the kind he used to grow.

"I heard you were killed, Michio."

"I was . . . near the Arno River.
Nazi machine gun and mortar fire
were tearing us up . . . then nothing."

"What happened?"

"A mortar round hit me.
I hovered above the battlefield strewn with
wounded and dead Nisei soldiers,
the rest continuing the attack,
crawling forward, firing at the enemy.
I was proud, we were the 'Go For Broke' guys.
We proved our loyalty to America."

Riverside Writers

"You didn't have to prove it to me, Michio. I knew."

Smiling, he vanished in the dismal haze.

I looked through the shattered roof.
A shooting star flared the sky,
ricocheting into the cosmos.

There went Michio.

As the Lights Come On Again
(West Coast - Late Summer 1945)
by Rod Vanderhoof

In evening darkness
the city gasps for air
pulsing its blood
struggling to revive from a
wartime coma

Gone are
blackouts
air raid wardens
slotted headlight covers
sand buckets for incendiaries
rationing

Skyrockets erupt like
prize-winning chrysanthemums of
red
white
blue

Searchlights stir the mix of stars with
silvery shafts
creating a galaxy of living light

Once again
neon signs glow embers of color for
department stores
gas stations
taverns
shops

Yellow street lamps brighten
avenues
bridges
wharves along the harbor
arteries leading in and out

In the town square
a band plays Stars and Stripes Forever
then switches to Glenn Miller
throngs dance
celebrate

Tipsy soldiers and sailors
laugh
kiss girls

Across the bay
lights shimmer in
moist air
dream music plays on

Endless cars
stream through town
horns blaring a
raucous hullabaloo

Headlights adorn the city like
strands of
Tiffany pearls on
soft
purple
velvet

A Walk in the Park
by J. Allen Hill

John Powers navigated his old Chevy sedan belching black exhaust, through the one-way lanes and double lane corners in Marietta Square at a speed that guaranteed a ticket if a traffic cop had been watching. But none was on this warm June afternoon. Finally breaking free of the Square without taking out any of the lunch addled tourists, the car reached Marietta Highway, speeding through the first three traffic lights just as they turned red, before traffic forced him to slow down.

He hated his junk car. He hated his job. He hated his life. All he asked on his day off was to watch the track meets on TV and be left alone to wallow in *mighta-beens*. Watching the kid was not his job. Buckled tightly into his car seat, the baby chortled a loud spitty raspberry.

"Don't complain to me, Little Bud. I didn't want this trip either—your Mom's idea. How the hell far is this park anyway?" Bobby banged his fist on the tray of the car seat, screeched and rubbed his eyes with grubby fists. "Right on, Bobby. Your Dad is a loser. Nearly two years back from Nam and still just a broken down old desk jockey. Fat and fucking worthless. Even that slug, T. Eddy Williams, is coaching high school track.

"Not me. Not ol' shit-for-brains, Big Man on Campus, John Robert Powers. Did I use my good grade immunity? Did I run to Canada? Naw, not me. I got a feather up my butt and volunteered. Volunteered, for Christ's sake!'"

Bobby's answer was to blow curdled milk and chopped carrots down the front of his shirt and produce an ominous burble from his bottom that foretold the stench soon filling the car.

"Damn it, Bobby. Couldn't you wait 'til we got home?" The child began to cry. John pressed down on the gas pedal. "Eff the cops." He was now doing 70 on a stretch zoned for 45.

"Where is that damn park?" There—Cheatham Hill Road— *Kennesaw Mountain National Battlefield Park.* John slammed the brakes, jerked the steering wheel sharply left, and laying skid marks on the black park road, he slid the car against a grassy bank.

"Shut up, shut up, shut up. I'll clean you. Just shut up." The smell gagged him—the sour yellow-orange vomit, the soft ooze of the diaper. He flashed on spilling intestines white and wet and split and leaking, red and orange and green. On oily brown excrement smeared on bloody legs, on dirty faces. He slammed his fist into his forehead.

"Hold still, Bobby. It's okay. Dad just gets freaked sometimes." He wiped the plump little butt with Redi-Wipes, taped on a new diaper and redressed the child. Then he wiped his own hands, his face and neck, his arms—his hands again— and breathed deeply of the soft damp air of this June day. "Let's take a walk."

A hard rain had fallen that morning, but now the sun was high in the sky and every tree leaf and bush sparkled with raindrops full of rainbows. He bundled Bobby into a backpack and hefted it to his shoulders, stumbling beneath the weight and the slight drag of his right leg.

Rising in the distance behind them were Kennesaw Mountain and its companions, Lost and Pine Mountain, hiding in the lingering low-lying wisps of cloud.

"Some mountains! Might as well be Everest. Can't haul my sorry ass up there, much less you too, kid." Out of breath in the first five minutes, John cursed his lack of fitness and his poor choice of parking—the trailhead was out of sight. He rested.

Lush fields where once was forest lay to the right and left of the road, crisscrossed by a curious herringbone pattern of dirt mounds and ditches—earthworks—laid at deadly angles to the enemy's flank. Catch them unawares. Cut them down. He remembered reading about the hundreds of Union wounded fallen here as the woodlands were set ablaze. *No wonder*, he thought, *the trees grow so tall, Fairy Lily grows so thick. Blood and bones make good fertilizer.*

And he was back in the mire of the rice fields south of Danang. The fields there were enriched with human manure. Three murderous days held down in that damn field. God, it stank. He would never forget that stink. Or the jackhammer pounding of the enemy barrage. And the rain. Never ending rain. Only one helicopter got through to evacuate the wounded. One guy—little guy from Ohio—never did get out. Sank right into that muck. *Probably still there.* Fertilizer.

At the trailhead, John studied the posted trail maps and chose to walk the short and level loop at Cheatham Hill. He plucked a brochure from a sheltered rack, its glossy pages offering a short history of the battles of Kennesaw Mountain.

> The Atlanta campaign started at Kennesaw Mountain. Some of the heaviest fighting occurred here on a sweltering hot Monday, June 27, 1864. General William Tecumseh Sherman led 8,000 Union infantrymen in five brigades against the two best divisions in General Joseph Johnston's Confederate army commanded by Generals Patrick R. Cleburne and Benjamin Franklin Cheatham. Most of the northern assault waves were shot down until several regiments broke through and engaged in brutal hand-to-hand fighting on top of the defenders' earthworks. It is estimated that Sherman lost nearly 3,000 men. The Confederates, 5,350.

Slowly John began to walk the path curling gently through woodland, soft with delicate new green marred here and there by blackened tree trunks—old warriors, their tops sheared clean away, blunt but alive, leafing this day a dark and damaged green.

He approached a monument looming beside the trail—tall white stone elaborately carved and peopled with bronze figures—a memorial to 500 simple men of Illinois slaughtered here. He circled the site atop a low ridge overlooking a broad meadow, a staging ground for blue troops—formed into close-packed columns, massed regiments, human battering rams, rushing uphill straight into the guns of the Confederates.

He could almost see them advancing. Waves of blue turning the green valley into a heaving sea, sweeping forward and falling back. Sweeping forward, falling back – shot, bayoneted, clubbed, carpeting the field in bodies. Damn, it seemed so real. He thought he could even hear the bap-bap-bap of rifle fire.

"Guys in gray had the advantage here," he said aloud as though Bobby could understand. "They held the day. Lotta good it did them. Sherman's boys just picked themselves up and marched right on to Atlanta. Grays couldn't know this wasn't to be their war."

He wondered if any of those troops even knew why they were here. "Probably no more'n we did at Thuybo." The hooch. The smack. The napalm. Raggedy little thatch huts burning like tinder. Shooting bent over old grandfathers, women, little kids just because they ran away. Leaving them twisted and silent in the dust. Or screaming. Didn't take too much of that kind of stuff, he couldn't picture home anymore. Couldn't remember why he was there.

He paused to sit upon a Confederate redoubt still protecting its two-cannon battery. Slipping the straps of the backpack from his shoulders and freeing Bobby from its hold, he lay against the hard earthen barricade as the delighted boy toddled into the grass. John located the site on the map in his brochure and read:

> Site of Mebane's Tennessee Battery. Under orders not to fire until the Federals were upon them, these

two cannon tore into advancing bluecoats at point blank range.

Who would press forward straight into sure death? What kept them coming?

"Effin' fools!" John snorted. *What fools slogged like blind men through jungle muck into the unseen, looking for the unknown?* He remembered the thick black enveloping darkness where every shadow could be a sniper. Every bending branch, pebble rolling, earth slithering, silence vibrating on the air held terror. He felt the putrid mud rotting the shoes from his feet, and the clinging sucking leeches, the mosquitoes, the spiders, the centipedes. He heard the exploding dog turd and booby-trapped rice basket. He felt the fear. He dripped with the sweat.

Bobby's shrill screech brought John to his feet, shaking his head to rid it of ghosts. The little boy had tripped on a tree root and tumbled into the moldering leaves and bark beneath the rotting trunk of a fallen tree.

John brushed dirt and leaves from Bobby's face and hands, dislodging a small object from one chubby fist. Small and round—its metal sheen and clasp locked in corrosion—it was a locket pushed from its hiding place by time and erosion. John opened it and drew out a corkscrew of soft golden brown hair, one end tied with faded blue ribbon. That was all. Just a lock of hair. How soft. How carefully ribboned. Sent into hell by a sweetheart. Carried into hell by her lover over 100 years ago. And he remembered a lock of hair lost somewhere in the madness of Danang.

Bobby was curled in his lap, thumb in his mouth, spit dripping from his elbow, snoring softly. John let the peace and quiet of the woodland envelop him. He remembered this used to be Cherokee land—homeland, sacred land, battleground, burial ground. A land rife with death—of men who wore deerskin and the rough homespun of militia, of red coats and of blue and gray.

It has always been. When old men call, young men answer; marching bravely into fire without question. Every father has a war to pass on. Was this to be the fearsome legacy he would give his son?

It was too much. Too much death. The trees were closing in on him. "I gotta get outa here." He grabbed Bobby and began to run.

Suddenly he heard the unmistakable pounding of cannon, the staccato sound of rifle fire, the drumming sound of many pounding feet, shouts of "Charge!" and "Fire when ready, boys!" Panicked, John looked for cover and tumbled into a rifle trench beside the path. His leg buckled and failed. He gulped for air. His heart pounded. Bobby was pinned beneath him. He tried to release his son, screaming and dirty – his little body smeared in soft red mud.

"Steve, where are you Steve?" All he could see was the great, red sucking well in his friend's chest, red bubbling, red flowing, red seeping into the earth, and the earth was red. He saw his own leg, ending in white shredded fringe like the edge of a New Year's Eve party honker. He wondered where his boot had gone. The roar of overhead shells burst in his head numbing his ears, freezing his flesh, deadening his senses. He could not hear his own scream.

"You okay, Bud?" Rough hands were shaking him. He could see sun again and southern hardwoods. He saw the raindrops had dried from the branches. There was a warm breeze and it carried the sweet pungent smell of wood smoke.

He could feel his hands. He could feel the pain in his knee where the prosthesis had torn away. But where was he? The man who stood before him wore a captain's uniform of dark blue wool with brass buttons and epaulets edged in gold. Another, wearing gray with sergeant's stripes, held an old .58 caliber rifle musket, a "Springfield". A bag of mini balls hung from his belt.

John's eyes glazed, his mouth gaped open. The soldier in gray grinned large.

"Lemme give you a hand, pal. We're practicing for a re-enactment—anniversary of the Battle of Cheatham Hill. You have a flashback?"

"Guess so," said John and rubbed his eyes.

"Nice shoulder patch you got there—old 9th *MEF* devil's pitchfork. We Jarheads gotta stick together." He retrieved John's prosthesis and helped him reattach it. "I was at Hué. I still get them flashbacks once in a while. It gets better."

"Thanks, Sergeant. Hope so. Can't take much more of that hell."

The blue-clad Captain handed Bobby to his father.

John wiped tears from the small anguished face and kissed the blond hair that dripped with red mud. The blood-red mud of Georgia.

"We fought a good fight, Bud."

"At what cost?" whispered John, hugging his child tightly. "At what cost?"

PTSD
by Ron Russis

Like artillery, the thunder roared,
a great rolling noise, a barrage
of sound. And the lightning
reminded me of flares, of willy-
peter, of drifting white umbrellas.
And then came the rain— strafing
everything in sight, flattening the grass,
tearing free the leaves from trees,
drilling holes in dirt and making me
believe I was back in 'the Nam,'
back in Saigon, in the Tet of '68,
when the shit got bad and half
the guys I knew got Purple Hearts
and the other half got plastic bags…
then the F-14s came in, laid napalm
down to set the world ablaze and set us
free of interlocking fires. They told me,
later, the Chinooks came in and took us out…

And all the while my wife pulled at my sleeve,
saying, "Come in John; come in.
It's begun to rain, we're getting wet."

The Man He Might Have Been
by Juanita Dyer Roush

She saw him walking down the street,
and joy welled up within;
his camo'd back turned to her--
the man he might have been.

She ran, caught up, took his arm
and as he turned his face
she felt her heart crushed once again,
a stranger stood in his place.

Her face crumbled; tears escaped
the pain she thought she hid,
but the soldier saw inside her,
"I'm sorry, Miss," he said.

He saw the pain, he felt the hurt.
And it touched something deep within
for he had seen it all before—
the man he might have been.

She held his sleeve, looked up at him,
his eyes wished to console.
Images flashed through his mind
of the war that took its toll.

And in her mind, the memories played:
the wedding gown, white, unworn;
all the plans that might have been,
the babies left unborn.

Oh, the things that might have been,
but his uniform took him away;
he did what he thought was right
for his nation and his way.

Riverside Writers

A hometown hero, small town boy
whose passion within grew
never captain of the football team,
he worked to make his dream come true.

But now he is a hero
to all the ones he left
and now her heart feels sadness
but he did his very best.

Day after day, year after year
her hope is growing dim
looking at every uniform—
for the man he might have been.

Seeking Something More

Ophidian Vanity
by Anne Heard Flythe

I dream of shedding
this thin mottled skin,
like a serpent
I'd emerge

enamel bright and new.
A long strong muscle,
aware of every nuance
in the grass, the warm

scurry of a field mouse,
the clicking of the smallest
beetle's carapace.
Restored, alert,

I'd discard the dry
empty garment
of my life
and glide away.

That Brass Ring
by Ummie

Always reaching, hanging half off
Reaching, reaching trying to grab
Stretching, trying to touch
Life as it is
Whizzes and Whirls by
Grabbing air
Occasionally making contact
With a precious thing or a precious someone
Sometimes
On rare occasions
You grab it, you catch that brass ring
Shouting
I got it! I won it!
Causing life for you
To sing, sing, sing
Never lasted
Had to hang it back up
And start all over again

Among the Anthropophagi
by Larry Turner

> It was my hint to speak—such was the process;
> And of the Cannibals that each other eat,
> The Anthropophagi, and men whose heads
> Do grow beneath their shoulders.
>   William Shakespeare, *Othello*

All day I feel a burning in my bones.
The people here all victims of a curse.
I know within, this place is not my home.

The wealthy do not hear the poor man's groans
Though there's enough for all within their purse.
It causes me a burning in my bones.

They let fear dominate, those wretched clones,
Abandon freedom for some fear they nurse.
I know within, this place is not my home.

They love this land, this city of their own.
Despising those of others is perverse.
It causes me a burning in my bones.

There may be some dispute among the thrones.
But war won't solve it. War itself is worse.
I know within, this place is not my home.

Where is the land that long ago I roamed?
And how do I go back? What place to search?
All day I feel a burning in my bones.
How can I find the place that is my home?

Forbidden Planet
by Jim Gaines

Just another brave new body
Nothing to do but throw
Rocks at tin cans and you
Have to bring your own
But still the Almighty makes gorgeous
Worlds surely man could grow to love
Boundless in enthusiasm to create
New life far from scurry and strife

Yes, son, we're seeing it again
Instead of mad robot cartoons
It's more than what your Mom says
A knockoff of The Tempest
It's a parable, a poem
A dream of what may come

Yet some dark incomprehensible
Force sly and irresistible
Lurks close at hand only
Waiting to be reinvoked
For murder devilish in our nights
Do you hear some big breathing
Or shall we have less dreaming on this ship

You ask where's Caliban
He's neither fish nor circuit board
Unseeable and still unseen
You'll find someday
Evil's more than a night's mistake
More than a pawn of incantation

Oh, rank doth have its privilege
Being perfect specimens so fine
Exceptions all but divine our eyes
Almost afire we're not so harmless
The view to our desire
Looks just like heaven
Touching lips so silly is that
All there is to it no
Feeling no emotion
What is wrong with this theory

The woman seems a jewel in the flower
So innocent she charms the unicorn
And pure enough to dull the tiger's claws
But the price of that thrill is some added doom
For the former virgin draws more rage
To the faithless interloper so curious
To know beyond the sea of ages

Tiger tiger dying bright into atoms
In the dark epitaph for Anyman
Forbidden to behold
Gorgon's face and live
Unfit yet to receive
Such portions of the power

Can you beware of what you think
Before the murder becomes palpable
Or use proportion's mirror to deflect
A buried angel's fiendish destiny

The metal toy tinkered together
Cannot destroy what's locked in its own
Electrical dilemma where monsters from
The Id are nightmares anywhere
Mindless primitive man-beasts we
Refuse to face and therefore cannot flee
Or with rough magic place
Two thousand centuries
One hundred million miles of space
Between us and the terror
Other with us ever to recall
We are not God after all

My Time with the Cosmic Forces
by Joe Metz

Of course, Momma had her way. She called and got me an appointment with Dr. Harry. Fifty dollars for one hour. That's about what I make doing odd jobs some weeks. "Plain silly," I thought. But Momma said she'd pay for it. Said I needed to find out what my future looked like. Said a forty-year old shouldn't be just piddling his life away doing odd jobs. So I told her I'd go find out what Dr. Harry had to say. She thinks he's a real smart man. Thinks he's nice looking too. I couldn't see why gray hair, a big belly, and walking with a cane make somebody look nice. Except he's about Momma's age. I guess that makes him look different in her mind.

Anyway, on Wednesday I walked over to his office. It's about three blocks away from where Momma and I live in my doublewide trailer. The sign on his door said "Open," so I walked right on in. There was this tiny lobby with a couple saggy chairs. Looked like they was supposed to be leather. Looked like they'd been set on a lot, too. Coffee table had some magazines scattered on it. Wasn't any that I knew about. Some important looking papers in black frames was hanging on one wall. One said "Dwayne Eugene Harrington" completed a "Program of Spiritual Advocacy and Insight" and was awarded a degree of "Doctor of Spiritual Counseling." I was about to look at the other ones when the big orange curtain opened. There stood Dr. Harry, belly, cane and all. Had on a yellow shirt. Big purple tie. "Come in. Come in," he said. And I did, sure hoping I'd get my fifty dollars worth.

There was lots of things in the room. Big posters of stars and suns. Rows of books with gold letters. A big neon sign said, "WE ARE CHILDREN OF THE UNIVERSE." Two big yellow chairs, next to each other, got my attention most. Dr. Harry said for me to take a seat in one. I did. He leaned on his cane and plopped down in the other one. Then he said, "Well, Lester, let's see about where you're headed with your life." Him knowing my name impressed me right off. Then I thought about it. Momma had told him making my appointment. He reached over and took my hand real tight. I jerked it away in a hurry.

"Now, Lester, just loosen up, son. We need to let the cosmic forces flow through our bodies. Our hands will bond us to share their energies." He took my hand again. I felt all sweaty doing it but left it there. He said he could feel the forces coming right then into his body. Said how cosmic winds were blowing truth about my future into the room here. Seemed more to me he'd just turned on a big fan in the back of us. All of a sudden he asked me, "Are you ready for tomorrow?" Well, since I had some jobs already lined up, I just said, "Yessir, I sure am."

"That's good, Lester, because it'll be a new beginning for you. Tomorrow will be the start of a new life." I couldn't see how it'd all happen so quick, so I just stayed quiet. Then he asked me how old I was. I said, "Forty-two next May." He said, "Yes," just like he knew I'd say that. All of a sudden he jumped out of his chair and stood right in front of me. He took my head in both

Riverside Writers 271

his hands. Started going on about everything. About me finding my way in life. About how having money don't matter much in the bigness of the universe. That time don't get wasted, even if you got a small job. How we're born to be what we think we're bound to be. And just on like that for about ten minutes or so. With him breathing right there in my face, I guessed Dr. Harry had had him a shot or two of gin before I came. "Do you feel it, Lester? The forces, son? Here in this room? Here in my hands?"

Some lights that spread bright colors all over the room come on. He was rubbing his hands through my hair like giving somebody a shampoo. "It's all in front of me now," he almost shouted. "It's all clear to me." I think I felt real good about that. Mostly it was because I didn't hardly have no idea what the hell Dr. Harry was talking about. Noticed though a couple buttons on that yellow shirt had popped open.

He pointed his cane at a big number chart on the wall. "See there?" I said I could. "Three. Think of that number, son. Three." I did. First, he said a woman in my life would be leaving me soon. I wouldn't imagine it'd be my girlfriend, Judy. We'd been going together ever since I got out of the Navy. That was two, three years ago. Was it Momma? She'd stayed with me there in my doublewide for a couple years. So I asked, "Is it my Momma?" Dr. Harry went right on like he never heard me. Then he said, real loud, "The cosmic energies are in a new orbit now. They tell me you'll find a new job. Wait. A new kind of job. Here. Right in our own town."

Now, I appreciated Dr. Harry's degrees and all. But I thought, "Well, damn, being a handyman I get all kinds of new jobs." It started to not sound like fifty dollars worth of cosmic forces to me. I tried to straighten out my hair some and asked, "Like what kind of new job, Dr. Harry?" That seemed to peeve him off a bit. He put his fingers on his temples. "Opportunities. Grand opportunities you cannot pass by." Momma's been saying that's what I need, so I smiled. Dr. Harry put his hands on my head again. Wished I'd brought my comb. Remembered it was in my other work pants.

"Finally! Oh yes, there it is. Remember the three. Yes, Lester boy, the venues of space tell me, show me right here, you're due to come into some money. No, wait. Let me listen." Dr. Harry pushed his ears toward whatever he was thinking he heard. "No, not some, Lester. Lots. Looks like soon too." Now having lots of money would likely make me, Momma, and Judy a whole lot happier. I'd done paid off my doublewide and used truck. But there sure wasn't much left to enjoy on anything for fun. I grabbed Dr. Harry's hand and shook it as hard as I could. "That's real great, Dr. Harry. We sure can use it. How soon's it coming?"

Looking all worn out, he started back to his yellow chair. About halfway down he got up and said, "I need to go back and consult my cosmic icons." He remembered to pick up his cane, then went someplace behind our yellow chairs. He came back soon, wiping his mouth and smiling. "The, ah, icons say it'll be all relative. Sometimes it's sooner. Sometimes it's later. Your spirit will know when it's time. The signs of the forces will appear." I thought there wasn't much sense planning to buy nothing special right away. Dr. Harry got a bad case of hiccups but kept right on with that big smile. I was ready to quit. I'd had about as much of cosmic forces as I could put up with.

"And one more thing now, Lester." Dr. Harry came over face to face again. It smelled like his cosmic icons had let him get a couple other shots of gin. "This is just all between you and I. We must not violate the vicissitudes of the universal spirit. We must stay confined within the circumstances of the cosmic icons. We cannot betray their trust. Understand, Lester?" Well, some of it I did, but mostly I didn't. To me it all depended on what happened once I walked out his door. I told him I did. He did something on the side of his chair and the "cosmic winds" went off.

Dr. Harry had told Momma he just took cash, so I handed over five tens. "Thank you, Lester. Just remember the number we said. 'Three'." When I left, some young girl was waiting in that little lobby. Blonde-headed and cute. Looked like one I'd seen along side of Dr. Harry riding in the Fourth of July parade. Looked too like she was four or five months expecting. "Hi," she said real nice. I tipped my baseball cap and opened up the door. Dr. Harry came through the curtain, this time without his cane. Appeared he was trying to hold in his belly a little. "Jennifer, come in. Please do come in, dear. The cosmic forces await us." He took her hand and they went behind that big orange curtain. I closed the door and started back home. Couldn't help then but wonder what them cosmic forces might bring up for Miss Jennifer.

* * * * *

Dr. Harry's "three" all came to be about true. First, Momma told me about her boyfriend. Said they'd been going together for about a year. Now he wanted her to come live in his apartment over by the ballpark. So, hugging me hard and lots of tears, she moved out. Said she hoped I understood. Two days after she was gone, I asked Judy if she'd think about moving in the doublewide with me. She thought on it for a couple days. Came over one night and said she would. First of that "three" worked out for a lot of good times.

Second then, about the new job. I had a blowout on the pickup truck. Went to "Eddy's Tire Shop" to get a used tire. Eddy asked if I was still doing odd jobs. Told him of course I sure was. He said if I liked, he'd give me a couple of months work. Putting on winter tires for his customers. I said, "Yeah, sure." Driving home though I hoped this wasn't one of the grand cosmic opportunities Dr. Harry had said would come. I'd been hoping for more of something steady. Year around.

Then there was number three. About the money. I'm hoping Dr. Harry's right about the part where it'd be still all relative. That there'd be some come sooner, some later. The Thursday after I saw him, I won a hundred-and-fifty dollar on a "fill-your-card" bingo game at the American Legion. Right after that, I bought some scratch-off tickets at the store where me and Judy buy most of our groceries. I won twenty more dollars. I'm figuring that both of them was the "sooner" part of the lots of money he'd talked about. So far, the "later" part didn't get one more cent in it. I thought maybe I should take Dr. Harry some good gin or something. Might help his cosmic icons tell me how much more's coming later on. From my way of thinking, it's way past time.

Judy and me keep hoping the cosmic forces think so too. She's expecting. Dr. Harry was sure right telling me to think about three. Believe it, Judy and me do a lot. Got to the point yesterday we went and bought us a big floor fan at the Salvation Army. And two pretty nice lean-back chairs. Didn't have yellow. Put all them in a place we cleared right inside the doublewide. Near the big neon sign we already had hung over the window. Says, "Coors Light." We figured it'd be a lot cheaper blowing in our own cosmic forces. We're trying it out tonight. Soon as Judy gets back. She went to get us a half-pint of gin. Thought we'd try and stay on the good side of them icons. Like Dr. Harry does.

Your Beliefs Can Sabotage Your Relationships
by Chuck Hillig

During my 30 years as a Marriage and Family Therapist, I've noticed that many couples in distress often have the same erroneous beliefs.

Belief #1: By far, the most commonly-held myth is that other people and situations can, quite literally, make you feel some emotion. This widely-held falsehood probably creates more strife in relationships than all of the other myths combined.

Let's look at this more closely. When you've gotten upset in the past, did you believe that it was because someone had hurt your feelings, or because they had made you angry? If so, then you've got a lot of company. Every day, I used to hear my clients making that very same complaint about each other.

However, here's the big problem: If you believe that the true source of your emotional discomfort is somewhere outside of yourself, then you're putting someone (or something) else in the driver's seat of your life. Instead of accepting personal responsibility for creating your own painful experiences, you see yourself as being unfairly victimized by forces that are far beyond your control.

Once that sense of victimization kicks in, it's downhill from there. In order to get revenge, for example, you might even start to blame others for your own acting-out behavior. For example, if I can point to my wife and say, *I got drunk last night because YOU made me angry,* then I'm trying to get off the responsibility hook by putting my wife on it.

Belief #1 is so widespread because it's been constantly reinforced through our culture and the media. For example, millions of us firmly believe that soap operas can make us feel sad, that wearing old clothes can make us feel embarrassed and that traffic jams can make us feel angry.

The simple truth, though, is that external situations and circumstances can't really make anyone feel anything.

In the end, after all, it's not what happens to you that really matters. It's only what YOU say about what happens to you that makes a difference. In other words, it's always the interpretation or the spin that *you*, yourself, put on what's happening that ends up coloring your experience of it. And, since you're always able to choose your own responses, you're, ultimately, response-able (i.e. responsible) for creating your own feelings. Period.

So, just how did this long-standing, erroneous belief become so widely accepted as an undisputed fact?

Well, before we were in kindergarten, probably 99% of us were indirectly conditioned by our parents to believe that we could, magically, control other peoples' feelings. For example, I remember my mom often saying things like this: *Don't tell Aunt Kate that you don't like her present because you'll hurt her feelings.* Or she might say, *Don't tell Grandpa that he has bad breath. You'll make him feel bad.*

So my mother's message to my 3-year old mind was that, even though I was the youngest member in the family, I still possessed some kind of magical power to actually hurt these bigger people. However, of course, this strange ability to hurt others also came with a big downside, too. If *I* possessed this power, then other people also possessed it, too. In short, if I could hurt *their* feelings through my words, then they could also hurt *mine*.

The actual reality, however, is that we humans simply don't have the power to literally *force* one another into feeling ANY emotion…either negative OR positive. After all, no one is physically getting inside our brains and re-wiring our synapses and neural pathways in order to *make* us feel anything. In short, no one out there is doing it to you. You've always been doing it to yourself. When you abdicate your personal responsibility for creating your *own* emotional life, then you're setting yourself up to feel used, powerless and victimized.

Of course, it's obvious that significant others (e.g. family, friends, etc.) can make it much *easier* for us to choose to create some emotion, but the final decision (as well as the full responsibility for it) is still ultimately ours and ours alone. Significant others can, in a sense, "invite" you to feel something, but *you* are the only one who ultimately decides whether or not to take them up on their offer.

Actually there's great power in acknowledging that you're sourcing all of your own emotions. Whatever feelings you create, you can also *un-create,* too. If, on the other hand, you believe that all of these upsets have been happening TO you instead of happening BY you, then you're going to be stuck with them until others choose to stop upsetting you.

Belief #2 is a common myth that says you should always have a good reason for feeling what you're feeling. On top of that, you should also be able to explain and justify all of your feelings both to yourself and to others.

But what happens when you're just not able to come up with a reasonable explanation about how you're feeling? Well, oftentimes, you might just ignore those concerns or, worse yet, even deny their presence. However, when your outside presentation to the world doesn't match your inside reality, you're sacrificing both your authenticity and your personal integrity. In short, when you lack the courage to tell others the unvarnished truth about what's so for you emotionally, then you're probably just trying to look good.

The only recourse is to always give yourself complete permission to fully embrace whatever feelings arise in you, moment to moment. Why? Because if you don't own those feelings, then, eventually, those negative feelings will end up owning YOU.

It's helpful to remember the acronym J.U.D.E. In short, you don't have to Justify, Understand, Defend or Explain your feelings to either yourself or to anyone else. It's not a prerequisite that you first figure out your feelings before you actually go ahead and just feel them. Instead, it's much healthier if you just give yourself permission to be with whatever arises in you instead of trying to push any of it away.

Suppose, for example, a man begins to feel envious of his wife's sudden financial success. Although he has an excellent job himself, his wife's recent career advancements have now become inwardly threatening to him. However, he can't come up with any good reason to justify his growing fear of, say, her possible abandonment. So, instead of sharing his vulnerability and concerns with his wife, he starts to repress these feelings and unconsciously denies that there's anything wrong.

His own personal myth that he's a good guy simply won't allow him to feel fearful and envious about his wife's new successes in her career. However, these powerful feelings still have to go somewhere. If they're not acknowledged and owned, they'll stay internalized and will eventually create a kind of psychic constipation. If the husband continues to lie to his wife about what's really so, his emotional blockage will only get worse which will likely trigger still more fear and further withdrawal.

But, in the long run, a feeling is just a feeling is just a feeling. If we don't acknowledge the presence of ALL of our negative feelings when they arise, we're likely to unconsciously cover them over with what we think are more acceptable ones. In truth, our feelings don't hassle us as much as the relationship that we set up in our own heads between what we *are* feeling and what we think we *should* be feeling, instead.

Belief # 3 holds that, because they care about me, my friends and family should automatically know what I want from them…*without me actually having to ask them for it.* This kind of irrational thinking places on your significant others the impossible burden of having to, magically, read your mind. The danger is, of course, when they fail to correctly divine your wishes, (no matter *how* obvious they may be to you), you might then mistakenly conclude that, perhaps, *they don't really care about you.* In short, you might end up experiencing a rejection that was never actually occurring.

For example, let's say I'm sitting next to my wife who's reading a new novel. Then I start rubbing my shoulders and complaining out loud about some neck pain. However, maybe she's not fully listening to me and is still into reading her own book. So, I might take it up a notch and suggest out loud that a neck massage would feel really good. She nods absentmindedly, but she just doesn't respond. Please notice, however, that I still haven't actually asked her directly for what I want (i.e. the neck massage).

Now, if she still doesn't pick up my hints, I could easily feel very hurt and angry from this perceived rejection. *She knows exactly what I want,* I might conclude, *but she's not giving it to me.* What I've done, though, is to relieve myself of the personal responsibility to ask her directly for a neck massage. Instead, I'm now unfairly requiring her to do something quite impossible: mind reading. Remember, of course, that all of my turmoil is self-induced and has only been happening inside of *me*.

It's best to always give yourself permission to ask 100% of the people you know for 100% of what you want, 100% of the time. If you don't clearly and directly ask others for what you want in life, then what you're going to get is what's left over after everyone else gets what *they* want.

Remember, though, if someone says NO to one of your requests, (no matter how reasonable) and you get angry behind that, then you weren't really making a request of them at all. You were actually making a *demand*. If you're making an honest and mature request, however, then you're willing to hear from them either a YES or a NO. If you're only willing to hear a YES to all of your so-called requests, then you're acting narcissistically.

I've even heard many clients say, in effect, *If my spouse REALLY loved me, they would always do what I want*. And then, when you couple that very unrealistic expectation with an unspoken demand that your spouse also be able to read your mind, you've got a perfect recipe for some serious marital conflict.

The desire to have our wishes divined by our loved ones probably has its origins in our unconscious memories as infants. However, those basic human needs back then (e.g. food, clean diapers, sleep, etc.) were both obvious and predictable. For most of us, there were benevolent caretakers who, miraculously, predicted what we wanted and made it available for us.

Amazingly, though, many grown adults still expect that same kind of insightful awareness from their significant others. However, demanding that your mate automatically understand and fulfill your current needs in the same magical way that your parents did when you were an infant is an *unreasonable expectation*. Instead, you need to find the courage to openly and clearly ask others for what you want, and then to be willing to hear from them either a YES or a NO.

Unfortunately, we don't often recognize that these three beliefs are *not* infallible truths at all, but, instead, are only unconscious habits that have their roots in our earlier conditioning. In order to become emotionally mature, however, many of our bio-computers could probably use some serious updating.

So, ask yourself three questions: 1) Do I believe that the *source* of my emotions is somewhere outside of me; or am I willing to take 100% responsibility for everything that I think, feel, say and do? 2) Do I believe that I first need to justify, understand, defend or explain my feelings; or am I willing to fully acknowledge, experience and share my emotions as they arise in me, moment to moment? 3) Do I believe that the people who love me should magically know what I need from them; or do I have the courage to clearly and directly ask them for what I want and then be willing to accept either a YES or a NO?

By openly challenging and deconstructing these three erroneous beliefs, you can remove some of the major obstacles that prevent you from enjoying stronger and healthier relationships.

Bump in the Night
by Larry Turner

Herb thought he heard a noise downstairs and was instantly wide awake. He was certain he had fastened and locked the iron grate over the windows and doors of the delicatessen as he did every night. So if someone had broken in, it was not a casual prowler. He heard the sounds again, vaguely like footsteps plus something else, and got up quietly so as not to awaken Rose. He slipped into his robe and, after giving it some thought, put his pistol in the pocket. Not knowing what was down there, he didn't know whether he'd be better or worse off with the gun.

He silently left the bedroom, shutting the door behind him. He paused at the top of the stairs but did not turn on the light.

When as newlyweds he and Rose had opened the delicatessen, they had no choice but to live above the store. Later, as the business prospered, they talked of moving to a better apartment, condominium or house, but didn't like the thought of commuting, and so they stayed. Later still, as the neighborhood began to change and profits dropped off, they had no choice but to stay in those few rooms—no choice, that is, but to do as their family and friends advised, sell the business and live off their savings or start again elsewhere.

But Herb had a great loyalty to the neighborhood where he grew up and which had treated them so well for so many years. Also there was something he scarcely admitted to himself, let alone to his cynical friends. Despite constant annoyance and occasional danger, deep down he truly believed in this multicultural neighborhood. If different races and ethnicities couldn't get along here, what hope was there they could do so in the wider world?

He heard something down below falling and started down the stairs. His dark-adapted eyes could easily see by the illumination from the streetlights outside. But what did he see? Even with all the lights on, even with searchlights brought in, he wouldn't have recognized the creature before him; it looked like a hairy, humpless camel.

Without thought he blurted out, "Who—What are you, and what are you doing here?"

The creature jumped, turned to him and spoke in a voice like a chant. "Oh, I'm sorry. I never intended to startle you. Please, don't be anxious. I'm proud of what you're doing here in the neighborhood, and I wanted to come by and wish you peace and tranquility."

"Yes, but who are you?"

"Didn't I introduce myself? I'm the Deli Llama."

Hallelujah Carol
(modeled on Leonard Cohen's "Hallelujah")
by Larry Turner

(one voice) In the hills, the shepherds hark.
The air is cold, the night is dark,
The wind so sharp and cruel it cuts right through you.
Then up above, the rush of wings,
A choir of joyful angels sings,
A heavenly chorus singing Hallelujah.
    Voices singing Hallelujah.
    Angels bringing Hallelujah.

(men) How can you sing this song of grace
At such a time, in such a place
Where tyranny and poverty undo you?
We've lost all hope, we're ruled by Rome,
Injustice sits upon the throne,
making mockery of Hallelujah.
    Why embrace this Hallelujah?
    Out of place, this Hallelujah.

(women) In Bethlehem, the prophets said,
An infant in a manger bed
Would come to God's own people and renew you.
For he's the one who came along
To give you hope, to right each wrong.
Come join us in our mighty Hallelujah.
    In the manger, Hallelujah.
    Holy stranger, Hallelujah.

(all) Now twenty centuries have passed.
Tyrants and injustice last.
Heartache and despair keep coming to you.
But come to Bethlehem again
And join the angels' glad refrain,
A mighty and redeeming Hallelujah.
    Angels beaming Hallelujah.
    A redeeming Hallelujah.

The Apostle Peter
by Joe Metz

I think there is too much focus on the denial:
bad judgment, but only a small part of my life
with the person I called "Lord" and "Savior."
How can I not remember the rooster's cry
that night? Not remember the tearful sorrow
I felt as He was led away to be crucified?

But He was only one of many Jews crucified,
one of many who had no chance for denial,
for lamenting the weight of their sorrow,
for enjoying the mystic lore of Judaic life.
Had I the tongue today, I would gladly cry,
"These too share a Kingdom with Our Savior!"

Among the Galileans in search of a savior,
Andrew and I felt our lives often crucified
only by the raging sea, the dark, desolate cry
from fishermen with empty nets, their denial
of a daily catch wrenching God from our life.
How long, we asked, must we subsist in sorrow?

But a time came for the ending of our sorrow.
Andrew told me, "We have found our Savior.
Come with me; let us find in Him a new life."
He named me Cephas, his "Rock." Crucified
no longer by each day's longing, by denial
of loss, "Comes the Kingdom!" I could cry.

Now I fished for men. Listening for the cry
of multitudes, I lifted their grief, their sorrow,
offering them a God of love. I dissolved denial
of their faith and longing. I offered a Savior
with a Kingdom of Peace for those crucified
by terror, humiliation; One who brought new life.

Riverside Writers

He was the Son who became the Spirit of my life,
Prophet for my people. Could I do other than cry,
"You know I love you!" after He had been crucified,
returning still to feed us, lifting our veil of sorrow?
I followed Him as a man, worshiped Him as a Savior.
With His life He dealt sin, death their lasting denial.

An Apostle of compassionate life,
I shed my cloth of personal sorrow,
heeding sinners' cry for mercy, forgiveness.
In the name of my Savior,
I too crucified, cried for His mercy,
forgiveness for my craven act of denial.

Of People and Flowers
by J. R. Robert-Saavedra

You have to be like,
    The lily pad:
Moving to where the wind,
    And current takes you,
Yet not losing yourself,
    By their murmurs and whispers.

Keep blooming,
    Even though the water stinks,
Keep nature's colors,
    Although the pond is crystal clear,
Do not change your nature,
    Try as the stream may to drown you.

You must be what you are,
    What God and nature made you,
Blossom, bloom and smile unto the world,
    Dark as it might be,
Look up and see the sun,
    And not the stagnant waters beneath you.

Life's Cellar
by J. R. Robert-Saavedra

In the cellar of life,
Everyone is a bottle!
Filled with grape juice....

Some of us turn into wine,
And some of us turn into vinegar;
Yet others, turn into the finest champagne!

The Unknowable
by Rod Vanderhoof

At three in the morning
all is wrong.

I pace for hours wondering
how to make things right.

I sit on the edge of my bed
unable to get chaos out of my head.
I panic, scream and swirl downward,
trapped in a
terrifying nightmare.

If only I'd known the unknowable
and done better,
but now that's impossible.

My bad choices are made
and
reality lies ahead.

Overlooking the Aegean
by Anne Heard Flythe

Who ever built the last
temple standing wins.
Layers of worship lie
beneath stone pillars
supporting sky.

Laminations of belief,
gods and doctrines
older than memory
marble on rock on stone,
rubble topped with wood
or shells or bones.

Each judged heretic
by sequential architects,
an ecclesiastic midden,
an empty reliquary.

Nothing Personal Just Business
by Fred Fanning

    The smell of Lavender and Chamomile hung in the air as Beethoven's Bagatelle played lightly in the background. Susie slipped into the hot water of the tub releasing the stress from her body as she warmed. As she lay there listening to her favorite music and smelling her favorite bubble bath, her thoughts began to wander. She took the razor blade and cut both wrists allowing her arms to settle into the water. As the water filled with blood, she sank into a soft sleep.
    "It is over," she said softly.
    She awoke in a grassy field with the sun on her. Warmth and relaxation took over her body. Lying there

not moving or thinking felt safe. Just then a man spoke to her. She raised her head to see a beautiful man sitting on a blanket next to her. His voice was calming and soothing.

"Hello," she said.

The man was wearing khaki pants, deck shoes, and a half-opened white shirt. His skin was the color of bronze and his hair the color of gold.

"Hello," he said. "Won't you join me for a glass of wine?"

"I'd love to."

She raised herself to her feet, walked closer and sat next to him on the blanket. He poured her a glass of wine that she sipped slowly. It was the best wine she had ever tasted.

"This is delicious, what type of wine is it?" she asked.

"This is what they call ice wine, made from frozen grapes," he explained. "I just picked it up in Mosel Valley in Germany."

"It is exquisite," she said.

"By the way, I'm Lucifer, but my friends call me Luke," he said with a smile.

"It is nice to meet you Luke; my name is Suzanne, but my friends call me Susie," she replied.

"I hear you like music?" Luke asked.

As if on cue the song "White Rabbit" by Jefferson Starship began playing out of nowhere. The sound was lovely and enchanting.

"This is my favorite song," said Luke.

"I usually prefer classical music, but it is attractive."

As the song played, a group of dancers could be seen across the field dancing to the enchanting rhythm. Their dance was mesmerizing as they swayed to the rhythm of the music, circling each other sometimes reaching out and touching hands. As the dancers drew closer, Susie noticed they were skeletons dressed in beautiful lace gowns. The sound of the music was all around them as they danced in a spellbinding motion. Susie felt drunk from the experience.

"I don't know what to make of this," she said.

"Oh, it is not much really," said Luke.

Dark clouds raced across the sky; lightning flashed; thunder roared. The whole spectacle was very frightening. Indeed. Susie began to sway with the music as she sipped the wine. She became lost in the moment. As the song ended the dancers moved away, and the weather returned to a warm blue sky and gentle winds.

"I must have died and gone to heaven," said Susie.

"Oh, I am afraid not, my dear," said Luke. "You have gone the other way."

"How can that be when everything here is excellent?"

"Hell is what you make of it," said Luke. He snapped his fingers and a lizard man in a tuxedo appeared holding a chilled bottle of wine. The demon refilled their glasses and disappeared in the blink of an eye. Then the Toccata and Fugue began to play as a second troupe of dancers appeared in dark and depressing costumes.

"What music is this?" Susie asked.

"Ahh, this is the Toccata and Fugue, written by Johann Sebastian Bach," said Luke. "It is another favorite of mine."

"I seem to have heard it before."

"You certainly could have; it was the song played by the character Captain Nemo in the movie 20,000 Leagues under the Sea," Luke said.

"Oh my, yes, I do remember it now," Susie said.

The hypnotic music swirled around them while the skeleton dancers were joined by demons dressed in tuxedos. They danced to the music with perfection. As they danced the weather again changed with the music.

"Do you know I am a musician?" Susie asked.

"You were a musician."

"What did you say?"

Riverside Writers

"I said you were a musician. Remember now you're dead."

"You're right; I was a musician," she sighed.

She closed her eyes and laid back. It was all coming back to her now. She laid there quietly listening. The tune changed to the Egmont Overture by Ludwig Van Beethoven. This music was not as depressing, and she relaxed a bit. As the song played, memories of her life flashed through her mind. She was here now; this was what she deserved. As she thought about the pain, a tear ran down her cheek. Just then a Mozart Serenade began to play. She smiled; this was a piece she knew well.

Suddenly and without warning she was jerked back on the ground as if she were being shocked. There were bright lights and whiteness all around her. Then it was all gone; the serenade played again in her ears. She was back. She was shaken, but didn't tell Luke what had just happened. She thought it must be some sort of side effect.

"If this is hell, why isn't it bad?" she asked.

"Oh, it is bad, but you've just arrived."

She sat up, wondering what he meant by that. Before she could say anything Luke transformed into the most hideous creature she could imagine. She jumped back in fright. The grass died, and the leaves fell off the trees. The sky became cloudy with a sharp cold wind. Then on cue the world around her became black and white. She became frightened and began to cry.

"What have I done?" she cried. As she knelt down she continued to sob and cry. Luke grew taller and hideous with every moment. The dancing skeletons reappeared in rags with rotting skin on their bones, and they danced to the most horrific music she had ever heard. She saw people being torn apart by rabid dogs. Close around her she saw people being poked and stabbed with long sharpened poles. She began to scream and yell, hoping someone would come to her aid. No one did; she had made her choice.

Suddenly and without warning she was jerked back on the ground again as if she were being shocked. The bright lights returned creating whiteness all around her. Then it was all gone and she was back in the horrid scene. She was shaken that it had happened again, but dared not tell Luke this time either.

"Hey Luke," a man said as he walked toward them from a distance.

Luke looked and began to return to his previous attractive appearance. The demons, skeletons, and people disappeared and the sky opened up to blue. The approaching man wore a warm smile.

"Luke, how you been, old buddy?" he asked. The man was tall, tanned, and nearly as beautiful as Luke.

"Hey Mike, I've been okay. What brings you here?"

"Oh, you know me just wandering around looking for trouble," Mike said.

Luke looked down at Susie and said, "Susie, this is my good friend Michael; our friends call him Mike".

"Help me, please help me!" she cried.

"Whoa, hold on young lady what is going on Luke?" Mike asked.

Susie screamed out, "You must save me from this hell!"

"Calm down young lady, let Luke explain,"

"Well Mike you know just business, nothing personal," Luke said.

Luke's company was fire and brimstone, and business was good lately. He tormented humanity for the duration of their life on earth and those chosen after death. Despite his claim to the contrary this was all personal, he loved his job dearly. He had a great job, not to mention the power he wielded and the demons he oversaw.

"Luke I know it is just business, but I really came here to speak to you, Susie," Mike said.

"Damn Mike, not another mistake," yelled Luke.

/ / /

June walked back into the house and up to the bathroom to grab her glasses on the counter. That was odd; she couldn't remember locking the bathroom door.

"Susie, you in there?" she yelled to no response, "Susie if you're in there let me get my glasses."

Suddenly she became panicked and felt something was terribly wrong. She stepped back and with all her might rammed the door with her shoulder breaking it open. There in front of her was the most horrible sight in the world, her only child floating in a bath tub of blood.

"Susie!" she screamed loudly. June threw open the window and yelled to her husband in the car to come quickly. Then she pulled Susie from the tub and immediately wrapped her wrists with hand towels to stop the bleeding.

"Call 911! Susie cut her wrists and isn't breathing!" June yelled as her husband Glen appeared at the bathroom door.

As June gave Susie CPR, she cried and screamed at her. "Susie, what in the hell were you thinking? Don't you die on me!"

Susie was June's only daughter and she loved her more than life herself. As she continued to work on her daughter, she could hear the sirens of the ambulance pulling up the driveway. The emergency medical technicians crashed into the house, and Glen motioned for them to go upstairs. They scrambled up the stairway banging the railing and walls with their equipment. Once in the bathroom they pushed June aside and began to work on the lifeless young girl. They performed CPR and applied bandages to both her wrists. They still couldn't get a pulse. The medical technicians contacted the doctor at the emergency room, who ordered them to provide an electrical shock to save the girl's life. The EMT worked frantically. As the button was pushed, Susie's back arched in response to the shock.

As they worked on her daughter, June stepped from the bathroom into the upstairs hallway. Glen rushed to her side. They both stood there in disbelief. Their only child had tried to kill herself. What reason could she possibly have had? Why would she do this? They had a million questions running in their heads. Just then one of the emergency medical technicians yelled out that he had a weak pulse. Both technicians scrambled to get her on a stretcher and out of the bathroom and down the stairs. They looked like ballet dancers as they negotiated furniture and leaped out the front door. Before anyone realized it, the ambulance raced off to the hospital.

The emergency room was prepared for Susie's arrival. Nurses ran to meet the ambulance as the driver backed it up to the door. A trauma team was standing by. They all gathered around her and began to work. Like an orchestra, their movements were in unison working with each other to save this young girl.

"I have no pulse," yelled the nurse.

"Clear for shock," yelled the doctor.

"I got a weak pulse now," said the nurse.

June and Glen arrived and were led to a waiting room beside the emergency room. They both paced the floor crying and sighing.

"She has to make it!" Glen said.

"Oh God, please let her live!" said June.

As she spoke the hospital pastor walked up to them. "You must be Glen and June. I am Pastor James," he said.

"Pastor, thank you for coming," said Glen.

"Why don't we all sit down. May I get you both something to drink?" Pastor James asked.

"No, thanks, I am too nervous and upset," said June.

Just as they began to describe the horror of the past few hours a doctor walked in.

"Hello, are you Susie's parents?" the doctor asked.

They nodded their heads.

"Your daughter has lost a lot of blood, but she is stable now, and we are giving her transfusions."

"Will, will…will she make it?" June asked.

Riverside Writers

"It is too early to tell and we won't know much for a few more hours."

But June and Glen could hear the lack of confidence in his voice. In spite of the doctor's trepidation, it was enough. All they wanted was a chance. If they just had that, they knew, Susie could make a full recovery. A complete physical recovery that is, because there would be a lot of mental recovery needed.

/ / /

"Mike you guys have got to get a better process in place," said Luke. "You can't keep coming down here and taking people back."

"I know, Luke, but you know how it works."

"Oh yeah, I know how it works all right," said Luke sarcastically.

"I'll tell everyone you said hello," Mike said.

"Mike, I'll get her yet!" yelled Luke as they walked away.

"Luke you just may at that," said Mike.

As he walked away, Mike snapped his fingers and Bach's "Jesu, Joy of Mans' Desire" began to play. Mike waved his arms in time with the music as bluebirds flew around him to the sound of the music. All Luke could do was shake his head. *Nothing personal just business*, he thought.

Heavenly Gardens
(for Sandy Hook Elementary)
by Michelle O'Hearn

Soft, bare soles
running across the lush
green lawn
playground swings flying
merry-go-round spinning
Giggles
Laughter

Re-living the happiness
of smiles awaiting the gifts
of Christmas.
No memory of how they
arrived on the fourteenth day
of December 2012.

Instead, flowers of God
laughing with them;
Angels cradling them here.
Trim hedges protecting
their eyes and surrounding
them with petals
of bright color
and pleasant dreams.

Sonnet of the Imperishable Minimum
by Steven P. Pody

Myriad people skitter across this scrummy crust of earth
in the here and now of proto-point time inertial.
Of tales, sagas and personal trials, there is no want or dearth
of reenacting and renewing love's theme eternal.

But from the sum of sweaty vows and seeking hearts
    triumphant;
amongst the lonely multitude of billions, there is you and
    there is me.
And though the body of humanity be super-abundant,
we are, in microcosm, the sum and worth of history.

For within vast evolutions of times and seas and dust
and the turbulent stirring pot of countless interactions,
obscured by mass, hard-wired quests of basic lust,
thrive melding duets of magnificently shared abstraction.

In the mega-scheme, what meaningful love exists seems
    fragile stuff:
Two is a tiny sum in such a world. But it is enough.

Contributors

Madalin E. Bickel (pen name m. e. jackson) Madalin's first published work was *Discovering Astronomy* in 1987. Although she began writing both poetry and music at an early age, most of her life has been devoted to developing curriculum and teaching units. Finally retired after forty years of teaching, Madalin is pursuing her first love, poetry. Her first book of poetry, *The Wolf at the Door,* is currently seeking a publisher. At sixty-seven she believes she is really just a novice. Madalin is currently a member of The Academy of American Poets, Poetry Society of Virginia, Riverside Writers, and the Virginia Writers Club. She is from West Virginia, and her poem "Collapse of the Silver Bridge" won a third place prize in the Poetry Society of Virginia's 2011 contest. She has poems in three of Riverside Writers anthologies and an anthology by Bridgewater College.

Darrin E. Chambers is a member of Riverside Writers.

S. Kelley Chambers is a member of Riverside Writers.

Maxine M. Clark grew up as a military brat. Experiences while traveling with her family fuels the content of her memoir that is currently in revision. Her memoir is both a personal story and a reflection on the social issues confronting the United States during the 1950s and the 1960s. In another life, Ms. Clark has been billed a community activist. Her activism caught the attention of *The Wall Street Journal, Business Week,* and the *NBC Today Show*. She is the founder of two book clubs: Women of Words and Ladies of Literature. With her husband in Fredericksburg, Maxine supports *The Fredericksburg Jazz Collective*'s efforts to create cultural awareness and enjoyment of jazz within the community. She is a gardener, an art collector, and a keeper of family and friends. Maxine graduated from Hampton University and The College of William and Mary. She retired from Fairfax County Public Schools.

Jill Austin Deming has written articles on wildlife rehabilitation and animal massage and bodywork for various publications. Recently she has turned to poetry to express her appreciation for the outdoors. Riverside Writers and The Virginia Writer's Club have been a great help in that endeavor.

Fred Fanning is a successful and well respected program and project manager. He traveled widely and lived in seven U.S. states and Guam as the child of a US Air Force veteran. As an adult, Fred lived and worked in Germany for over nine years. He is an avid reader and writer. Fred began writing as a non-fiction author with books, chapters and articles published. His new goal is to break into fiction. Fred has completed a few short stories and is working on a novel. In addition to his published work, he has presented seven technical papers before national audiences. Fred served two years as the editor of the Prospective Newsletter and is currently the newsletter editor of the Northern Virginia Chapter of the American Society of Safety Engineers. Fred is a member of The Virginia Writers Club and the Riverside Writers.

Anne Heard Flythe, a navy brat, attended 16 schools and won senior prizes in art and poetry. Her poems have won second in Mid-Atlantic Writers Conference, a first in the Poetry Society of Virginia state wide-contest (2008), third prize in the 2010 Golden Nib contest. All of the Riverside Writers anthologies include her work; she is proudest of the one dedicated to her in 2008. She studied art at the Corcoran and Phillips galleries in Washington DC. In 1947 she produced a weekly WMAL TV show in Washington DC sandwiched between Jimmy Dean and the evening news. She crewed and cooked on a 75 ft. schooner for a year from Maine to Granada via Bermuda. She has two sons and a granddaughter. Widowed, Anne lives on and manages Rebel Yell Tree Farm, a Loblolly plantation in Spotsylvania County. Surprised to be 89, she remains fascinated by the beauty and complexity of life and people.

Besides his creative writing, **Jim Gaines** has taught world literature, French language, English, and social sciences for over forty years at the university and high school level in Michigan, Pennsylvania, France, Louisiana, and most recently in Virginia. He is the author of six scholarly books and edited the Sociocriticism monograph series for Peter Lang Publishing. His first collection of poetry, *Downriver Waltz*, is scheduled to be released in the coming year. He is collaborating with his son, John, on a science fiction novel entitled *Life Sentence.*

Born in Liverpool, England, **Jennifer Anne Gregory** is an author, freelance writer and public speaking consultant. A former actress, Jennifer has appeared in several B.B.C television dramas, alongside writing, directing and producing for her own theater company. Jennifer holds a Bsc. (Hons) in social science, in addition to associate memberships to the London College of Music and Dramatic Art, and the London Academy of Music and Dramatic Art. Jennifer also holds a Certificate in Public Speaking from the Guildhall School of Music and Drama, London. Recently, Jennifer was interviewed on Virginia Living Television, discussing her 2010 paranormal/ fantasy novel *Among Other Edens* written under the pseudonym Guinevere Edern. *Dark Core*, the sequel to *Among Other Edens,* has just been completed and is scheduled for release in 2014. Jennifer also runs creative writing workshops for Germanna Community College department of Workforce and Community Development.

Thomas J. Higgins was born and has lived in Fredericksburg, Virginia all of his life. He has been active for over twenty years as a teacher in a Sunday school class for the mentally handicapped at Fredericksburg Baptist Church and a board member of a day program, run by the local Community Services Board that serves special needs folks. He and his wife became supervisors for two group homes for the mentally handicapped, owned by Fredericksburg Baptist Church. They worked there for 14 years. Tom published a book titled *How Far is it From Richmond to Heaven?* It tells of the wonderful experiences working with these folks. In 2010 he was recognized for his long term service by receiving two awards. The Fredericksburg Jaycees presented him with the Distinguished Service Award and the Rappahannock Community Services Board presented him with the 2010 Distinguished Intellectual Disability Volunteer Award.

Chuck Hillig was born in Chicago and has two Masters degrees. He has enjoyed successful careers as a Naval Officer, Social Worker, college Instructor and County Probation Officer. After living in Ohio, Missouri, Rhode Island, Virginia and Pennsylvania, he moved to San Francisco during the late 1960's. Between 1978 and 2006, Chuck worked as a state-licensed psychotherapist in California. His five books, combining eastern philosophy and western psychology, are currently available on Amazon.com. Several years ago, Chuck was interviewed for the movie *Leap! Finale.* His writings and interviews have been published in nine languages, and he has been a guest on many radio and TV programs. Chuck travels frequently to speak at conferences and to conduct workshops about his books. He invites you to visit his website at www.chuckhillig.com

J. Allen Hill (pen name of **Judy Hill**) was born in downstate Illinois but now considers herself an "east coaster" having lived not far from Atlantic beaches for over forty years. She has written to keep body and soul together as a Fairfax County School administrator, a Pentagon based training and documentation Project Manager and MENTOR's data manager. There have been many delightful paid and volunteer interludes involving writing, the arts and history: crew for Signature, a Tony Award-winning regional theater; usher at Arena Stage in Washington DC; docent for James Madison's Montpelier; Toastmaster governor; participating editor of many organizational newsletters, including Fairfax County, VA Parks. Currently she concentrates on short stories, a little poetry and a recently published historical novel, *The Secret Diary of Ewan Macrae*, available on Amazon in paperback and Kindle format. Encouragement and support has come from family, friends and membership in The Writer's Center, Bethesda, MD, Playwright's Forum, Washington, DC, Riverside Writers, Fredericksburg, VA and Virginia Writers, Inc.

Joe Metz and his wife, Susan, live in Spotsylvania, Virginia. They enjoy the rural atmosphere and, as Master Gardeners, work at turning Virginia red clay into soil that supports the growth of plants, shrubs, and vegetables. They've had some successes. Joe has been working with words most of his life. His prized possession is a copy of *Bambi* awarded to him in second grade for spelling achievement. He now relies on Spell-Check. Joe's a sporadic writer, sometimes exploring the intricacies of poetic forms; sometimes crafting the characters and dialogues of the short story; often attempting to master the disciplines of playwriting; sometimes dawdling over his keyboard hoping for an injection of inspiration. In 2007, Joe self-published (Infinity) a collection of short stories, *A Layman in Space*. He hopes to complete an autobiographical novel, *Sonny Boy*, by his eighty-fifth birthday. This is a four-year timeframe, during which he dare not dawdle.

Greg Miller was born in Ft. Sill, OK, the youngest child of Lt. Col. Robert Miller and his wife, Patricia. Most of his formative years were spent in Galesburg, IL, where he was educated holistically about the realities of life. In 1986, he moved with his wife and daughter to Fredericksburg, VA to begin a 22 year career as an IT expert and advanced technology report writer. During that time, and more emphatically afterwards, he pursued writing as a hobby and second career. He has participated in NanoWriMo (winning in 2012), and maintains a blog, and is a member of the Riverside Writers. Two of his works appear in this anthology.

Michelle O'Hearn (aka **MiCKi**), born and raised in Virginia, is a poet, songwriter, and multi-media artist while working as a business professional during the day. MiCKi released two solo music albums, several poetry chapbooks and small works from 2007-2012 after various stints with Philly and DC rock bands such as Cobalt Blue, Forbidden Youth and Sexsist. Michelle reached the last Semi-Final rounds in both the 2012 and 2013 Country Idol competitions held in Fredericksburg, VA after fighting her way back from a surgery that took her voice. She is currently preparing a wedding performance for a dear friend and mentor while continuing work on two novels and other new works of music and poetry. Some of her works can be found in the Special Collections Library at the University of Virginia.

Kelly Patterson reports, "A young seventy-year old man, I have been a poet for about twenty years. I love to write and have been published about ten times in anthologies. Historic Fredericksburg, Virginia is my home. I am a retired home builder, twenty years in business. Currently, I write only a few poems a year and have recently started to write my first novel, quite different from poetry. However, I enjoy learning new things about writing and people. I have learned: There is not a dime's worth of difference in any of us."

Julie Phend, a retired middle school teacher and writing tutor, loves everything about books: reading, writing, discussing, speaking, and teaching about them. Her first book, *D-Day and Beyond: A True Story of Escape and POW Survival,* tells the story of Stanley Edwards, a young pilot shot down over Normandy on D-Day. She has recently completed a historical romance, *Sculptor and Spy,* which takes place during the American Revolution. The book is based on the true story of Betsy Wright, a wax artist and spy in George III's court, and Ebenezer (Eb) Platt, a member of the Sons of Liberty. Julie belongs to the Society of Children's Book Writers and Illustrators, Riverside Writers, and Lake Authors Club, and is active in two writing critique groups.

Steven P. Pody, a native of Delaware, served four years with the U.S. Air Force in Alaska. In addition to ten total years in Alaska, 1.5 years in the Middle East, and 4.5 years in Africa, Steven has logged various adventures and travels across the globe. His total tally stands at 51 countries and 48 U.S. states visited, including crossing the Arctic Circle four times. Africa time was mostly with the U.S. Peace Corps. Steven met his wife, Beate, at an archaeological dig in the Golan Heights of Israel. They have three children. Steve has contributed two works for this anthology, including "The Thorny Branch," winning, in 2009, competitive publication in Volume 33 of

"Watershed," the literary journal of California State University. He has been writing poetry between latitudes and longitudes since 1969, and has published a well-regarded volume of verse, entitled *The Panoptikon*.

Norma E. Redfern was born in Shreveport, Louisiana in 1943. A military brat, she moved from Shreveport to Japan, Georgia, Alaska, and at last to Virginia, where she lived with her family at Ft. Belvoir. Norma met her high school sweetheart when both attended Mount Vernon High School. They were married in December, 1961. Norma worked for the federal government for five years after high school. After having three sons, she and her family moved to Fredericksburg, Virginia. She went to work for the government in Quantico, Virginia in 1978 as a military pay clerk, later promoted to military pay supervisor, verifying and auditing all facets of pay and allowances. Norma retired after twenty five years in the pay field in June, 2003. She joined Riverside Writers in 2001. She writes poetry and short stories.

Andrea Williams Reed is a member of the Riverside Writers group; her writing experience began with writing and developing curriculum for Work Ready Workshops and Family and Consumer Science school curriculum. She now enjoys writing poems and short stories. In 2013 her poems "New Shoes" and "Waiting" appeared in the Voices on the Wind Poetry Journal. She won third prize in the Virginia Golden Nib Tier I for poetry in 2012 for her poem, "We Endure". In 2011, her poem, "The Stationary Family" appeared in the Riverside Writers group's anthology, *Rappahannock Review*. A native of Gloucester County, Virginia she now makes her home in Fredericksburg, Virginia with her husband John.

J. R. Robert-Saavedra (pen name of **Jorge Rafael Robert-Saavedra) was** born in San Juan, Puerto Rico. He is an alumnus from the University of Notre Dame

(BBA) and the California State University—Stanislaus (MBA). Mr. Robert lived three years in Germany and one in South Korea. After 27 years of service he retired from the Department of Defense. One of his last assignments was as an International Audit Manager where he traveled extensively overseas. He is also retired as a Captain from the U. S. Army Reserves with 32 years of service. From 1998 to 2007 Mr. Robert worked as a federal government efficiency consultant. He presently works as a Realtor. Mr. Robert published his poetry book, *Poems by El Capitan,* in 2012. Jorge volunteers in various local associations and enjoys the stock market, writing, travel and photography. Much time is now spent with family and friends at sidewalk cafes.

Juanita Dyer Roush is a native Virginian with a husband of 43 years, a grown son, and a grandpup. She has worked in the Orange County Public Schools for 30 years. Her goal is to do something that she has never done before in every decade of her life. In her 20's she got married and became a Christian. In her 30's she adopted her son. In her 40's she learned that she was going deaf and started writing, and in her 50's she walked ½ marathons in Philadelphia and New York City. In her 60's she is volunteering at Point Lookout Lighthouse which is under preservation. She can hardly wait to see what life has in store from here on out!

C. A. Rowland (pen name of **Carolyn Rowland**) is originally from Texas but has resided in Virginia for eight years. She started writing at a young age but put that aside for college and law school. A history major, Carolyn has always been fascinated with ancient civilizations and their architecture. She has volunteered her time in many ways: Smithsonian Women's Committee, Quilts of Valor, and Project Linus quilts. Carolyn's law practice focuses on transactions, including historic rehabilitations such as the RJ Reynolds aluminum foil packaging plant in Richmond, Virginia. Currently Carolyn is working on short stories, is a regular blogger on www.mostlymystery.com, and is finishing her first humorous mystery novel. She is a member of the Society of Children's Book Writers and Illustrators, Virginia Writer's Club, Inc., Riverside Writers, and The Writer's Center. "An Interview with a Rabbit" was originally published in 2013 in the e-magazine, *Kings River Life*.

Ron Russis's first profession was as a U.S. Marine, retiring as a Master Sergeant after twenty-three years of service. Following retirement he renewed his formal education, graduating first from Mary Washington College with a B.S. (Psychology Specialization) and then from Goddard College with a MFA in Creative Writing. His writing typically addresses topics of rural interest.

Elizabeth Talbot relies on her travels and interest in developing technology to write "Second Chances," an exploration of the seamier side of the Internet. She has lived in Fredericksburg for over a decade while spending most of her adult working life in Washington D.C. after she graduated from Georgetown University. "Breaking Good" is based on some of her personal experiences during the government shutdown of October 2013. The piece also pays tribute to the hit AMC series "Breaking Bad" after her two daughters introduced her to the show. She is grateful to the Riverside Writers for the camaraderie and the opportunity to polish her craft.

D.P. Tolan (pen name of **Don Rowe**) was born and raised in Maine before a Navy career spanning almost 28 years with the most challenging in NAM and Arabia. He has published family research for over 20 years and blogs current results with cousins worldwide. He was deeply involved with Scouting for 15 years, and volunteers at the Regional Library in Fredericksburg assisting patrons with local history and genealogy. His first novel, *Golden Gate*, is available as an eBook from Barnes & Noble and Amazon.com. The second novel of the Tessera Trilogy, *Sooley Base*, will soon be available. His "A tour of duty recalled" illustrated with photos and maps of experiences in Vietnam, is held by the Naval Historical Center. His novels are based on Navy experiences including a 28 month tour in Arabia and technical contractor jobs. His works reflect help from family, friends ... and foes, and the Riverside Writers.

Stanley B. Trice's stories have been published in over a dozen national and international literary journals. He is a member of several writing groups that have been great sources of information and support. You can find him listed in *Poet and Writers'* "Directory for Writers." Stanley grew up on a dairy farm in Spotsylvania, VA and continues to live in the Fredericksburg, VA area where he commutes by train to Northern Virginia to work on budgets and legislative issues.

Donna H. Turner and her husband Larry moved to Fredericksburg in 2001 to be closer to their three sons and their families. She has a BA from Earlham College in Music, Art and Drama and an MA in Theatre from Northern Illinois University. She taught English in middle school and worked as a professional director for community and professional theatre groups in America and England. Currently she is directing for a dinner theater and teaching English as a Second Language at Peace Methodist Church in Fredericksburg. Her children's book, *Thanzaloria Sticks Her Neck Out*, was published in 1996 by University Editions. She has written dozens of short dramas used in church services, some of which have been published. "Valentine's Day Surprise" and "Growing Up with Dreams" won first prizes for fiction and nonfiction respectively in the Tier 1 Golden Nib competition in 2013.

Larry Turner moved to Fredericksburg after retiring from a career in college physics teaching and research in the USA and England. His poetry has appeared repeatedly in *The Lyric* and in the online journal *Voices on the Wind*. He has published two books of poetry, *Stops on the Way to Eden and Beyond* (1992) and *Eden and Other Addresses* (2005), and a collection of poems, stories and dramas, *Wanderer* (2011). He edited this anthology and the three previous ones for Riverside Writers. He served as president of Riverside Writers, and earlier as president of the Illinois State Poetry Society and regional vice-president of the Poetry Society of Virginia. "Six Children" and "Shape Up, Sylvia" won first prizes in national contests and were published in *The Lyric*. "Miracle," "Triceratops" and "How Do Mermaids Mate" were published in *Voices on the Wind*.

Ummie (pen name of **Sylvia Higgins**) was born and raised in Smyrna, Delaware, by her grandmother. Writing became a cathartic vehicle to escape feelings of unworthiness. The marriage between her pencil and yellow legal pad has been a quiet, revealing and rewarding relationship. A computer sneaked into the relationship, and they are peaceful with the help of six grandchildren and one great-grandchild. Inspiration comes from God, her five plus one senses and the whispers of her ancestors. After fifty-six years of living in Philadelphia, raising three children and thirty-six years of teaching in public schools, she retired and relocated to Spotsylvania, Va. Her life is full with family, church, exercising, knitting, reading, writing, facilitating a poetry gathering at the Fredericksburg Center for the Creative Arts and membership in Riverside Writers. She is eternally grateful to God for His gift and allowing her to give it a voice.

Rod Vanderhoof grew up in the Puget Sound region of the Pacific Northwest and was educated at Washington and Stanford. He authored a novel, T*he Cry of the Shidepoke,* plus numerous short stories. He was coeditor of four literary anthologies. Rod won the Virginia Writers Golden Nib Award for Poetry, 2009, for his highly acclaimed, "Yellow Heat." Other wins include the Riverside Writers Best Fiction, 2008, for his short story, "I Send My Regrets," and the Best Nonfiction, 2010, for his essay, "The General Who Saved Gettysburg." His poem, "Father and Son," won second prize in the 2013 Welsh Society contest judged by Pulitzer Prize winner and Virginia Poet Laureate, Claudia Emerson.

L.D. (Dan) Walker taught English and creative writing for 40 years, retiring in 2011 from a position at the Commonwealth Governor's School, a regional school for the gifted in north central Virginia. He is currently an adjunct instructor at the University of Mary Washington and the Virginia Community Colleges' Career-Switcher program. He is the author of nonfiction books and articles on English education and of several novels including *Huckleberry Finn in Love and War: The Lost Journals*, a sequel to Twain's original novel and the *Iron John Trilogy,* to his knowledge the only trilogy in two volumes—for reasons so hard to explain you'd have to read the books to understand. He has also received awards for short fiction and poetry. He and his wife of 42 years live on a small farm in Spotsylvania County with twelve (or so) cats, four dogs, three horses, two chickens, and pear tree with (so far) no partridges in it.

John M. Wills is an award-winning author, freelance writer, and journalist. Writing in a variety of genres, including fiction, non-fiction, technical, short stories, and poetry, he credits this multi-discipline approach for improving his novels. Wills also writes book reviews for the New York Journal of Books, and is a member of the National Book Critics Circle. A former Chicago police officer and retired FBI agent, he has published more than 150 articles, relating to police officer safety and training. His monthly articles are on Officer.com. His latest novel, *The Year without Christmas* is available on Amazon. He is working on a new novel, *Healer*, about a young boy who receives the gift of healing. Visit John at: http://www.johnmwills.com/, or at his blog: http://jwillsbooks.com/blog-2/.

Index

Author	Title
Bickel, Madalin	Ain't Nothin' Left, 188
	Cold January, 156
	Collapse of the Silver Bridge, 189
	Route 66, 177
	The Album, 32
	The Five and Dime Fork, 144
Chambers, Darrin E.	First Damned Day, 234
Chambers, S. Kelley	Family Night, 93
Clark, Maxine	The Clay Girl, 90
Deming, Jill Austin	The Goose, 124
	The Pond, 165
	The Quickening, 160
Fanning, Fred	Dreadlocks and the Three Fishermen, 108
	Nothing Personal, Just Business, 289
Flythe, Anne Heard	Acorns as Vocabulary, 121
	Matters of Gravity, 167
	Ophidian Vanity, 265
	Overlooking the Aegean, 289
	The Profane Egg, 81
Gaines, Jim	A Whimper and a Bang, 214
	Beachcombers, 175
	Forbidden Planet, 268
	Lines on the Iowa Writers Workshop, 220
	Long Distance, 174
	Pastime, 170
	Play Time, 85
Gregory, Jennifer Anne	Chuckles, 61
Higgins, Tom	Danny the Cowboy, 49
	This Is It?, 44
	While Walking through the Park, 51
Hill, J. Allen	A Walk in the Park, 253
	Metamorphosis, 19
Hillig, Chuck	Your Beliefs Can Sabotage Relationships, 276

Metz, Joe	Ballad of the L & D Diner, 57
	Casey's Part: A Fantasy, 209
	Dern Hills–the Aftermath, 26
	My Time with the Cosmic Forces, 270
	The Apostle Peter, 285
Miller, Greg	Betsy and George, 182
	Sink or Swim, 95
O'Hearn, Michelle	A Moment to Own It, 127
	At Home with Mrs. Madison, 186
	Doomsday Daddy, 36
	Heavenly Gardens, 297
	Her Flowering Audience, 206
	Icicle Days, 119
	In Different Places, 75
	Old Rag Cottonwood Stag, 158
	Yopo Experience, 11
Patterson, Kelly	Frisky, 169
	Night Chase, 157
	The Actress, 207
Phend, Julie	Babies Burp, 4
	Camping in the Woods of Wisconsin, 164
	When I Get to Be a Composer, 201
Pody, Steven P.	Sonnet of the Imperishable Minimum, 298
	The Thorny Branch, 180
Redfern, Norma	Midwestern Corn, 151
	They Called Her Violet, 52
Reed, Andrea Williams	Blood and Sugar, 33
	House on Route 17, 148
	The In-Law, 111
	We Endure, 25
Robert-Saavedra, J.R.	As Death Works, 37
	I Want to Kiss You, 73
	Ignored, 163
	Life's Cellar, 287
	Of People and Flowers, 287
	Sunrise, 162
	The Fifth and Last Winter, 56
	The Tree, 161
	The Vagabond, 53
	Time, 3
	To Claudia, 74
	Towards the End, 34
Roush, Juanita Dyer	The Man He Might Have Been, 261
	Today I'm Deaf, 29
	You Call That a Massage?, 128

Rowland, C.A.	Interview with a Rabbit, 113
Russis, Ron	Bill and I Knew, 54
	Closing Days, 112
	Coming Down, 12
	Go Fetch a Switch, 88
	Heels, 76
	In the End, I Couldn't Sell, 149
	Michael McDonald's Reading, 216
	Now That You Ask…, 120
	PTSD, 260
	Signs, 122
	Sunday Swimming, 86
	Two Pints a Day, 55
Talbot, Elizabeth	Breaking Good, 221
	Second Chances, 236
Tolan, D.P.	Passages of Josephus, 190
Trice, Stanley B.	Boxcars, 128
	Sisters, 100
Turner, Donna H.	Growing Up with Dreams, 13
	Valentine's Day Surprise, 77
Turner, Larry	Among the Anthropophagi, 267
	Bump in the Night, 282
	Hallelujah Carol, 284
	How Do Mermaids Mate?, 59
	Miracle, 17
	Shape Up, Sylvia!, 215
	Six Children, 18
	Stickers for Grandma, 41
	Stories the Night Before Jim's Funeral, 38
	Triceratops, 122
Ummie	Birth of a Nation, 182
	Hit and Run, 72
	Portrait, 159
	Rebirth, 16
	Seed Planting, 71
	That Brass Ring, 266
	Way Back, 205
Vanderhoof, Rod	As the Lights Come On Again, 251
	Father and Son, 152
	Hawaiian Surfer, 176
	How I Became a Poet, 219
	My Evening with Igor Stravinsky, 202
	My Man in Pamplona,, 179
	My Summer on the Prairie, 6
	Only in America, 173

	Private First Class Michio Kobiashi, 249
	The Girl with the Curly Hair, 4
	The Unknowable, 288
	The Water Skier, 9
Walker, Dan	The Structure of the Poop, 63
Wills, John M.	Black Mask, 231
	Our Hearts, 15
	Why I Became a Cop, 243

CPSIA information can be obtained at www.ICGtesting.com
Printed in the USA
BVOW05s0513250314

348597BV00003B/3/P